WINNER Takes All

Also by Emily Martin

Five Ways to Fall Out of Love

The Year We Fell Apart

WINNER
Takes All

A NOVEL

EMILY MARTIN

EMILY BESTLER BOOKS

ATRIA

New York Amsterdam/Antwerp London
Toronto Sydney/Melbourne New Delhi

ATRIA

An Imprint of Simon & Schuster, LLC
1230 Avenue of the Americas
New York, NY 10020

First Emily Bestler Books/Atria Paperback edition June 2026

EMILY BESTLER BOOKS/ATRIA PAPERBACK and colophon are registered trademarks of Simon & Schuster, LLC

Interior design by Davina Mock-Maniscalco

Manufactured in the United States of America

1 3 5 7 9 10 8 6 4 2

Library of Congress Control Number: 2025046913

ISBN 978-1-6680-9520-1 (pbk)
ISBN 978-1-6680-9521-8 (ebook)

This one goes out to my group chat.

CHAPTER ONE

ELEANOR

Most musicians I know have a preshow ritual. They drink tea with honey, or they huddle up with their band and say a prayer. Or, in the case of one particularly eccentric indie artist I signed a while back, they scramble an egg on a hot plate backstage and hand-feed it to their bichon frise, Ringo.

For nights like this, I have a ritual of my own. One that involves getting my hair blown out, a single glass of white wine at the hotel bar, and the Louboutin stilettos I splurged on after I negotiated my first major contract at the label. The shoes make me want to saw off my own toes, but they also make my legs look incredible and are therefore perfect for meetings that have me feeling like I'm the one about to step onstage.

I have to sign this band.

Not just because I genuinely love their music and know I can help take them to the next level, but because I am desperate for a win. And Dempsey is a sure bet. They already have a solid fan base, have proven they can bring money in. Word has spread that they're unhappy with their current label. If I can close them, it will make up for every underperforming EP and personal failure of the past year.

I drain the last sip of my wine and put a tip down on the bar, then make my way outside to where my Uber driver is waiting. As he pulls away from my hotel and onto the Strip, I pop my earbuds in. Ninety percent of the time I'm listening to new music, demos my reps send me or unmastered tracks from an artist already on my roster. But right now I find my favorite playlist, full of familiar songs that demand I think only about what I was doing, what I was feeling, the first time I heard them. Songs that drive out every other thought in my head within a few beats. Which is what I need—a distraction. No irritating little voice reminding me I already had a chance to sign this band five years ago and failed.

Barely three songs later, we're pulling up to the posh steak house where I'm having dinner with Dempsey.

"Thank you," I say as I reach for the door.

"Have a good night, ma'am."

Ma'am. I pause and glance down at my outfit—a black leather pencil skirt and cream silk blouse. Is it giving ma'am energy? That is . . . less than ideal. It's too late to go back and change my clothes at this point, so I choose to believe he addresses every woman over the age of twenty that way.

"You too." One last deep breath, and I'm out of the car, heading toward the ornate double doors. I rub a finger over my front teeth in case of any rogue lipstick and smooth a hand over my hair.

Inside, my heels click against the marble tiles as I approach the hostess stand to give my name. The entrance is lavishly decorated with metallic wallpaper and gold leaf trim. Ostentatious, like the rest of Las Vegas. Before I have a chance to take it all in, I'm being led to a large curved booth along the edge of the dining room.

The two Dempsey siblings and their two bandmates are all seated on the crimson velvet upholstered booth, while their manager sits on one of the matching armchairs tucked in across the table.

"Hey, everyone," I say when I reach them, and Freddie Dempsey stands up first to give me the handshake/bro-hug combo that never gets any less awkward, no matter how many guys greet me that way. I work my way down the line, exchanging handshakes and air-kisses with Freddie's sister Sheridan and the band's manager, Fiona. Curtis Kennedy and Ralph Winters—drummer and bassist, respectively—are trapped in the middle of the booth, so I settle for over-the-table handshakes before finally taking a seat in the armchair next to Fiona's.

A server comes by to take my drink order—another glass of white wine, which I plan to nurse until this dinner is over.

"How does everyone feel about getting some pulpo for the table?" Ralph asks.

"Sounds great," I tell him. "I love pulpo."

I have no idea what pulpo is. But I flew to Las Vegas prepared to give these guys whatever they wanted. Which is why I chose this place, even though this dinner wasn't entirely sanctioned by my boss. Wining and dining artists is part of my job, but going over budget is a big part of why I'm on the chopping block. Josie will be pissed when I turn in my expense report, but as long as I have a signed contract to accompany it, I'll be fine.

The waitress tells us the food will be right out, and Ralph grins broadly before tipping his head back to take in the massive crystal chandelier dripping like rain from the ceiling above the bar. He's practically vibrating with excitement, and it reminds me of the way a toddler would dance in their high chair at dinnertime. This is why I've always been fond of Ralph—no matter how successful his band gets, he's still basically a goldendoodle, endlessly pleased just to be along for the ride.

And then there's Freddie, who is manspreading so much I have to keep my legs tightly crossed and my feet tucked under my chair to avoid unintentionally playing footsie with him. The family resemblance between him and Sher is strong—same jet-black hair and fine features. Same style when it comes to playing the guitar, even. Between the two of them, Sher is more talented. She has a better range and a purer voice, whereas Freddie already has a bit of vocal fry. She's a star. But Freddie has the bigger ego. So I turn to give him my full attention. "How do you feel, now that the tour is wrapping up?"

"Tired, mostly. I'm so ready to sleep in my own bed again."

"I believe it."

"Antsy to get moving on the next thing too."

Across the table from him, Sheridan sighs loudly. "Some of us would like a break."

Freddie rolls his eyes. "We all want a break, Sher. But we have ten tracks ready to lay down. We should keep up our momentum, is all I'm saying."

I'm momentarily distracted by the arrival of my wine and the appetizer—it turns out *pulpo* is a fancy word for octopus. Fantastic—then, my brain catches up: "Wait, ten new songs?"

"I wouldn't say they're ready to lay down, exactly." This comes from Curtis, who tilts his head as though he's saying it mostly to Sheridan.

"Uh, yeah. I wouldn't either." Sheridan adjusts the front of her lurex jumpsuit—it looks vintage, probably from the '70s. Her style is so fierce. "They also don't all belong on the same album."

Perhaps sensing the rising tension between the siblings, Fiona jumps in: "Which is exactly why we're looking to land somewhere that offers more creative control."

I smile, grateful for the opening. "Absolutely. That's something I can offer. More artistic freedom, and a more relaxed time frame for putting out work. If you finish an EP ahead of schedule, great. But at Blue Sky, we don't have the expectation that our artists churn out an album every year."

While this sinks in, I take a bite of pulpo and try to ignore the texture of the literal tentacle in my mouth, the way the suction cups attempt to latch on to my tongue in the process. I chase it with a generous sip of my wine and begin to wonder if I'll be able to make this glass last all the way through dinner after all.

"That's good to hear," Sheridan says. "We don't want to lose momentum, like Freddie said. But two albums in three years has been . . . strenuous."

From what Fiona hinted at during our last call, it was more than strenuous. I get the sense there's been a lot of discord among the band members ever since they launched their sophomore album. Touring hasn't helped, because it never does. Artists always come off tour underfed and sleep-deprived.

The server returns to take our entrée orders, and I wait for her to leave before continuing my pitch:

"I think it's smart that you don't want to keep fans waiting too long, but you need to be strategic, and make sure the entire team is happy with where the album is at before we launch."

Freddie shares a look with the others, before leaning forward to rest his tattooed forearms against the table. "We just want to be sure you mean what you say. That there won't be drama down the line if one person at the label doesn't like a song, or a cover concept, or whatever else."

"That's understandable." I match Freddie's posture, perching my wrists on top of the table. "My priority is to help you put out the best album possible, and I promise to do everything in my power to give you guys back some control—of pace and decision-making."

"Well, in that case . . ." Sheridan smirks at the others before continuing: "Now seems like a good time to mention we plan to announce who we're signing with at the wrap party."

I blink. Turn to Fiona and blink again. Back when I tried to sign Dempsey the first time, Fiona was still green. Dempsey was the only band she managed at the time, and in meetings she never concealed her emotions. But now we're all older and more seasoned and her face has become impossible to read.

I know Fiona is in my corner—we kept in touch over the years, and she remembers how hard I fought for Dempsey before. She did me a solid, tipping me off months ago that Dempsey would be looking to move on once their current deal was up. But this is the third meeting I've had with the band since Fiona reached out, and it's the first time they've indicated a decision date. Which, evidently, is tomorrow night.

"Wow. Well, that's exciting." My pulse kicks up a notch,

and I work to keep my voice level and calm. "Not that I wasn't already excited to come to your show."

Tomorrow marks the final show of their monthslong tour. I anticipated it being a blowout, celebrating not only the end of their tour but the official end of their contract with Sin City Sound. But I can't say I expected them to finalize their next move so soon.

I glance around the table at each of them in turn. Curtis is predictably drumming his fingers against the wood, nodding along to the beat inside his head. I am only half-convinced he's following our conversation. Ralph is still eating pulpo with a blissed-out expression, but flashes me a smile once he swallows his bite. Freddie seems quietly content as well, slouched back against the luxe velvet booth again, the picture of someone who's well aware the world is his oyster.

I'm not naive enough to think I'm the only rep Dempsey has met with. I'm sure they've had plenty of interest, from every major label out there. But for the first time, I let myself believe I have this in the bag.

Our food arrives, and I dial back on the hard sell, and between bites I ask about the songs they've written and visions for their next album, what they'd like to do differently next time in terms of promotion.

By the time our plates are cleared, I'm buzzing with endorphins and the exact right amount of wine. I feel like I could sprint all the way back to my hotel, devil shoes be damned.

While I wait for the server to return with my company card, I allow my gaze to wander. This place is bougie enough to attract a certain crowd—namely, celebrities and people who are willing to pay exorbitant amounts of money for the chance to be in close proximity to celebrities. I've lived in LA for long enough now that I consider myself somewhat immune to the thrill of a celebrity sighting, never mind that it's patently uncool to be caught staring at anyone famous, so when I cast a look around the room it's more perfunctory than anything. Until my eyes land on one familiar face in particular.

Adam Shaw is sitting across the room at the bar. I look away before he spots me, instinctively slouching a bit in my seat before realizing how unattractive that posture will make me look. I straighten again and sign the bill with a flourish as soon as it's placed in front of me. But even as I make small talk with the group as they finish their drinks, I can't stop myself from surreptitiously glancing at Adam every few seconds until, inevitably, I look up to find him already watching me. I tense, half expecting him to immediately come over, but the only reaction he gives me is a slight nod. As minutes pass and he stays seated, I'm able to incrementally relax.

It's not easy to ignore his presence, though, especially because I can't shake the suspicion it's no coincidence, him being here.

I pull my phone out and shoot off a text to my assistant, Nora:

Any idea why a rep from Exeter would be at this restaurant?

Despite the late hour, she replies almost immediately:

???

I drop my phone back into my bag and down the dregs of my wine. I can feel the faint vibrations of my assistant texting a couple more times, but don't bother to read her messages, because now Adam actually is making his way over.

As if it's not bad enough for a rep from another label to be interrupting this meeting, of course it has to be someone from Exeter who was there to witness it when my life blew up four years ago. And of course it has to be *Adam*, who has already stolen one recording artist from me this past year.

"Eleanor. Long time no see."

My shoulders tighten, and I consciously force them to relax. To make myself look laid-back and unfazed. "Of all the steak houses in all the towns," I bite out. I shake the hand he offers, squeezing as hard as I dare. "What brings you to Vegas?"

Adam offers an easy shrug. "Meeting someone for dinner."

"Small world."

His hazel eyes flicker around the table, then return to hold my gaze, expectant. This fucking guy.

Six months ago he signed my favorite artist out from under me. The musicians I work with are probably meant to be like my nonexistent children—I'm supposed to love them all equally in spite of their shortcomings or attitudes or how prolific they are. But Maya was a gold mine. She was driven, and professional, and she had a sound unlike anyone else out there. She was my favorite, and I was just as upset as she was that her last album didn't hit the way we wanted. But I had a plan. A strategy to make sure her next one would succeed. Only she didn't give me the chance—she took Adam's bait and wouldn't even come to the table to renegotiate. Now he's standing here looking to do it again, and he's actually going to make me introduce him.

I clench my jaw, then suck in a breath and smile big as I lean back in my seat. "Guys, this is Adam Shaw. He's an A&R rep at Exeter Records. Adam, this is—"

"You guys need no introduction," he cuts in to say, already offering his hand first to Freddie, then the others. "I'm a huge fan."

"Thanks, man," Ralph says.

"You said you're with Exeter?" Fiona asks.

"That's right. Eleanor and I worked there together before she left for Blue Sky. But I'm actually a manager now."

And doesn't he look the part? An expensive, perfectly tailored wool suit has replaced the ill-fitting poly-blend polos he used to wear to work. Back then, Adam looked like he was playacting at being a grown-up. His hair was always shaggy, so the ends curled over the shells of his ears, but now he's got a big-boy haircut, styled with pomade and everything. His jawline is sharper, his shoulders broader, and it's hard to ignore the fact that this definitely qualifies as a glow-up.

I run my tongue over my teeth. "Manager, huh? Congratulations."

"Thanks. So far, so good—I've got some exciting stuff in the pipeline."

Now he's just poking the bear.

Fiona's eyes narrow. "Adam Shaw . . ."

Wait for it . . .

"Aren't you Atlas Shaw's son?"

And there it is.

"I am." Over the years, Adam has perfected his reaction to this question. A casual smile, like the fact that his father was a goddamn legend is neither here nor there. He even manages to look a touch embarrassed, like he can't believe Fiona figured out the connection. Which is hilarious, because the fact that he had a famous father was one of the first things I learned about Adam when we met.

"I was sorry to hear about your old man," Freddie offers. "He was a hell of a guitarist."

Adam nods, a bit stiffly. "Thank you." He clears his throat and gestures over his shoulder. "I'm actually here with an old friend. You guys know Chris Edwards?"

For fuck's sake. Is he serious? Rock & Roll Hall of Famer Chris Edwards. Of course that's who he's having dinner with.

Sheridan and Ralph scramble to get a better look, both of them elbowing Curtis out of the way as they try to turn in the booth.

Even Freddie lets out an awed laugh, which is somewhat alarming. Unlike Ralph, who is and always has been an overexcitable puppy, or Curtis, who is so impassive all the time I low-key suspect he might be a robot, Freddie has curated a too-cool-for-school persona since getting a taste of fame.

"He'd love to meet you all if you have a moment."

Oh, he's good. Positioning it as a favor they're doing him, even though Dempsey has cited Chris as an influence in more than one interview. I'm more certain than ever that Adam planned all of this. I'm generally great on my feet, but right now I've got nothing.

Especially when Ralph turns to me with his mop of blond curls and big doe eyes, like he's waiting for my permission. What am I, his mother? Dinner is over. I've made my pitch. I'm in no position to tell them they can't go over and meet their idol. The best I can do is attempt to intervene by tagging along.

"I'd love to meet him, too, if that's cool."

"Of course." Adam steps back to give everyone room to slide out of the booth.

With a promise to be in touch tomorrow, Fiona takes the opportunity to make her exit. Though she's only a couple of years older than me and the band, she's a new mom and I can imagine the peace and quiet of a hotel room is more appealing to her than partying with a bunch of other industry folks. We wave her off, and the rest of us trail Adam across the restaurant like some perverse game of follow the leader. At the bar, he introduces each of us to Chris. Conversation flows easily between all the musicians, leaving Adam and me decidedly on the outside. Adam orders an old-fashioned and lifts the glass toward me in a silent *cheers* before he takes a sip.

"How did you know I'd be here?" I ask, quiet enough I won't be overheard by the others.

He swirls the ice around his glass. The sound makes me want to smack the drink out of his hand. "I didn't know you'd be here."

"Really," I say flatly. "You expect me to believe it's a total coincidence?"

He smiles blandly at me, exuding don't-give-a-fuck energy. "Honestly, I'm not very concerned about what you believe."

His sudden inability to meet my eye feels like a tell. An amateur one, at that. If he's going to crash my meeting, he should at least have the balls to own it.

Freddie steps back to catch my attention. "Hey. So, I think we're going to head over to a club with Chris."

It's quite clear this is my cue to leave, for us to do another handshake / bro hug and promise to speak tomorrow after the show, while Adam accompanies them to the club because Chris is his friend or guest or possibly some guy he now owes a favor. But instead I turn to Adam. I grab him above the elbow and smile like we're best buds and say, "The place you were just telling me about? That sounds great. Let's go."

Adam's gaze flickers down to my hand on his arm, then up to meet mine. He puts on a fake smile of his own. "Ready when you are."

Under no circumstances am I going to allow the band to be alone with Adam tonight. Josie made it clear: I have until the end of the month to turn my revenue stream around, or I'm finished at Blue Sky.

Dempsey is my lifeline. I've put all my eggs in this basket, and I will do whatever it takes to prevent Adam from swooping in and signing them out from under me.

Which is how I wind up squeezed into the back of a limo next to him, pretending I can match men who are twice my size drink for drink.

I'm not going down without a fight.

CHAPTER TWO

ADAM

Before I'm even fully awake, I know I've fucked up. It's a bone-deep feeling, accompanied by a blinding headache and the desire to pull the pillow over my face and will my body back to sleep. But that ship sails when the mattress dips and my eyes shoot open to find Eleanor beside me in bed.

She's propped up on her elbows, clutching the crisp white sheet to her chest with one hand, staring at me like she's seen a ghost.

I blink once, twice, trying to clear my cloudy vision. My eyelids are like sandpaper. It takes me a second to realize I slept in my contacts. "Eleanor?" My voice comes out low and gritty. "Why are you in my bed?"

"This is *my* bed," she hisses. And . . . huh. Upon closer inspection, this does not appear to be my hotel room. The color palette is blue and gold, whereas mine was beige and green. The desk and nightstands are made of clear Lucite instead of wood, the overall aesthetic is much more modern, and the layout is completely different. I don't even think this room is in the same hotel as mine. I sit up, ignoring the pulse of nausea that follows, and try to get my bearings. Only I don't get much of a chance, because next thing I know, Eleanor kicks me out of bed. Literally. Her foot connects with my shoulder, and I hit the ground with a thud.

The sheet still tangled around one of my legs is tugged away, and I hear her scramble off the other side of the bed.

". . . Sorry," she says a moment later.

I groan. Then press the heels of my hands against my brow bones, hard. It feels like there's shrapnel in my brain.

"Are you naked?"

My hands flop back down to my sides. I frown and lift my head enough to peek down my body and confirm that I am, in fact, wearing boxer briefs. As well as one sock. "No." Alarm bells start to go off in my head. "Are *you* naked?"

"No," she answers quickly, her tone almost offended.

The alarm bells won't shut up, though. They've turned into more of a blaring siren. I roll onto my side, and with great effort manage to push up onto my hands and knees. I hear Eleanor moving, too, and we look at each other over the bed at the same time.

Christ, my eyeballs are fucking *burning*. I blink hard a few more times, bringing Eleanor into focus. Her hair is a mess and her mascara is smudged all over her eyes, but she's still wearing her blouse from yesterday. That seems like a good sign.

"You don't think we . . . I mean, we didn't have sex. Right?"

I half expect her to laugh. To tell me there is no world in which she would ever sleep with me. Instead, Eleanor's gaze drops down to the rumpled bed between us. "No. I don't think so."

"Wouldn't you be able to tell?"

She cuts me a look. I can't figure out if she's annoyed or confused. "Excuse me?"

I'm still on my knees. I rock my weight from one to the other. "Women are supposed to be able to tell, I thought."

"Who told you that?"

I shrug. "A friend."

It was a girl I went to college with, who lived down the hall from me freshman year. It came up after we'd gone to a party together, only to get blackout drunk and separated before the night was over. Thankfully, it turned out her roommate had taken her home after she puked in the middle of a game of beer pong, but when I checked on her the morning after, I remember her saying she would have been able to feel if something had happened to her anyway. At eighteen that seemed perfectly believable. But I also used to believe running bottom-shelf vodka through a water filter would make it taste better. So.

Eleanor slowly shakes her head. "Okay, well, no. As amazing as my vagina is, it is not all-knowing."

I lock my gaze onto her face, resist the urge to let it travel south. She flatly holds my stare for a few beats, then pushes to her feet with a sigh. She's in her underwear, lacy and black. Her top isn't quite long enough to completely cover her ass when she turns around. I swallow and try not to creep on her as she moves around the room, checking the trash bin under the Lucite desk, then disappearing into the bathroom. I'm about to ask what she's doing when she comes back out and shakes her head again.

"Nothing happened. No used condom or wrapper, and I probably *would* know if we'd been stupid enough to fuck without one. We're good."

Thank the lord for that. Because if we were too wasted to remember how we wound up sleeping in the same bed, we were *definitely* too drunk to fully consent to anything else.

Though I'm fairly confident that after the amount I drank last night, my dick wouldn't have worked even if we'd tried.

"Good. That's good."

"Agreed," she says. And then the room is quiet, aside from the faint whir of the air-conditioning and muted traffic noises from however many floors down below, and though neither of us is naked, I am suddenly very aware that we're not fully dressed either.

"I should find my pants." I use the bed for leverage and push up to my feet. Then I have to take a moment to breathe through my mouth before I'm capable of casting a look around. The pants and my shirt turn up near the foot of the bed. My other sock proves more difficult to locate, and I'm frankly too hungover to bother with it. I sit on the end of the bed and dress.

If Eleanor and I *had* slept together last night, this would be the part where I'd suggest getting breakfast. But as we've established, that did not happen. Of course it didn't. She may not have outright laughed in my face at the idea, but evidence suggests I am not Eleanor Thompson's type. Which is fine, because Eleanor isn't my type either. I mean, sure, back when we were interns together I thought she was cute. I remember we liked a lot of the same artists—how she'd take her headphones off to talk to someone and I'd hear Alabama Shakes or Lorde blasting out of them. Once upon a time I might've even considered asking her out for a drink. But that was like seven years ago.

My eyes shift to the nightstand and I snag an empty bottle of booze from it. I inspect the label and hold it up for Eleanor to see. "This is Lagavulin 25."

She rubs the space between her brows. "That's scotch, right?"

"That's a twelve-hundred-dollar bottle of scotch," I say, a bit awed. I splurged on a glass of it once before, but never owned an entire bottle.

"Fuck me," Eleanor mumbles. "Who paid for that?"

I pull the cork and sniff it out of instinct, not taking into consideration my raging hangover and the fact that any alcohol—even the good shit—smells abhorrent to me right now. I fight off a gag and put the cap back on.

"No clue," I tell her. "Guess last night got away from us."

"Apparently." I look over my shoulder to find her buttoning the fly on a pair of denim cutoffs. Her neck's bent, her hair a curtain of tangled brown waves that hides her face from view.

I focus on doing up the buttons on my shirt. I'm about to ask if she remembers what happened after Dempsey and Chris turned in, because I for one do not, but the question dies on my tongue when I catch sight of the ring on my finger.

"The fuck?" I frown at my left hand for a long moment, confused. And possibly still a little bit drunk. Because even as my pulse starts to roar in my ears, I don't immediately connect the dots.

Then I'm on my feet so fast I have to bend back over, close my eyes, and plant my hands on my knees to avoid throwing up. Absurdly, despite being a twenty-eight-year-old grown-ass man, the first coherent thought I have is: *My mom is going to kill me.*

"You okay over there?"

I shake my head. Take a breath and—*slowly*—straighten. "Let me see your hand."

Eleanor makes a face and holds out her right hand, palm up.

"Other hand."

She huffs, then lifts her left hand, spotting the matching platinum band at the same time I do.

"Gah!" Eleanor covers her mouth with both hands, then wrenches her left one away, stretching her arm out like the ring is carrying an infectious disease. "What is that?"

"I think," I begin slowly as I wade through my hangover-muddled memories, "that we might have gotten married last night."

"No," she says flatly. She shakes her head and crosses the room to grab her phone off the nightstand. She breathes fast as she unlocks it and taps with her thumbs for a few seconds, then freezes. *"Noooo!"*

I wince. "So, yes?"

Her whole body deflates, arms falling and head hanging back in defeat. She sighs and holds the phone out so I can see the screen. Which has a picture of us, very obviously wasted, in front of a brightly lit chapel. I'm holding Eleanor bridal-style, her arms looped around my neck with one of her legs kicked out, a pose that feels pretty damning in this context.

My stomach sinks, heavy with guilt. It's not like I forced her into this. I don't think I could *make* Eleanor do anything. But historically Eleanor has always seemed indifferent toward me. Then I signed Maya, and am here to sign another act she wants on her roster, so I'm thinking *indifference* might be too generous a term for how she feels about me now. Compared to the short-lived attraction I had toward her in the early days of us interning together, and the fact that I have no fucking filter when I'm lit, I have to wonder if this whole mess might've been my idea.

"How did we even get that drunk?" she whines. "I was careful, and I drank a glass of water with my wine at dinner—"

"Well, it was probably the edibles that did you in."

". . . What?"

"The pizza," I say slowly.

"You're telling me I ate pizza with weed in it?" she asks, just this side of shrill.

"Yes? Chris took us to a cannabis lounge." Which was very clearly branded as such. The menu even stated how much THC was in every serving. "How did you miss the giant neon sign shaped like a pot leaf above the door?"

Eleanor glares down at the photo on her phone for another beat. Then, abruptly, that glare shifts to me. "This is all your fault."

Even though I had the same thought, I find myself getting defensive. "How do you figure?"

"Because you're *here*," she yells. "I have loved Dempsey's music for years, I know what they need to take it to the next level, and I was way more focused on them and my pitch and watching *you* to make sure you didn't pull any bullshit, so no, I did not notice the signage above the restaurant door—sue me. If you hadn't come to Vegas to fuck with me, I wouldn't have been in the position to make that mistake."

Oh man, I am way too hungover to handle being yelled at right now. Especially when she's dead wrong. I did not come here to fuck with Eleanor. I came because my mentor asked me to. Billy has known me pretty much my entire life—he was my father's old manager, and he gave me my first break when I was a sixteen-year-old, smart-mouthed kid. I owe him a lot. So it was a no-brainer to chase the lead when he tipped me off that Dempsey was looking to make a huge switch—new label, new publicist, maybe even a new manager.

Billy told me to focus on signing them, not to worry about putting in a word for him as a manager. But I know it could be great for Billy if it does happen. He's had a rough go of it lately, especially after the incident last summer. The DUI was bad, but made worse because he had a celebrity in the car with him, so of course *TMZ* picked it up. Since then he's gone through treatment and is sober, as far as I know, but he lost a handful of clients in the aftermath. Something like this would really help turn things around for him. And if I bring Dempsey on, that alone could be enough of a leg up for Billy because they know he and I work well together.

But none of this is any of Eleanor's business.

"I came here because Dempsey was going to be here," I say simply.

"And you knew damn well they were meeting with *me*. You somehow heard where we were having dinner—and don't think I won't figure out where you got that information—and you decided it was a perfect opportunity to swoop in and work your bullshit machinations to poach them like you poached Maya."

See, this right here is why Eleanor and I have never become friendly. She thinks she's in a league of her own. Even back when we were both bottom-feeders at the label, she acted so entitled. Like she shouldn't have to pay her dues, or actually *earn* her way up the ladder.

Eleanor may see my being here as a personal attack, but the truth is it had nothing to do with her. Yeah, I knew the band would be having dinner with a rep from another label, but I didn't know that rep was her, and it's like I told her—nothing is official until it's official. Just because Eleanor got an in with Dempsey first doesn't mean I shouldn't be allowed to throw my hat in the ring.

I shake my head with a dry laugh. "First of all, they're not your band. You haven't signed them. And you're not *going* to sign them, because I can offer better terms."

"You don't even know my terms," she says tightly.

"Second of all," I go on, watching her nostrils flare when I don't acknowledge her point, "I didn't poach Maya. I simply won."

"By playing dirty."

Oho, that is fucking rich. Everything that went down between her and Griffin Hastings when he was an executive at the label, and she's accusing *me* of playing dirty? I round the bed, closing in on her. "Are you really going to stand there and pretend you've always played by the rules?"

She holds my gaze, even as her jaw tightens. Her expression is hard to read, becoming more closed off with each passing second.

An itch crawls up my back, just out of reach. I roll my shoulders and look away first. Hastings has nothing to do with this. I'm not going to throw their relationship in her face so I can gain the upper hand in a stupid argument.

I scrub a hand over my hair and sigh. "Look. I don't exactly remember how it all went down last night. But I don't think either of us were dragged down the aisle against our will." What I vaguely remember is laughing. A lot. "Maybe the whole thing is a joke, anyway."

Eleanor holds her hand up again in response. "We are wearing *wedding bands*, Adam."

Well, yes. There is that. "What I mean is, we don't know if this is even legit. We need to figure out if the marriage is legal before we freak out or start tossing blame around."

"Fine." She crosses her arms. "So we'll go to the chapel and find out."

Since I am still missing a sock and in dire need of a shower and to brush the taste of bad choices out of my mouth, we agree to take forty-five minutes to get our respective shit together and meet back up to head over to the chapel. Which should be plenty of time, given that a peek out Eleanor's window reveals my hotel is right across the Strip.

Hopefully, showering and peeling these godforsaken contacts off my eyeballs will clear my head enough to check in with work before we meet back up too. This shitstorm couldn't have come at a worse time; I was planning on getting some work done this morning. I've been swamped ever since the promotion. I have two other contracts in negotiations, not to mention an A-list artist session to set up before the end of next week, the budget for which hasn't even been finalized yet. Not that I'm complaining. This is my dream job; it's everything I've worked for since I was sixteen and got my first internship shadowing Billy.

I'm not throwing in the towel because Eleanor called dibs, or whatever. That's not how business is done.

I double-check that I have my phone and wallet, and then pull on my shoes—which feels supremely weird given the whole missing sock situation—and head for the door. I've just stepped into the hallway when Eleanor stops me.

"Adam?"

I turn around to find her hovering in the doorway. "Yeah?"

Her gaze is contemplative, like she's debating asking whatever it is she wants to ask. "Who told you about the meeting?"

Not for the first time, facing off against Eleanor feels like a game of chicken. Like hell am I going to flinch first.

But I do hesitate for a moment. I glance down the long, ruby-carpeted hallway, then back to Eleanor. Barefoot, she seems much smaller than I ever realized. Almost vulnerable. Given the way she's looking up at me through her lashes, I get the feeling that's exactly how she wants to come across.

I lean forward and brace my forearm against the doorframe. "Listen . . . I know honesty is the foundation of a healthy marriage . . ." Her face hardens and she tightens her grip on the door. "But seeing as neither of us actually remembers the wedding, I think I'm gonna keep that one to myself."

I barely manage to move out of the way before she slams the door in my face.

CHAPTER THREE

ELEANOR

Logically, I know I can't be the first person to wake up in a Las Vegas hotel room with regrets. But that doesn't stop me from feeling like a singular screwup. The moment Adam and his little smirk are out of my sight, I shuffle back over to the bed and collapse face down for a pity party.

It's obvious I've entered a coma, or a parallel dimension, or maybe purgatory. Because how else do you explain going from being justifiably furious at Adam for crashing my dinner to willingly walking down the aisle and *marrying* the man?

I have no desire to get married. At least not anytime soon. And definitely not to anyone even remotely involved with the music industry.

I figured if it ever happened, it would be years from now, after I'd met the right guy and we'd dated for at least eighteen months followed by a long enough engagement to plan a low-maintenance but *legitimate* wedding. I'd have the vintage handkerchief my mom used at her own wedding tucked discreetly in my bra—my something old, borrowed, and blue. My sister, Iris, would be my maid of honor, because we made a pact when I was ten and I don't take that shit lightly. I would sip champagne but remain sober because in addition to being emetophobic and rarely having more than two drinks to avoid any chance of getting sick, I would want to be a classy bride. Elegant.

Hungover as I may be right now—and let's be clear, I am hungover as shit—I cannot fathom drinking enough to make any of what allegedly happened last night seem like a good idea. Intoxicated people eat too much Taco Bell and call up their exes and say cringey things they can't take back. They do not marry someone they haven't even had a full conversation with in years. Even if drunk me was trying to one-up Adam . . . it just doesn't track. This has the potential to hurt me as much as him. More, probably. Because Adam isn't the one who has spent the past few years trying to offset a reputation as someone who fucked their way to the top.

The kicker is, I can't remember exactly how I left things with the band. I have no idea if I'm supposed to call Fiona today, or if I'm supposed to do anything before the show tonight. I remember dinner, and Adam's limo taking us to a club across town, which apparently was actually a cannabis lounge. Everything after that point is hazy.

I roll over onto my back and pull my phone out to dial my office number. My assistant, Nora, answers after the first ring.

"Thank god," she says. "I've been dying here."

"Sounds like a super-rough morning for you," I deadpan.

Nora huffs and the line fills with rustling, followed by the click of a door closing. I suspect she's switched to Bluetooth and shut herself in my office for privacy. "How did it go? Did you sign them? Did you two-piece the guy from Exeter?"

I fiddle with my ring, twisting it around until abruptly I register what I'm doing, and tuck my fingers into a tight fist. "Not exactly."

"So then what happened?"

She sounds so earnest, my hand unclenches and my body releases some of the tension I've been holding all morning. It wasn't Nora. She's not Adam's source. Ever since last night I've wondered—with access to my calendar, she's the most obvious suspect, after all. But she wouldn't do that, would have no reason to.

"They haven't committed to anyone yet."

"Okay. So what are the next steps? What do you need from me?"

"Nothing at the moment. Do I have any messages?"

"A few . . . Most can wait until you're back, but Josie wanted an update."

This comes as no surprise. It's already after eleven, and she probably expected me to check in as soon as the office was open. Josie has kept me on a bit of a short leash lately, especially since learning about the times I skirted her budget cap by spending my own money to take artists out.

Josie might have lost some of her confidence in my ability to bring in new talent, but I know I can make this happen. Just like when I first signed Maya—I wasn't the only offer on the table then either. But I never let Josie see me sweat. I assured her I had it covered, and I took Maya out and I sold her on what we could accomplish together. That's what I'm doing with Dempsey. Josie will see.

"Can you let her know I'm on top of everything, and that I'll reach out after tonight's show?"

"No problem." A pause. "You're sure you don't want to check in now? I could transfer you over."

"I've got a few things to take care of right now. Tonight works better." For a moment, I consider telling Nora. Just to have *someone* to tell. But the fewer people who know, the better. Besides, Josie is technically her boss too. I won't put Nora in a position to lie for me. "Well, that's all I've got. Thanks, Nora."

We hang up and I poke around on my phone some more. I have a missed call from my sister, and I almost call her back. Iris is a personal trainer, so it's basically her job to motivate people. She honestly gives the best pep talks. The problem is, I can't lie to her, and she's getting married in a couple weeks. And I have a feeling telling her I drunkenly married some guy I can't stand fourteen days before her own wedding might not evoke the sort of sisterly support I'm accustomed to receiving from her.

Especially since she's still pissed at me for bailing on her engagement party. In my defense, I was there for the first hour. But she scheduled it on the same night as an important album launch party, and I don't possess the ability to be in two places at once.

Instead of calling Iris, I pull up my photos again. I spend a solid minute staring at the selfie in front of the chapel, trying to remember taking it. Eventually, I give up and scan the half-dozen other photos I took last night, noting that the time stamps start around one in the morning, which seems to be after Adam and I split from the group. It looks like we went from the chapel to some bar, but the rest of the photos were taken outside, the lights from the Strip blurry in the background.

As I swipe through the photo app, I notice my phone automatically created one of those custom slideshows with all the pictures I've taken in Vegas, set to sappy instrumental music. I cover my face with one hand and watch it through my fingers. In every single picture of Adam and me together, I'm wearing my biggest smile. One that crinkles my nose and does nothing to hide the fact that my two front teeth are a bit crooked because I never wore my retainer. It almost looks like I was enjoying Adam's company last night.

No. That can't be right. Drunk people grin all the time for no good reason. I once took a picture of my college roommate beaming at a broken cross-country ski she found on our walk home from a party.

I stare down at my phone until the slideshow ends and the screen locks again. I have to bite the bullet and call Fiona. I'll go crazy otherwise, not knowing where things stand.

She answers on the first ring. "Eleanor, how's it going?"

"Great," I say, rubbing my throat when my voice comes out raspy. "I wanted to touch base and see if Sher and the guys had any other questions for me."

"Yeah, I'm glad you called. I actually just got off the phone with Freddie. I know we originally told you we'd have a decision by tonight, but it's possible they're going to need some more time."

My grip tightens on my phone. I imagine my fingers are wrapped around Adam's neck instead. "Oh?"

"He says they want to think it over a bit after last night," she says, sounding almost apologetic.

Anxiety sets in as I rack my brain, trying to think of any

moment that might have tipped the scales. Swear to god, if I spouted off about being on my last leg with Josie, or gave them any sense of my own desperation, I will straight-up perish.

Of course, there's also the distinct possibility it wasn't anything *I* did. I tried my best to run interference, but it was loud and chaotic, and I couldn't catch every word Adam said. And there is so much he could've said.

Aside from his ability to pitch artists, which is absolutely one of his strengths, Adam also had a front-row seat to the start of everything with Griffin. I know the kind of gossip that was going on behind my back, especially among the interns. I can only imagine how much worse it got when I left, and Griffin was still at Exeter to control the narrative.

Another woman we interned with reached out to me last year, when Griffin was finally fired.

Sorry we were such assholes. Glad to see you're doing so well.

It meant a lot—the first indication I'd gotten that at least some people had come to see the situation in a different light.

Adam hasn't shown any signs of being in that camp.

My free hand clutches the front of my blouse, even though it's buttoned almost all the way up, because talking to Fiona while braless and on my back foot is excruciating. I want to be wearing a crisp Hillary Clinton pantsuit. I want to be as polished as Kate Middleton with weights sewn into the hem of her dress, skirt prevented from even shivering in the wind. I don't care that it's a high of ninety degrees today in

Nevada—I want to be suffocating in layers of fabric with modest Victorian necklines.

"Is Freddie free today? I'd love to help clear things up—"

"You're still coming to the show tonight, right? We'll talk then."

I nod and press my free hand to my forehead. "Yeah, sounds good. Can't wait. Thanks, Fiona."

I realize I'm shaking when I hang up and tuck my phone in my back pocket. Nausea comes in a hot-cold crawl up my spine, and with it a spike of anxiety. I glance at my windows to confirm they don't actually open. I need fresh air. I need a gallon of coffee. I need Pedialyte—my sister's hangover remedy of choice from her college days—and some dry toast to nibble on.

I had them. I *had* them. I promised Josie this trip would be worth it.

It hits me that we ordered bottle service last night, and I can only hope I didn't put it on the company card. Dinner I can justify expensing, even as exorbitantly pricey as the steak house was. It's not like Josie expects me to take prospective artists to Applebee's. But dinner *and* bottle service *and* travel expenses to Vegas is . . . a bit excessive.

Unless I sign them. Then everything will be forgiven. Everything will be fine, and the money spent on this trip will be well worth it, and Josie will remember why she can't run her company without me.

So I just have to ensure that still happens.

I can't do anything to change Freddie's mind until tonight. In the meantime, I have to focus on containing the collateral damage. No one can find out about Adam and me. When Josie hired me, she knew the circumstances that led to me leaving Exeter. At least, she knew the vague details that everyone seemed to know: that I'd gotten involved with an executive at Exeter, and subsequently gotten promoted, and soon after I was looking for a new place to work. She didn't hold it against me, or even ask many questions, which is something I remain grateful for to this day. She did, however, make it clear that she would be watching me. That I had better not step a toe out of line.

That was four years ago. And in that time, I have signed so many amazing artists, and I've made Josie so much goddamn money.

It's just that the last nine months or so have been a struggle. First it was a debut album tanking. Which happens sometimes—the market can be unpredictable, and it wasn't anyone's fault, per se. But it was also the most expensive album we released that quarter, so the numbers looked especially bad. Right after that, Maya—the highest-earning artist on my roster—signed with Adam instead of re-upping. Add in another group having artistic differences with their producer and subsequently going way over budget, and then me overspending while courting new talent . . . I can't exactly blame Josie for giving me until the end of this fiscal year to straighten out my profits versus losses.

My artists' streaming analytics and record sales have been trending up the past couple of months, but not enough. The projected earnings from bringing on a band like Dempsey, though? That would more than make up the difference.

Signing them means keeping my dream job. It means keeping my apartment, and my independence, and the dozen other talented artists on my roster who trusted me with their careers and their art and who will likely be dropped from the label if I get fired.

God. My head is pounding. I would give away my entire vinyl collection if I could go back to bed and not deal with any of this. Even the prospect of dragging myself into the shower is starting to feel like a pipe dream.

I can't decide if standing under hot water would make me feel better or worse. When I check the time I discover I have only twenty minutes left until I'm supposed to meet Adam, so that makes the decision for me. I crawl over to my suitcase instead. Sweet summer child that I was yesterday, I packed rather optimistically. I'd planned to spend the bulk of today reading romance novels by the pool. My first vacation day in almost a year—and it wasn't even going to be a full day off, when you factor in going to the show tonight. With a frown, I flick my bathing suit aside and continue to pick through the suitcase until I find a concert tee.

At some point last night I seem to have taken off my bra—something I'm very hopeful Adam didn't notice—but since I'm still wearing the same sleeveless blouse as yesterday, I'm choosing to believe I removed it without going topless. Now I yank the shirt off and pull on a lacy bralette. It's the kind without clasps that you have to put on over your head, and I immediately become tangled in the straps. I'm going to accidentally asphyxiate myself and the housekeeper who finds me will assume it was some sort of autoerotic thing. My obituary will read: *Eleanor Thompson, age 28, passed away in a Las Vegas hotel room that smelled like the hangover sweats. She leaves behind husband Adam Shaw, who recently signed the alt-rock band Dempsey to Exeter Records.*

I cannot abide.

I huff out a breath and calmly maneuver my bra into place. I throw on the T-shirt and grab my phone to turn on some music. I pull up Dempsey's debut album and go straight for track five. Though it's technically a breakup anthem, written and sung by Sheridan Dempsey, it's always worked to hype me up, make me feel in control of my own fate. If I were a professional baseball player, this would be the song they'd blast through the stadium speakers every time I stepped up to the plate. I take a moment to listen to Sheridan belt out the chorus, to let the lyrics work their magic, before I head into the en suite bathroom.

The hair gods must be smiling down on me because my blowout still looks decent once I run a brush through it. Other than that . . . yikes. I have the sort of deep-set brown eyes that make me look like I didn't get enough sleep even on my best day. This morning, I bear a strong resemblance to Uncle Fester. Splashing cold water on my face does absolutely nothing to help. With a heavy sigh, I reach for my makeup bag.

After slathering on sunscreen and concealer, I grab the tube of mascara. My hands are shaking, either from the hangover or lingering anxiety, so I have to brace my elbow against the marble countertop to avoid getting it all over my eyelid.

Two coats later, I finally look slightly better than I feel.

I brush my teeth and confirm my mascara is dry before putting in a few drops of Visine. I remember how red Adam's eyes were when we woke up and think about bringing the eye drops with me for him to use, but ultimately decide Adam does not deserve itchy eye relief. Not from me, anyway.

Before stepping out of the bathroom, I rifle through my

toiletries for a bottle of Tylenol. I raid the minibar for a Coke and use it to chase down two pills. I snag a small can of Pringles, too, and wolf them down as I finish my soda. Once I'm done, I cast another longing glance toward my suitcase—the bikini and paperbacks tucked inside—before sliding my sunglasses into place and heading out to face the music.

CHAPTER FOUR

ADAM

I make it back to my own hotel more or less in one piece. It's rough for a minute there, and I did puke into a potted palm outside Eleanor's hotel, then once more in the shower halfway through washing myself. Fortunately, I feel better after that.

When I come out of the shower, I check my phone, and there's a message from Freddie, asking me to meet the band at a brewery near the venue after they finish sound check this afternoon.

It's great news, so I'm not sure why I feel uneasy as I type out a response. Maybe because I have no plans to drink again for the foreseeable future, and even thinking about that smell all breweries have is almost enough to make me head back into the bathroom.

But this will be hours from now. I'll get breakfast and some coffee and an annulment and be right as rain.

I text them back to let them know I'll be there, and then

begin the uphill battle of pulling myself the fuck together. I'm relatively new to the whole concept of a skin-care routine, and I wasted so many hours going down rabbit holes on skin-care subreddits that I feel strangely guilty when I skip even one step in it—the same feeling I get when I go to a dentist appointment knowing I haven't been flossing as religiously as I should be. So instead I skip shaving and apply the vitamin C serum, which as far as I can tell has absolutely no effect whatsoever on my skin, followed by mineral sunscreen, which takes forever to rub in, especially with my five-o'clock shadow.

It's not until I start getting dressed that I realize my shoes were in the splash zone when I got sick earlier. I attempt to wipe them down with a hotel towel, but that makes me gag almost immediately. No way I'm walking around in these. I open the closet and find a robe hanging, and a pair of slippers neatly lined up beneath them. I tell myself it's better than going down to the lobby in my socks, and slip them on, making a mental note to put them back after I acquire new shoes so that I don't get slammed with some exorbitant charge for them when I check out later.

Before heading downstairs, I sit down on my bed—still perfectly made, since I haven't slept in it yet—and plug my phone in to charge for a few minutes. I've got a text from my mom asking how my trip is going, which I ignore for the time being, because picturing her disapproval at hearing I had a drunken, quickie wedding still makes me want to die a little. More messages are waiting in my group chat with some of the guys from the office. Everyone is hitting a bar after work tonight, because for all of them, this is a totally normal Friday. I tap out a reply telling them to have fun without me, then close the messaging app so I can check my email. One of my reps sent a follow-up about a band they scouted. They've got a unique sound, but as I've already told my rep twice now, they're almost *too* distinctive. I can't sign every artist my reps send me, no matter how good they are. It's a business—I have to cherry-pick the ones that are sure to make the label money.

I flag the message to respond later and tap through my phone to pull up Billy Draper's contact info.

"Hey kid," he answers on the third ring. "How's Sin City treating you?"

The decision to lie through my teeth is automatic. "So far so good."

"Last night go according to plan?"

A loaded question if I've ever heard one.

"That's actually what I wanted to talk to you about." I rub the back of my neck. "Why didn't you tell me the meeting was with Eleanor Thompson?"

"I didn't think it really mattered," he says.

He's right. It shouldn't have mattered. If he'd told me ahead of time it was Eleanor's meeting, I wouldn't have backed off. It wouldn't have changed a thing. Except maybe I could've been more prepared, been able to prevent her from getting under my skin last night. And then maybe I wouldn't have had so much to drink. And then *maybe* we wouldn't have wound up wearing wedding rings.

Can't really blame Billy for that part, though.

"No, you're right. Just took me by surprise." I think about the way my stomach twisted when I spotted her at the restaurant, the first time we'd been in the same room in years. "She and I have butted heads a few times in the past."

Billy makes a considering noise. "She give you trouble?"

More than he could possibly know. But again, I'm not

going to admit that to Billy. Not when he practically spoon-fed me this opportunity. Disappointing him has always felt akin to what I imagine it feels like to disappoint your dad, for someone who has a healthy relationship with their father.

"No trouble." I rub my jaw, stubble scratching against my palm. I really could use a shave, but it's just as well I don't have the time. I'd probably nick myself if I tried to wield a razor in my current condition. "She is putting up a good fight, though."

Billy laughs. "She's scrappy—I'll give her that. But you know as well as I do that she only got where she is because she sucked off Griffin Hastings."

I frown at the gray carpet underfoot, an uncomfortable heat snaking up my neck. At the time, yeah, I was annoyed she was getting special treatment from Hastings. That she was promoted so young, and without a relevant degree. But whether that was Eleanor's reason for getting involved with him or not, it doesn't change the fact that Griffin was older, and in a position of power over Eleanor, and it was just . . . not all on Eleanor, the way Billy is making it out to be.

I'm not under any illusions about Billy. Alcoholism aside, he's no saint. He has a reputation for being a bit of a prick, and I've known him long enough to recognize it's well earned. He doesn't mince his words, and that rubs a lot of people the wrong way. It tends not to bother me, personally—you don't succeed in a cutthroat industry like ours by playing nice or worrying whether everyone likes you. Besides, this is the man who fostered my love of music. He was the first person I called when I got my acceptance letter to Berklee College of Music. Four years later, he flew across the country to see me graduate. My dad didn't show up, but Billy was there, sitting right next to my mom, looking proud as hell when I accepted my diploma. So yeah, I let a lot of his more indelicate comments slide.

But every now and then shit like this comes out of his mouth, and even I can see why several big names have cut ties with him in recent years.

"You think she'll try to talk her way into Freddie's pants?"

My mind immediately rejects the idea, lip curling in distaste. "She wouldn't do that," I bite out.

Billy grunts. He doesn't sound entirely convinced. "Either way, I'm sure it won't take much to poison the well against her."

Given that Atlas never offered me any fatherly advice, good or bad, I've always appreciated guidance from Billy. I like that he feels close enough to me to share his unadulterated opinions. That said, Billy came up in a different era. So sometimes, like right now, it's shit advice that I fully intend to blow off, same way I probably would with my actual dad, if he were alive and interested in giving his thoughts on my career. It's just nice to know Billy cares enough to weigh in. I don't need all of his suggestions to be winners. And I definitely don't need to talk shit about Eleanor to close this band.

"Yeah." I clear my throat. "I'll keep you posted."

"Go get 'em, kid."

I hang up and scrub my hands over my face, psyching myself up for the day ahead. It's overwhelming, trying to wrap my head around everything that needs to be done. I have to narrow my focus: Coffee. Breakfast. Annulment. Then close this deal and be done with Vegas.

Done with Eleanor Thompson too.

CHAPTER FIVE

ELEANOR

I'm in the cab on the way to pick Adam up when I realize I'm still wearing the wedding ring. For a moment I'm mesmerized by the shine, the way it looks on my finger. It's a simple, timeless metal band. I have no idea whether I picked it out or if Adam did, but it's exactly my style, the sort of ring I could see myself wearing every day for the rest of my life. If it were given to me by someone else, that is.

I mutter a harsh curse, which draws the driver's gaze to his rearview mirror. I meet his eye and shoot him a tight smile before dropping my gaze back to my hand. I tug at the ring. It doesn't move. I try surreptitiously licking it and twisting harder, but it will. Not. Budge.

We pull onto the palm-lined drive leading up to the resort, and I force myself to give the ring a rest as the front entrance comes into view. It occurs to me that I don't have Adam's number, but thankfully he's already waiting outside with a drink tray balanced in one hand, so I'm able to wave him over easily.

He slides into the back seat and wordlessly passes a Starbucks cup to me.

"Oh." I grab the cup and frown at it for a moment. It's a nice gesture. Like, *weirdly* nice. Makes me feel like an asshole for not bringing him the eye drops. "Thank you."

He nods and holds out a small bottle of pink raw coconut water. "Got these too."

I've never been a fan of coconut water. Even the expensive stuff tastes like melted plastic mixed with a bath bomb to me. I'm a little slower to accept this drink from him. "You can take the guy out of LA, huh?"

"You're dehydrated. It'll help."

It may also make me puke, which I am determined not to do. But he's right, I am dehydrated.

"Thanks," I say again. "This was thoughtful."

He grunts in response, already tipping his head back like he's going to try to sneak in a nap. Since his eyes are closed, I take advantage of the opportunity to look him over. It's obvious he showered, his hair neatly combed and slightly damp. His stubble seems to have intensified in the past hour, but I can't say the scruff is a bad look on him. I'm almost annoyed by how well he's managed to pull himself together, but then I notice he's inexplicably swapped his shoes for fuzzy white slippers. I stare at them for a long moment before shaking my head and lifting my gaze back to his face. He's also wearing glasses. I've never seen him in glasses before. I didn't even realize he wore contacts. It feels like the Superman effect in reverse—like I'm seeing Clark Kent for the first time—and it's unnerving.

The driver pulls my attention away. "Where are we headed next?"

I give him the address of the chapel, which happens to be named Happily Ever After.

Hahaha, *fuck my life*.

According to my phone, it should take about ten minutes to get there. It is also, evidently, the top-rated chapel in a one-mile radius. Five stars on Yelp.

Good to know drunk Eleanor still has some standards.

My phone lights up in my lap—another call from Iris. A sharp needle of guilt hits me as I send her to voicemail. Almost immediately, it starts buzzing again with a series of texts.

I'm having a minor crisis.

You know how Henry's friend Craig was supposed to walk Duchess down the aisle?

Well, apparently he sprained his ankle

He's going to be on crutches at the wedding

I was sort of hoping you'd be able to take over?

Duchess loves you, and you know how stubborn she can be on a leash. Plus, you're the only one in the bridal party without a date, so it's kind of perfect—

I sigh and exit out of the messages without reading the rest. I'm obviously going to say yes. I'm going to escort my sister's smelly, partially blind, elderly Chihuahua down the aisle. And then presumably be charged with taking care of her the rest of the night.

I just . . . can't message her back right now. I can't start a conversation with my sister, because as soon as we start talking I'll want to spill everything that's happened on this trip, and I can't do that either. Not because she might get angry. If I'm honest, that's pretty unlikely to even be her reaction. No, Iris would be worried about me, which is worse.

For the longest time after Griffin, my mother and Iris acted like I was this fragile thing, a dried flower liable to crumble unless handled with kid gloves. I won't let this be another reason for them to treat me that way.

My gaze slides back over to Adam. He seems to have given up on napping now that the car is in motion. He sips his coconut water, and I watch his throat move as he swallows. Aside from the slippers, he's wearing a light blue polo and khaki shorts. I can't decide if he looks more like a frat bro or a boomer at a country club.

"When's your tee time?"

Adam pauses mid-sip. "Huh?"

I hide my smile behind my own coffee cup. He glances down, fingers plucking at the front of his polo, and then he turns back to me with a scowl.

"Seriously, though, what's with the slippers?" I ask, pointing my chin toward his feet. They're even embroidered with his hotel's insignia.

Adam's cheeks go ruddy and he nudges his glasses up the bridge of his nose. "The walk back to my hotel earlier was a bit rough."

I don't know what that means, which must be apparent in my expression, because Adam elaborates with a huff.

"I threw up on my shoes."

My lips curl in. That is truly foul. And a visual I could have done without, considering I still feel like I'm white-knuckling my way through my own nausea. "Was that the only pair you brought?"

"Obviously. Why, how many pairs of shoes did you bring?"

I wore flats on the plane, the Louboutins last night, and right now I've got on Birkenstock sandals. "Three," I tell him.

"You packed three pairs of shoes for a two-day trip?"

I stare at him for a beat. "Says the man currently wearing terry cloth on his feet."

A shard of memory forces its way to the front of my mind—the two of us walking back to the hotel from some destination that is still fuzzy in my mind. It must have been late, but there were still plenty of people out and about, noise spilling out of each bar we passed. The sun had been set for long enough that the intense heat of the day had dissipated. We'd been shuffling along, not exactly leaning on each other, but not exactly walking independently, either, when Adam stopped abruptly.

"C'mon," he said, beckoning me with two fingers.

"What?"

He shifted in front of me and crouched down. "Hop on."

"You're offering me a piggyback ride?"

"Your feet hurt," he said. "I'm tired of hearing you whimper in pain with every step."

I blinked at him. Swayed on my feet. He wasn't wrong. Every step I took was like getting stabbed in the balls of my feet with dull knives. I shuffled forward and put one hand on his shoulder. “Okay, but don’t drop me.”

“I won’t.”

I leaned against him. “Just tell me if I’m too heavy, though, okay?”

He reached to curl his palms around the backs of my thighs, then hitched me up onto his back. My arms wrapped around his neck automatically, squeezing across his collarbone as he straightened his legs and started walking. “You’re not.”

“I’m not calling your masculinity into question. You’re a very tough, strong man, with manly muscles.”

“Aw, thanks for noticing.”

“But if you face-plant—”

“Will you relax?” He did a little hop to adjust his hold on me, which did not help me relax. “I’m not going to drop you.”

By the time we made it back to my hotel lobby, my muscles were loose and my face was smooshed into the crook of Adam’s neck, right where his cologne was strongest. I was too drunk to decipher any of the specific scent notes, but I remember liking the way he smelled. Warm, and a bit spicy, and very nice. He had to pat my thigh to get me to release my octopus hold on him.

Realizing how long I’ve been frozen in thought, I quickly shift to look out the window and pray my sunglasses prevented Adam from noticing my stare. I don’t know how to reconcile that memory—or him bringing me not one, but *two* drinks this morning—with the fact that he came to Vegas with the obvious intention of ruining my day.

“There was probably somewhere you could’ve bought new shoes back at your hotel,” I say, because despite his olive branch, I’m still in a vindictive mood.

"I tried," he says shortly. "My credit card was declined. I think my account's frozen. I have to call them."

I shake my coffee cup. "How'd you pay for this, then?"

"Company card," he answers, eyeing my shirt like he's trying to come up with something insulting to say about it. It's vintage, from David Bowie's Serious Moonlight tour. It belonged to my mother, but after the third time I stole it from her closet back in high school, she gave it to me.

I cock an eyebrow and wait.

Adam's lips purse and he huffs through his nose, wisely choosing to keep his mouth shut. He sulks in silence for the span of five blocks. I can't tell if he's genuinely distraught over our current predicament or just grumpy about his shoes, but I've always pegged him as someone with the emotional depth of a birdbath, so I would not be shocked to hear it's the latter.

"Can you silence your phone?" he grouses when yet another text comes through. "That buzzing is driving me nuts."

I roll my eyes and dump the phone into my bag without silencing it—Iris will run out of things to text me eventually. Besides, the driver is playing some great music.

"Would you mind turning that up?" I lean forward to ask.

He twists the volume dial, and Joe Cocker's "With a Little Help From My Friends" blasts through the speakers, plenty loud enough to drown out my phone. I face Adam and pointedly sing along. When he ignores me, I lean closer and sing louder, until finally Adam cracks and belts out the chorus along with me.

"Greatest cover of all time," I say as the cab pulls up to the curb outside the chapel and the driver turns the volume back down again.

"Debatable," Adam argues. "It's great, but best ever? What about Jimi Hendrix's 'All Along the Watchtower'? Or Aretha's version of 'Respect,' for that matter."

"Fair," I say as I swipe my debit card. The payment goes through, and I try not to think about how close I am to overdrafting.

Adam gets out first, and I scoot across the back seat after him. Once on the sidewalk, I pause to grimace up at the neon sign.

I am not someone who has spent a lot of time fantasizing about my dream wedding. But like anyone who read *Twilight* at an impressionable age, I've imagined getting married in the lush forests of the Pacific Northwest. I've also had the passing thought of getting married in the backyard of the house I grew up in, despite the fact that my mom sold it when Iris and I graduated high school. My last serious relationship was with Griffin, and the only time marriage came up was when we were visiting a vineyard in Napa. A bride and groom were having their photos taken nearby, and I made some innocuous comment about it being a nice place for a wedding, and then Griffin had scoffed and sipped his wine and said that when we got married, it wouldn't be in a place as overdone as Napa.

The point is, never once did I picture my wedding taking place in a squat building just off a major road, with a sign that buzzes if you listen hard enough.

Resentment swarms inside my chest because I hate thinking about Griffin, and I wouldn't have to if Adam hadn't come to Las Vegas. I wouldn't be remembering that day in Napa if I hadn't come to this chapel with a different music executive I had no desire to marry. I've worked hard to banish these kinds of memories, and Adam being here is forcing them all to the surface.

I cut a sidelong glare at Adam and discover he looks as miserable standing here as I feel. Good.

"Let's get this over with," I say with a scowl.

He blows out a big, disgruntled breath before following me toward the chapel.

Based on the signage and general aesthetic of . . . the entire city of Las Vegas, I expect it to look something like a cheesy Valentine's Day party. Like Cupid threw up on the walls. Hot-pink carpet and curtains made of the same cheap red satin you'd find on a heart-shaped, coin-operated bed in some sleazy motel. Or . . . I don't know . . . a rack of polyester veils you can rent for the occasion that they sanitize with Lysol spray after each ceremony, like bowling shoes.

Instead, what I find is a waiting area tastefully decorated in a woodland fairy-tale theme. A rustic flagstone fireplace sits in one corner, and while it isn't lit, an abundance of very realistic LED pillar candles in staggered heights are arranged inside. The doorway leading to the chapel itself is adorned in a twig garland and tiny lights, the kind that look like fireflies. Right now the chapel is empty, and I catch a glimpse of the altar.

I try to picture Adam standing under the wooden arch, delicate flowers dangling over his head while I walked—or perhaps stumbled—down the aisle. I'm hit with a whole-body pang, and I blink hard, cursing my hangover as I drag my focus back to the walls of the waiting area, which are painted a soothing shade of cream. The desk, which appears to be antique, has one of those cute little brass bells on it to get someone's attention. Not that we need it, because a petite gray-haired woman in a blush pantsuit is already standing behind the desk, smiling at us like we're long-lost friends.

"Thought I might see the two of you again."

Adam and I exchange a questioning look. "We were here last night."

The woman—Beatrice, according to her name tag—smiles brightly, oblivious to the question hidden in Adam's statement. "Yes, you ran off before I could give you your marriage license and photo package."

"Photo package?" I propel myself forward and peer over the desk as she flips through a stack of papers.

"Of course, I understand your eagerness to get on with enjoying your wedding night."

She shoots me a wink, and I shake my head vehemently. "No, not—that's not—"

"Ah, here we are. I'm so glad you came back for them!"

Oh my. The photo package apparently includes an 8 x 10 glossy print of us standing at the altar. It's tucked into a flimsy card stock matting with the words "Happily Ever After" embossed in gold along the bottom.

It takes several seconds for my brain to process that Adam is kissing me. Not a chaste little peck on the cheek either. This kiss involves Adam's hands gripping my waist, holding me close to his body. My arm is slung around his neck, opposite hand cupping his jaw, like I want him to kiss me deeper. Make it last longer. And I guess I should have realized the likelihood that we kissed at some point last night, what with the whole *you may now kiss the bride* thing generally being part of the process. But I didn't, or I chose to ignore that possibility, and looking at this photo, all I can think is: *What a shame I don't remember.*

It's just, the way he's gently dipping me, that one dark piece of hair curling over his forehead like Prince Charming . . . it's very fitting with the whole vibe of this place. And I haven't been properly kissed in a long time. If I ignore the fact that it's Adam doing the kissing, it seems like it might have maybe been enjoyable.

Adam peers over my shoulder to get a good look at the photo. His body is a hard line of heat against my back, and it doesn't take much to imagine his hands on me like they were in the picture, just this side of possessive.

Then Adam recoils from the counter wearing a pinched expression, like he's suffering from another bout of nausea, courtesy of this photograph. I snatch it off the desktop and stuff it roughly into my bag. Poor Beatrice winces, hand fluttering as though she was tempted to lunge across the desk and take the picture back, smooth it out, and lecture me about putting it into a proper frame with UV glass. I've clearly offended her, but come on. Read the room, Beatrice.

"So this is real." Adam points at the license. "We're married. Legally married."

Beatrice appears baffled by this question. "Yes. Of course it's legal." She dips her chin and peers between us over the rim of her glasses. "Did you . . . not know Las Vegas weddings were legally binding?"

Adam's scowl is so severe there might as well be a cartoon rain cloud hovering above his head. "I need fresh air," he announces, and walks toward the exit without another word.

I shoot Beatrice an apologetic smile and thank her for the pictures before following him outside, tucking the license inside my bag on the way. I find Adam standing at the edge of the sidewalk watching traffic with his hands laced together on top of his head. I sidle up next to him and slide my sunglasses back on. I miss the air-conditioning of the chapel. I'm desperate enough to cool off that I pull my unopened coconut water out of my bag and take a sip.

Which I promptly spit back into the bottle. I grimace and glance sideways in time to catch Adam's lips twitch. "How do you drink this stuff?"

He shrugs. "I like it."

"Do you really? Or is it another thing you actually hate, but started pretending to like once it became popular?"

Adam huffs a dry laugh and turns to face me fully. "Gee, Eleanor, it almost sounds like you're not talking about coconut water anymore."

I purse my lips and look away first, back toward the chapel entrance. Giving Adam a hard time about Dempsey is pointless. He likes them, he doesn't like them—it's a waste of energy arguing about it. Either way, it won't stop Adam from signing them if I can't convince Freddie I'm the best option.

"Let's just put our bullshit aside until we get this sorted out, okay?"

After a moment, Adam offers a tight nod. "Fine."

"I know it's not what we were hoping to hear, but we knew the marriage was probably real. Honestly, I'm more disappointed that the ceremony didn't involve an Elvis impersonator. What's the point of getting married in Vegas if it's not officiated by Elvis?"

He shoots me a glare that reads: *You're the worst.*

My answering smile says: *Right back at you.*

"I'm sure it's a quick fix," I say, composing my face back

into a mask of indifference. "We'll get an annulment, and no one but us will ever know."

A breeze kicks up, more stifling than refreshing. Adam runs a hand through his hair and nods. "Guess we need to find an attorney."

A name pops into my head, unbidden. *Oh, fuck.* Tyler and I go way back, but the idea of him helping me with this brings both relief and dread.

Adam is squinting at the chapel entrance, clearly unaware that I've been frozen to the spot at the mention of the word *attorney*. "We could probably ask Beatrice for a name. She must have some references, right?"

"Actually . . ." I clear my throat. "I know a guy." At least, I think I do. The last time I saw him—several years ago, now—he hadn't finished law school yet. I'd actually sort of forgotten he even became an attorney. I pull out my phone. A quick Google search proves that the guy who taught me how to make a bong out of a Pringles can did, in fact, pass the bar. And now owns the web domain StripLawyer.com.

"You just happen to know a guy who practices law in Las Vegas?"

He says it with this skeptical yet unsurprised tone in his voice that has me clenching my molars. I wonder, not for the first time, what kinds of things Adam has said about me behind my back. What kinds of things he might have told Freddie about my past, or my character, or my ability to do my job without someone like Griffin there to prop me up.

I unclench my jaw and answer evenly: "He's a friend from college." Or, he was. We lost touch after his last visit out to LA.

Admittedly, it is a bit difficult to reconcile my memories of Tyler—most of which involve sharing a bowl in one of our dorm rooms—with the idea of a suited-up lawyer. Then again, Tyler always did have a knack for talking himself out of trouble.

"And he'll be discreet." Despite my cool tone, my pulse starts to race when I hit the call button. Adam Shaw of all people does not get to judge me or my dealer-turned-attorney pal—but also, I don't relish the thought of Adam witnessing it if Tyler answers just to tell me to go to hell. Tyler was always the kindest, the chillest, the most understanding . . . and I still might deserve to be sent to voicemail.

I turn away from Adam as I listen to it ring.

"Tyler Malarkey."

"Tyler, hey! It's Eleanor." There's a beat of silence. I squeeze my eyes shut and add: "Thompson."

"No shit. Eleanor? What's it been, like four years?"

His voice is neutral. Guarded. He doesn't sound especially happy to hear from me, but he hasn't hung up on me yet, so I'll take the win. "Yeah. Been a while. I'm actually in Las Vegas. Are you free today? I was hoping you'd be able to help me out with something."

"I'm not dealing anymore, but I've got my own stash if you want to catch up in person. I'm mostly vaping these days—easier on the lungs. Or I could recommend a couple of local dispensaries?"

"No . . ." I press the phone harder against my ear and click the volume button down with my thumb, just in case Adam has supernatural hearing. "That's not what I meant. I actually have a legal situation I could use your help with."

"Oh, damn. This isn't your one call, is it?"

"No. I haven't been arrested. It's actually . . . I need to get an annulment."

Another heavy silence stretches between us. Then, his voice more serious than I've ever heard it, "From him?"

Heat floods my face. He means Griffin. "No," I say quickly. "No, that's been over awhile. It's this guy from work. Sort of. We aren't even dating." I feel Adam staring at me and ignore him, focusing instead on a pair of Vegas showgirls with big, feathered headpieces crossing the street. "Can we actually have this conversation in private? I'm literally standing outside a wedding chapel right now."

A pause, then Tyler starts laughing his ass off. I run my tongue over my teeth and wait for him to stop.

"Okay," he says, making an effort to contain himself. He clears his throat and puts on what I assume is his lawyer voice. "Yes, I can help with that." He lets out another amused breath. "Why don't you come by my office? We'll get you all fixed up."

"Great. Text me the address and we'll make our way over."

"Done," he says, and I can hear the smile in his voice. It's offensive how cheerful he sounds when he adds, "Can't wait to see you again and meet the mister."

CHAPTER SIX

ADAM

The maps app is open on Eleanor's phone, telling us we've arrived at our destination. I glance between the screen and the neon sign hanging that reads "Deja Vu." A smaller sign beside it advertises topless dancers.

"This is the address he gave you?"

"Yeah." She says this like it's normal to meet your attorney at a strip club. Of course Eleanor is cool with this—before this morning I've never seen her get remotely frazzled over anything. Generally, she could be summed up with the word *unruffled*. Any perceived slight or bit of constructive criticism rolls right off her. You just know she goes to bed at night and falls asleep the moment her head hits the pillow. She's never stared at her ceiling for hours replaying every awkward thing she did that day, writing scripts for conversations she wishes she could do over, or revisiting the time in ninth-grade gym class when she tripped over absolutely nothing in front of everyone. Which is why finding out that the dinner last night was Eleanor's put a pit in my stomach. There's something unnerving about someone who isn't bothered by anything.

"So, he works . . . here." It's that, or he gave us the wrong address. I'm not sold on his competence either way. I drag a hand down my face and shake my head. "No."

"What do you mean, 'no'?"

I gesture to the sign, incredulous. I really feel like this situation requires no further explanation. "We need to find a legitimate attorney, not Saul fucking Goodman."

Eleanor narrows her eyes. "Saul Goodman won, like, *all* of his cases. He was a great lawyer; his life was ruined because of the money laundering."

Before I can argue further, the door under the awning opens and a man I can only assume is Eleanor's friend saunters out. At first glance it seems like he might actually be somewhat reputable after all, dressed in a suit and tie despite the heat. Then he gets close enough for me to notice he's wearing Converse and his tie has the X-Men symbol printed all over it.

"Ellie!"

The guy envelopes her in a bear hug as soon as she's within reach. She returns the embrace and lets out a little squeak when he lifts her off the ground.

"Damn, dude," he says when he sets her back down. "Adulthood looks good on you."

"Me? Look at you! You're wearing a suit."

My gaze flicks back and forth between them, trying to figure out why Eleanor is staring at this guy like he hung the moon. His jacket is at least one size too big for his lanky frame, and his floppy hair is overdue for a cut, something he's unsuccessfully tried to hide with too much gel. Her standards cannot possibly be so low that this guy managing to dress himself semi-appropriately is enough to impress her.

He straightens his ridiculous tie with a smirk. "I know, right? I had to go to court this morning. Gotta look the part."

"The part of a lawyer who conducts business out of a strip club?" I cut in, and Eleanor scowls and smacks my arm.

Tyler seems to take it in stride. "Is there something wrong with working in a strip club?" he asks, head cocked as he gives me a once-over, lingering for a moment on my slippers.

"No, that's—I didn't . . ." I cast a look at Eleanor, who seems to be enjoying seeing me sputtering. "Obviously, there's nothing wrong with that."

Tyler hums in agreement. "Did you know the United States has more strip clubs than anywhere else in the world? But as a society we still perpetuate a stigma against sex workers, which in turn perpetuates a cycle of violence and bias held against them by police, judges, and juries. Which is why so many victims of sexual assault decline to even file reports."

I shuffle my feet, feeling distinctly cowed, but Tyler offers me an easygoing shrug. "The bulk of my clients are sex workers. They don't typically mind meeting me here." He turns the wattage up on his smile. "Plus, the girls give me free lap dances on my birthday!"

"Oh." I clear my throat. "That's . . . nice of them."

"We haven't been properly introduced. I'm Tyler."

I shake the hand Tyler is offering. "Adam."

"All right." Eleanor's hand finds Tyler's shoulder, turning him around and guiding him back toward the entrance. "Lead the way."

I avoid Eleanor's eye as we approach a large bouncer standing with arms crossed in front of a velvet curtain.

"They're with me," Tyler tells him, and the guy nods once and pulls the curtain aside.

It's half past noon, but inside the windowless club it's so dark you'd have no idea the sun was even up. I wouldn't have expected a place like this to even be open midday, but apparently this particular establishment fully caters to the lunch crowd. Which is . . . not the most charming of crowds. Mostly it's composed of older men who look like the types to get edged out of their companies with offers of early retirement, just so HR doesn't have to deal with any more sexual harassment complaints.

People like Griffin Hastings.

I don't know why I'm having so many intrusive thoughts about that asshole today. It's been almost a year since he was fired from Exeter. Long enough ago that no one at work really talks about him anymore. But I guess spending time with Eleanor and seeing all the ways she's changed since we first met reinforces how fucking *young* she was at twenty-two. And how messed up it was for Griffin, a fifteen-year veteran at the company, never mind a man pushing *forty*, to get involved with her. The fact that two other women reported him to HR for inappropriate comments leading up to his dismissal confirms what a creep the guy is.

Eleanor catches me looking at her, and like I'm afraid she'll somehow be able to read my thoughts, I turn my head away quick. Tyler is leading us past the stage, and I allow my gaze to land on the woman in six-inch platform heels and not much else swinging around a pole upside down.

It's not like I've never been to a strip club before. I've been to bachelor parties, done the cheering-up-a-friend-who-recently-got-dumped thing. And I know what people imagine the music industry to be like. Stereotypically, it's all about sex, drugs, and rock 'n roll. Except that really applies more to the artists themselves. Not the people responsible for the paperwork, the contracts and budgets and bookings. And there is something distinctly uncomfortable about coming to a place like this with someone you know through work.

Even if any semblance of a professional relationship between Eleanor and me is pretty much shot to shit at this point.

Thankfully, we don't linger on the club floor. I'm relieved when Tyler brings us backstage, but that relief is rather short-lived, because there are even more half-naked women gathered there, fixing their makeup in front of a wall of mirrors. One of the dancers is singing along to the Nicki Minaj song filtering in from the club. It feels invasive for me to be back here, uncomfortably voyeuristic to focus on them in their private space, so I keep my gaze glued to Eleanor's back as we walk through a cloud of cheap perfume and hairspray. I follow her down a hall and through an unmarked door, which Tyler closes behind us, blocking out the music from the club.

"Can I get you anything? Coffee?"

"Uh . . ." I weigh my caffeine craving against the likelihood that anything Tyler serves from this office will be potable. "Sure?"

"I'm good," Eleanor says.

The office is a tight fit—barely enough room for the wide metal desk and the two chairs in front of it. Tyler turns sideways and steps between us to squeeze around the desk. He takes off his suit jacket and drapes it over the back of his chair before taking a seat, gesturing for us to do the same.

I watch as he spins around in his chair and reaches for a ceramic mug sitting on top of a bookshelf, right beside a little potted plant that has to be fake, considering there is zero natural light in here. If not for the dampened bass thudding through the walls, you would never guess that we were inside a strip club. The vibe feels more similar to a school counselor's office—functional, if outdated and slightly depressing. All that's missing is a Hang in There! cat poster behind Tyler's desk and some pamphlets about cyberbullying.

"So, you want to tell me the story?" Tyler asks after he pours a cup from the coffeepot behind him and passes it across the desk to me.

Eleanor crosses her legs and huffs a breath out of her nose. "Probably one you've heard before. Got abducted-level drunk, stumbled into a chapel, woke up the next morning with more questions than answers."

Tyler seems surprised to hear this, even though it must be a pretty common scenario, like Eleanor said. "Well . . . you always were the life of the party."

That is . . . not the impression I have of Eleanor. It's not like I see her as some prudish stick-in-the-mud. We are sitting in the back office of a strip club because of her "connections," after all. She's a type, you know. Red lipstick, shoes that have got to be uncomfortable but admittedly make her ass look great. A stare that makes you want to look away first in deference. She is capital-C Cool, effortlessly so, and she knows it.

The thing is, being cool is not the same as being *fun*, which implies an easygoing nature that Eleanor never seemed to possess.

I hook my thumb in Eleanor's direction. "Her?"

Not once did she deign to come out to the bar or to a show with the rest of the interns when we worked together. I'll admit her standoffishness sort of intrigued me at first, made me want to get to know her all the more. But after a while—especially once everyone found out she was seeing Griffin—it felt like she thought she was too good for us lowly peasants. Never mind any embarrassment I may have felt personally for ever entertaining the thought of asking her out, when she clearly had her sights set on something higher.

"Oh yeah," Tyler says. "My top five nights in college all involved Ellie. God, remember that time we got baked and you decided to build a snowman orgy on the quad?"

I choke on a sip of coffee. Eleanor reaches over and slaps me between the shoulder blades, perhaps a bit harder than necessary, and shoots a warning glare across the desk at Tyler, who leans back again and starts laughing. It's this utterly delighted, nearly contagious giggle that has Eleanor visibly biting down on the inside of her cheek as she straightens up again.

My eyes are watering by the time I've caught my breath from the coughing fit, and I slip a finger under my glasses to wipe at them. "Snowman . . . orgy?"

Tyler's eyebrows draw into a little V, even as a playful smile continues to tug at his lips. "How do you guys know each other, again?"

"We used to work together," she tells him. "And now Adam here likes to pull underhanded shit and come after the artists I've scouted, because he has no ear."

"Oh, *what*? What was that?" I sputter. "Remind me, how many of *your* artists hit the Billboard Hot 100 list last year?"

Eleanor examines her nails, managing to look bored even

though she's the one who started this pissing contest in the first place. Tyler's gaze flickers between us with interest.

Not for the first time since waking up in Eleanor's bed, I wish I could go back in time and opt not to come to Vegas. I already have an incredible roster of artists, and at least a dozen more on my radar. But Dempsey is poised for a major breakout album. If I sign them and take them platinum, that's the kind of thing that will impress the powers that be, that will help me gain more influence at the label. Plus, I can't deny the draw of beating out a competitor. It's like a double win. Triple win, if things work out for Billy to become their new manager.

But more and more I'm questioning whether the juice is worth the squeeze. I can admit it wasn't the best etiquette, coming to Vegas and crashing Eleanor's meeting. It might even qualify as quote-unquote *underhanded shit*, just like she said. So maybe this is exactly what I deserve, for listening to Billy when he insisted I should fly here to speak with Dempsey in person, for chasing a band instead of playing it cool and making them chase me.

"Maybe we should get down to business," Tyler cuts in. I glare at Eleanor a beat longer, then turn back to Tyler when he continues: "In Nevada, the process for an uncontested annulment is pretty straightforward. I'll need to get some information from you guys, and then I can file the paperwork on your behalf."

"Great," I say, relieved that this is a relatively easy fix. Maybe my mom will never have to find out about this. "And we can get it submitted today, right?"

Tyler checks his watch and makes an agreeable face. "Don't see why not. You have your marriage license?"

Eleanor sighs and reaches into her bag. "Yeah."

She pulls out the crinkled piece of paper and passes it across the desk. As Tyler reads it over, Eleanor bends forward to put her head in her hands and starts breathing through her mouth in a very deliberate way. As someone who gets very carsick and has zero tolerance for carnival rides or airplane turbulence, I recognize the signs.

"Are you feeling okay?"

She grunts. "I haven't been this hungover in years."

Fair. I don't think I've *ever* been this hungover. The nausea is a constant hum through my body.

Tyler leans forward and rests both forearms on his desk. "Really? You drank *that* much?"

Again, there's this bewilderment in his expression that makes no sense to me, given his characterization of college Eleanor.

"I got cross-faded," she tells him. "Accidentally. We were hanging out with this band and they ordered pizza, and I didn't realize it had THC in it."

I bite back the same comment I made earlier, because how—especially as someone who evidently got high a lot in college—do you not realize there is weed in every single thing on the menu at a literal cannabis-tasting lounge. She uncrosses her legs, only to cross them again the other way. She's studiously avoiding my gaze, probably because she knows what I'm thinking.

"Is there somewhere to eat around here?" I ask. Maybe getting some food in our systems—some food without marijuana in it—would help.

"Oh!" Tyler rolls his chair back and pulls open the middle drawer of his desk. "I've got you covered."

He passes each of us a buffet voucher. As in, for the strip club's buffet.

". . . Thanks," I tell him.

"Sure thing. I always take care of my clients. You guys go ahead and grab some food. I'll start on the paperwork and come find you when it's time to sign on the dotted line."

I take both vouchers and try to pass one to Eleanor, but she shakes her head. "I'm good."

"If it helps, I eat here all the time," Tyler says, his voice turned gentle. "They never let the food sit too long."

Eleanor's expression is almost pained. "I can't right now."

"I could sneak into the kitchen and bring you something else?"

"No, you don't have to do that. I'm okay. Seriously." She offers him a smile—not her real smile, but one that's clearly meant to be reassuring. "I appreciate it, though."

Eleanor moves toward the office door, and I follow close behind, completely confused by their conversation. As we're passing through the doorway, Tyler calls out to me.

"Make sure to try the mac 'n cheese!"

I shoot him an awkward thumbs-up, which is a gesture I don't remember doing in my entire adult life, and then keep my gaze on my own feet until we've made it out of the changing area and back onto the floor, where they're blasting headache-inducing dubstep. Eleanor beelines for a table while I head to the buffet tucked in the back corner of the room.

My lips press into a flat line as I take in the spread. Skeptical as I was about dealing with an attorney who works out of a strip club, I'm twice as skeptical about eating at one. The fact that Eleanor passed is not reassuring either. But the food does look pretty decent, and surely Tyler wouldn't suggest his friend eat here if it wasn't completely sanitary and safe.

I grab a plate and pile it precariously high with fried chicken and buffalo wings. I add a scoop of mac 'n cheese because Tyler does not strike me as the sort of person to steer you wrong about munchies, and then I make my way over to Eleanor's table.

The club has gotten busier since we arrived, but at this hour, there are still an abundance of open spots. Eleanor has chosen one as close to the main stage as she can get. It feels vaguely like a test, like she wants to prove I'm not chill enough to be in the same room as a topless woman without ogling her like a creep. Joke is on her—all I have to do is keep my attention on Eleanor instead, and I'll pass her little test.

For her part, Eleanor watches the dancer, mouth tipped down into a slight frown. I'm fairly certain that the phrase *resting bitch face* is sexist, so I try to avoid using it. That said, I feel like it really sort of fits Eleanor perfectly. I imagine this is the face she makes whenever she's reviewing long contracts, or standing in line at a coffee shop, or washing her hair.

Not that I've ever imagined her in the shower.

The point is, she looks sort of pissed. But when I take the seat across from her, she shifts her focus and smooths her expression out to something neutral. She flags down one of the women working here—it's unclear to me whether she's a waitress or a dancer or both—and politely asks for a couple of waters. I focus on my own plate and take a small bite of macaroni. Which is all it takes to decide the inevitable food poisoning will be worth it. Tyler was right—it's amazing.

The next time I glance across the table, Eleanor has produced a paperback book from somewhere, and is reading. In a strip club. It's so unexpected and cute, I cough out a laugh. Her eyes flick up to meet mine, then immediately drop back down to the page.

I go back to my food, but I'm determined to pass her Chill Test, so I watch Eleanor more than the woman onstage—who, according to my peripheral vision, is currently squeezing the pole between her thighs and hanging upside down, so I think I deserve some credit for not gawking.

I sort of assumed the strippers working in the middle of the day might be the B squad. Like, the dancers who are new and still slightly uncoordinated, or recovering from a pole-related injury, or the ones who have been doing this for so long that they have no more fucks left to give. But from what I've seen, through my super-casual and non-lingering glances, I'd give the girl onstage a ten out of ten.

Meanwhile, Eleanor is biting her lip while she quietly reads, and it's . . . distracting. Knowing that we kissed last night is doing something to my brain. I'll admit I've thought about kissing her before, years ago. I never could've imagined getting to do it, and then not even remembering it afterward. I'm tempted to ask her if I can see that photo stashed away in her bag, but I'm pretty sure we're supposed to be pretending it doesn't exist. Also, looking at it again would probably only make me feel worse. It's kind of embarrassing. Photographic evidence that my long-dormant crush on Eleanor Thompson led to me making a complete fool of myself last night.

She drags her tongue across her bottom lip, and I can't seem to stop staring at her mouth, can't stop thinking about her full lips crushing into mine, about all the other things she could do with—

"You do realize there are half-naked ladies here, right?" she asks without looking up.

I blink hard and drop my gaze down to my plate, stabbing my fork into my macaroni and shoveling the bite into my mouth. Once I've chewed and swallowed I say: "I'm familiar with the concept of a strip club, yes."

She sets her book down, still open so she doesn't lose her page, and leans forward to plant her elbows on the table in a way that pushes her cleavage together.

To be clear, I'd really prefer not to find anything about Eleanor attractive. Unfortunately, it's out of my hands. She's smoking hot. It's just the truth.

Her lips twitch into a smile. It's another one of those calculating looks she has, the kind that makes you feel laid bare. "Then why do you keep staring at me instead of them?"

I ignore the heat rising up my neck. "I was wondering what your book is about."

"It's a romance."

"Yeah, the bare-chested guy on the cover clued me in. Gotta say, that's not what I would've expected you to be reading in your spare time."

"Oh? And what would you have expected me to read instead?" She rests her chin on top of her knuckles, waiting.

"Probably a pop psych book about how to make people like you more. Or maybe a business guide to help your flailing little indie label." She rolls her eyes and scowls, and I drag a hand across my jaw to wipe away the smile tugging at my lips. It's way too much fun, riling her up. "Guess I didn't picture you as a romantic, *Ellie*."

Her eyes narrow, and she's quiet for long enough that I grow uneasy. I play what I said over in my mind, and internally cringe at the implication I think about her in the first place.

"Don't call me that" is what she winds up saying.

I take a sip of water, let it cool me down. "Aw, how come Tyler gets to call you Ellie but I don't?"

"Because I actually like Tyler," she says with a biting smile.

A hand over my heart. "You wound me."

"I wish," she mumbles.

This time, I don't bother to hide my smirk as I stab another bite of macaroni with my fork. "You sure we can trust this guy?"

She shrugs, easy. "Of course. Tyler will get it done."

Of course. Why would I ever doubt her random stoner friend? Naturally, he is the best person for the job. "So you guys met in undergrad?"

"Yeah. The dorms, freshman year."

"Sounds like the two of you partied a lot."

Eleanor puts her book down again, this time seeming to give up on reading because she doesn't bother to mark her place. "I mean, it was college. We got high sometimes. Who didn't?"

"I didn't."

She makes a face as she tucks her book back into her bag. "Why does that not surprise me."

Offense taken. I set my fork down and fold my arms. "It's not like I'm totally square—"

"Uh, I'd argue anyone who uses the term *square* absolutely is."

My lips purse. "I didn't have time to fuck around."

Eleanor reaches for her water and stabs viciously at the

ice with her straw. "Right. Because you went to Berklee and no one there smokes pot."

"I didn't say that."

"No, I know what you meant. You were earning a music degree from a prestigious program, and I went to a state school and majored in business and smoked some weed, so obviously you're better than me."

I rear back. "Whoa. That is not what I meant at all."

She tilts her head. "No?"

"I do not think I'm better than you. Jesus. All I'm saying is that I took school really seriously. It was important to me to try to earn my place at a label."

"Whereas I had mine handed to me by Griffin." Eleanor states this in a flat voice, her face void of any emotion. But I can feel her anger simmering under the surface, ready to be unleashed on me as soon as I give her a reason.

Slowly, I blow out a breath. She's not totally off base, is the issue. I have thought that before. It never seemed fair, the way she leaped ahead of the rest of us, even though she objectively had less experience in the industry than most of the other interns. I've grown up enough in the time since to realize it wasn't that cut-and-dried.

I cock an eyebrow at her. "You know how many people think I only got where I am because I'm a nepo baby?"

It doesn't matter that I've been working my ass off since I was sixteen years old, or that I graduated from Berklee with honors, or that I've pulled countless all-nighters scavenging SoundCloud to find new talent. It doesn't matter that I chose to work for a label he never even recorded with. It's always been my primary identifier—Atlas Shaw's son.

"Well. You can't deny it gave you a leg up," Eleanor argues.

"Sure. Yes. But that's not something I've ever leaned on. The man bailed on me and my mom when I was six. I would've preferred if no one knew he was my dad, to be honest."

It was worst when I was first starting out. My dad hadn't put out new music in a while, but he was still very much part of the scene. I was always paranoid I'd run into him at a show or at a club, which of course never happened because he wasn't slumming it at the same venues as broke twenty-one-year-olds. That didn't stop the other interns from kissing my ass, like I was going to invite them over on the weekend and they'd find Atlas hanging around, eager to have a jam session with them. Eleanor was the only one who seemed unimpressed by my connection to a famous artist.

"Look, I don't pretend to know what exactly went on with you and Griffin," I say, choosing my words carefully. "But you did get promoted to a full-time A&R rep after less than six months of interning. Without a relevant degree. You're good at what you do, and I'm not saying you didn't deserve to be recognized for that. Or that I deserved it more. I'm just saying it was fast."

Eleanor's lips press into a flat line. "Yeah. It was fast," she agrees in a tight voice. We settle into silence for a moment, neither of us inclined to pull the thread any harder, I guess. Then her brow pinches. "You really wish people didn't know you were Atlas Shaw's son?"

"Most of the time, yeah." A lot of the time, I wish I weren't his son, period.

"But you kept his last name."

I shrug. "So did my mom. I didn't want a different last name than her."

She seems to consider this for a moment as she swirls her straw around in her water. "I figured . . . I mean, Billy Draper gave you your start."

And Billy was famously my dad's manager for a good chunk of his career. I get how easy it'd be to jump to the wrong conclusion there. "He did. Much to my mother's chagrin."

"Smart lady," Eleanor comments, with this flick of her eyebrow that tells me there's a whole lot more she wants to say.

My foot taps an agitated rhythm on the floor, completely out of sync with the Ice Spice song playing overhead. I'll readily admit that Billy is deeply flawed, but it pisses me off the way industry folks are piling on, bringing up shit he said years and years ago, trying to get him canceled. You'd think Eleanor, of all people, could relate. "He's really not a bad guy."

"*You don't know him like I do*," she mocks. She drinks some water and sets the glass back on the table before meeting my eye again. "I used to say the same thing about Griffin."

"Okay, let's not . . ." I lift both hands, palms out. "I know Billy can be a bit . . . problematic, but they are not the same."

Eleanor picks up her water again and brings the straw to her lips. She takes a sip and holds my stare, completely unmoved.

"Look, Atlas sucked at being a father. We hadn't exchanged more than a handful of words since I was thirteen. But obviously when I was younger, I still wanted him to be in my life. The year after he moved out, my mom wanted to throw me a party for my seventh birthday, but I begged her to let me spend the day with my dad instead. I'd asked him to give me a guitar lesson. My mom hated taking me to his house, but it was my one fucking wish, so they set up a time and she drove me over. But either he forgot, or blew me off for something better—either way I sat there in my mom's car, waiting behind the gate at the bottom of his driveway, for like an hour before my mom convinced me to give up and go home.

"The next day Billy showed up at my mom's house with a guitar from his own collection. He sat down with me and spent the entire afternoon teaching me chords. Then he arranged for me to take lessons. Paid for them until I decided to quit a few years later. I don't even know how he found out Atlas had let me down—my mom didn't tell him, that's for sure. But he stepped in, and he has consistently shown up for me since. Birthdays, school band concerts, and yes, my first job. He's been there, even after my dad fired him and he had no reason to keep in touch."

Eleanor's expression softens a bit, but her response is as pointed as ever: "So you're saying he's your disreputable fairy godfather."

I huff loudly, the sound somewhere between a laugh and a sigh. "That's your takeaway from my very personal and heartwarming story?" The worst part is realizing her description is not wildly off the mark. Billy sort of did become my fucked-up fairy godfather.

"I just think it's a mistake to dismiss professional indiscretions because of your own personal history with someone."

It's not that I *dismiss* anything. I'm fully aware of when Billy steps out of bounds, but I'm capable of being objective. Of using my own judgment.

That said, it's hard to deny that there has been some overlap between my personal and professional relationships with Billy.

I clear my throat and push some of the food around my plate with my fork. "Well. Anyway, it wasn't all about Billy—my mom's disapproval. She didn't want me going to Berklee either."

"Really?"

"She was proud, don't get me wrong. But she tried her best to shield me from the entertainment industry. She would've preferred if I became a doctor, let's put it that way."

Eleanor straightens in her seat. "I know your relationship with Atlas was complicated, but I'm, you know. Sorry for your loss."

I appreciate the fact that she referred to him as *Atlas* instead of *your dad* as much as I appreciate the sentiment. "Thanks." I shrug, trying to convey that I still don't totally know how I feel about it. About all the biographies and articles that keep coming out dissecting his legacy, his music. All the things that made him great, and all the probably true rumors about him being a misogynistic asshole behind the scenes.

Back when I used to get anxious about running into him around LA, I dreaded it and hoped for it in equal measure. Because even when I hated the guy, there was always some tiny part of me that wanted him to not hate me back. Guess that kind of longing is inevitable when your dad walks out on you before you even get a chance to know him. Now he's unavoidable, his picture popping up every time I scroll social media.

"Was he the reason you decided to study music?"

I tip my head back and forth. "Part of it. He got me into music really young."

Admittedly, my memories of quality time with the man

are sparse, given how long ago he peaced out of my life. But music was the only thing he ever cared about, so of course the few memories I do have of spending time with him are centered around that.

"Did you ever want to be a musician yourself?"

"Maybe when I was really little," I say, "but doesn't everyone want to be a rock star when they're that young?" Eventually, I realized I'd inherited most of my dad's features and precisely none of his musical talent. I've always found the behind-the-scenes stuff more interesting anyway. "What about you? What made you want to get into the industry?"

"Oh, I fully wanted to be a pop star," she says with a laugh. "My sister and I stanned the Disney Channel singers so hard. Growing up, my mom put us in pageants and stuff—"

Picturing Eleanor as a pageant girl kind of breaks my brain. "Wait, like, with the frilly dresses? And the creepy doll hair and makeup? And the tiaras?"

"Tiaras are for winners," she says sardonically. "My sister placed first a couple times, but the best I ever got was second runner-up." She waves her hands. "Point is, I quickly realized that I actually hate being the center of attention that way."

I lean back in my seat, overlaying the idea of Eleanor I had in my head with this new information. In a weird way, it tracks. Eleanor commands attention. She's nice to look at and difficult to ignore, and she has that aura of confidence that's sort of . . . captivating. But it never feels like she's actively *trying* to get anyone's attention.

"Always loved music, though. I would spend all the money I was supposed to be saving for college on concert tickets."

"What was the first concert you ever went to?"

Her lips purse. The longer she hesitates, the more excited I get, because clearly the answer is embarrassing.

Finally, her eyes flick somewhere over my shoulder and she huffs and says: "It was Justin Bieber."

"Oh, Eleanor," I say, voice full of mock disappointment.

"I was a literal child, okay?"

"Bieber, though? Really?"

"I mostly went because Iris was really into him—"

Food forgotten, I lean forward and prop my forearms on the table. "Did you have a poster of him in your room?"

Her jaw shifts. "I shared a room with Iris."

"So yes."

"It was *hers*."

"Sure it was." My grin stretches impossibly wider. "Did you fantasize about marrying him? You did, didn't you?"

"My tastes have evolved, is the moral of the story."

"Obviously." I gesture to myself as I lean back again, which earns me one hell of an eye roll. "So why A&R? Instead of becoming a talent manager or producer or something like that?"

She tips her head side to side, considering. "My first boyfriend was in a band."

"And you were a Belieber?"

"The horse is dead already," she says dryly. "They were alt-rock, and he was the drummer."

"Ah." I snap my fingers. "That was my second guess."

"*Anyway*, I essentially acted as his band's manager. It was around then that I started to think about discovering artists and getting to be the one to offer contracts that make someone's dream come true."

It's a straightforward answer, but it throws me all the same. It's just so . . . wholesome. *Making dreams come true.*

I think about the unanswered email sitting in my inbox, the band my rep keeps begging me to take a chance on. I had more time to seek out new artists myself before I got promoted, and I loved that part of the job. But even when I was young and overeager—desperately trying to get someone higher up the food chain to sign an artist I believed in—there was still a certain amount of ego involved. I wanted to be able to say, *I discovered them. I made that happen.*

Eleanor makes it sound like ego has nothing to do with it. Like money and recognition and validation are all incidental to her. I can't figure out if her motives have changed since we were interns or if I had her pegged all wrong before now.

"That makes sense." The dancer onstage finishes, and while one of the bouncers collects the stray bills scattered around the platform, the ambient lighting shifts from red to purple. As another bass-heavy song starts playing and a new girl steps up to the pole, I lean closer to Eleanor and add: "For the record, I don't have a problem with weed. It's just never been my thing."

I've seen too many people fuck up their lives thanks to drugs—my father included—and so I've always stayed away. But last night is proof enough that I'm as susceptible to over-indulging as the next guy.

"Fair enough," Eleanor says. She hesitates for a moment, visibly debating whether to tell me this next bit: "I'm emetophobic. So I'm usually a lot more careful not to get too buzzed."

"Emetophobic," I repeat. "What is that?"

Her shoulders tense, and I get the impression talking about this makes her uncomfortable. Though I'm not sure if that's because it's triggering, or because she feels defensive about it. "It's a fear of vomiting. People tend to think I'm being overdramatic, but it can be sort of debilitating. When I was younger I couldn't even talk about it without spiraling into a panic attack. Tyler actually helped a lot with that. I was terrified of trying weed because I didn't know if it would make me nauseous or what, but he sort of eased me into it. Offered a controlled environment, and it wound up really helping with my anxiety. But yeah, that's why I never would have knowingly mixed alcohol with weed. And why I'm not touching that buffet with a ten-foot pole."

I look down at my own plate. Then I shrug and pick up a chicken wing. "Makes sense."

Eleanor eyes me, wary, like she's waiting for me to tease her, or *well, actually* her about her own phobia, or pull some other dick move. Her opinion of me still isn't very high, I'm pretty sure. Which shouldn't matter, because in all likelihood I won't interact with her again for years, maybe ever, once we leave Vegas and finalize the annulment.

It's a bit of a chronic problem for me, caring too much what other people think.

But I've enjoyed bantering with Eleanor. Enjoyed talking about the heavier stuff too.

I suppose it's not completely out of the realm of possibility that we'll see each other again soon. I don't have a death wish, so I won't be going after any more of her artists. But there's always the chance she'll try to retaliate and come for one of mine. Or maybe we'll run into each other at an awards show. That wouldn't be so bad. It'd be a shame if after all this, we couldn't at least be amicable. Just—not sworn enemies is the main objective here.

I continue to eat in silence until my mouth is on fire from

the hot sauce, then I suck down some water and wipe my hands on a napkin. "So. What exactly does a snowman orgy entail, anyway?"

I'm not sure if it's the weird purple lighting in here, but I could swear she blushes, even as she waves her hand vaguely. "There were a lot of carrots."

This surprises a laugh out of me. Even more surprising—Eleanor returns my smile.

"And you say you don't party," I tease.

She smirks and turns to watch the dancer for a few moments, then glances back to me as I'm licking hot sauce from the pad of my thumb. "Enjoying your strip club meat?"

"Come on." I wipe my mouth and crumple another paper napkin in my fist. "Don't say it like that."

"Hey, you're the one eating it."

"It's actually delicious. Sure you don't want some?"

She looks at the chicken, then back to my face. "Hard pass."

I pick up another wing. "You're missing out."

"Pretty sure the only thing I'll be missing out on is a bout of vomiting in about six hours, but okay."

"Aside from it being strip club meat, I do think you'd like it. They're spicy. I remember you having a high tolerance for heat."

Before Griffin entered the picture and Eleanor stopped eating with the other interns, we would all get lunch from a nearby taco truck at least once a week. Eleanor always doused hers in hot sauce.

I catch her giving me this look, like she wants to comment on that, but before she gets a chance, Tyler is dropping into the empty chair between us.

"All right, kids. I'll just need to see Adam's ID and then we can start signing the forms."

I push my plate to the side and fish my wallet out of my back pocket. I flip it open, fingers stilling when I see the slot that always has my license in it is empty. I frown and start pulling out all the other cards, figuring it must've gotten tucked away in the wrong place. Except it isn't in any of the other card slots either. It isn't anywhere.

I clear my throat and lift my gaze to meet Eleanor's.

She seems to know what I'm going to say before I even open my mouth, and she shakes her head, as though that will somehow stop it from being true.

"So, slight problem. I seem to have misplaced my ID."

CHAPTER SEVEN

ELEANOR

"What do you mean, you *misplaced* your ID?" I ask in a measured voice. "Why isn't it in your wallet?"

"I don't know, Eleanor!" Adam shuffles through his wallet one more time. "There are a lot of things that don't make sense to me right now."

"Okay, well, let's not panic."

Adam is very clearly panicking. It's written all over the guy—he's practically breaking out into a cold sweat. And while this is admittedly the last thing we need right now, it's not quite the crisis Adam is making it out to be.

"Tyler, do you really even need to see it?" I ask. "I mean, you know us."

"I know *you*." He rubs the back of his neck, awkward, and it's all the answer I need. I may not always play by the rules, as Adam has been quick to point out, but I'm not going to put Tyler in a position he's uncomfortable with.

I turn back to Adam. "You didn't lose your wallet. Only the ID is missing, right?"

He nods.

"So most likely, you left it at a bar. We can retrace our steps and try to find it. Worst-case scenario, you'll get Tyler a copy in a few days."

I want this taken care of today as much as Adam does. But the reality is, it won't actually be processed today, whether it gets filed before the courts close in a couple hours or not. It'll take at least a week. I'm not sure if Adam understands that. Or if now is the time to mention it.

"Look, why don't you guys go ahead and sign the forms," Tyler says. "I'll hold on to the paperwork until you recover your ID. You can text me a picture of it for my records."

"Thanks, Ty." I take the pen he's offering and sign everywhere he points, trying not to think too hard about the fact that I'm signing annulment papers in the middle of a strip club because that's just asking for a depression spiral, and I do not have the time.

Adam signs after me, and Tyler taps the papers into a neat stack. "I'm going to take these to my office. I'll come back out in a few to say goodbye, okay?"

"Sounds good."

He heads backstage, back to the quiet of his office, and then there were two.

Adam's plate is nearly empty now, any remaining food gone cold. Without the distraction of Adam eating, and without Tyler here as a buffer, suddenly everything feels more surreal. Sitting here in a strip club with Adam, of all people.

"Thank you."

I lift my gaze to meet his. "For what?"

"Offering to help me track down my ID."

"I don't have much of a choice, do I?" We've cracked a few jokes, had a decent conversation, but that doesn't mean I'm going to drop my guard. It's in my best interest to stay on top of Adam and make sure he doesn't pull any more shit. Not that I can think of any scenario in which sabotaging this annulment would prove beneficial to him. The point is, Dempsey's show is just six hours away; I have to stay vigilant.

I shift my focus away from Adam's frown and watch as one of the dancers who performed earlier comes out to work the floor. She's clearly trying to tempt someone into a lap dance, or maybe a visit to one of the VIP areas behind the heavy velvet curtains toward the back.

She gives Adam a once-over as she saunters past our table, but he doesn't seem to notice. Too busy observing me with this contemplative expression on his face. Like he's trying to read my mind. Which is funny, because he's spent most of today acting as though he already has me figured out.

I've gotten used to that, since leaving Exeter. People hear the rumors, some bastardized version of what went down with Griffin, and that's all they need or want to know.

"I still appreciate it," Adam says. "Even if you don't want to be helping me."

I glance toward the men seated right up against the stage and watch them toss out a few singles. Then I heave a great big sigh and swivel back to face Adam. I don't know why he's picking at this, but if he's looking for confirmation, I'll give it to him. "It's not my first choice of activity. Can you blame me?"

"It's more than that. I get the feeling you still think I'm actively trying to screw you over." He leans forward again.

Elbows on the table, eyes boring into mine. "You may not believe this, but nothing I've done is personal. I really didn't know you were the one having dinner with the guys last night until I saw you there. And maybe crashing was bad form, but I saw an opportunity, and I took it. That's all there is to it. You would have done the same thing in my shoes."

I tap my fingertips against the table. Adam and I never had a rivalry, before he signed Maya. We've always been competitive, though. Even if a part of me had resented Adam for being born with a foot in the door of the music industry, it was plain as day that he worked hard to make a name for himself. We both did. And we both wanted to be the one to discover the next big thing.

I thought I'd done it when I first got my hands on Dempsey's demo. And I distinctly remember Adam's reaction to it.

"If I ask you something, will you give me an honest answer?"

"Maybe." Adam crooks a smile and nods. "Shoot."

"Why do you want to sign Dempsey?"

"What do you mean?" He's gone sort of shifty, no longer holding eye contact with me.

"You don't even like their music," I accuse. "So is it only because you know they can make you money?"

His gaze flashes back to mine. "No. That's—of course I like them."

I raise my eyebrow. "I tried to sign Dempsey for Exeter years ago," I say, pacing my words deliberately. "You said they were unoriginal. And I believe the word you used to describe Curtis's drumming was 'sloppy'?"

I know he remembers his comments as well as I do.

He takes a long drink of water, stalling. "I always liked them," he says eventually.

"You said Freddie Dempsey sounded like an off-brand Kurt Cobain."

Adam sighs through his nose, sounding sheepish. "When you brought in their demo I was just being . . ."

"Jealous?" I supply with a goading smile.

His jaw ticks. "Pretentious."

"That too."

No good can come from continuing to pick at this scab, so I pointedly shift my attention to the stage. The dancer fireman spins down the pole and squats when her heels hit the stage. Her hair is cropped into a blunt bob with bangs. It may or may not be a wig, but either way she's rocking it. And I know for a fact that haircut is not easy to pull off. Iris tried it last summer and spent the entire month of July looking like a thirteen-year-old boy who had just rolled out of bed. She's been desperately growing her bangs out for the wedding ever since.

Adam is still staring at me.

It's a heady thing, holding Adam's attention when there's a topless woman dancing fifteen feet to his left.

I grab my tote bag and push to my feet. "I'm going to use the restroom. Why don't you start looking through any pictures you have from last night, see if you can figure out the name of the bar we went to after the chapel."

Unsurprisingly, since I haven't seen a single woman on the floor besides those who work here, the ladies' room is unoccupied. I pee and wash my hands, and then press my damp palms to my neck. I linger a few extra moments in front of the sinks, if only because it's a momentary escape from the heavy bass and flashing lights and Adam's not-altogether-unflattering attention. It's not exactly an oasis in here, though, so I give myself a stern reminder that Adam is the competition and it's wholly irrelevant that his stare makes something spark across my skin, and then I head back to the table.

When I get there, Tyler is in Adam's seat. "Where's Adam?"

Tyler gestures behind him. "He needed to make a few calls to follow up on the ID. No phones allowed on the floor, so he went outside."

I nod and slide into the chair across from him. It's far from silent in here, but it feels distinctly uncomfortable all the same, now that Tyler and I are alone and without any specific business to discuss. He's ditched his tie and rolled his shirtsleeves up to his elbows, making him look decidedly more laid-back than I feel.

"Wow, I sort of wish we could get stoned right now."

"Technically, we could," Tyler offers, but he seems to know I'm not actually up for it.

"I'm sorry," I say after a moment. "That I didn't let you know I was going to be in town."

Tyler gives an easy shrug, slouched low in his chair. "No worries. I know you were here on business."

That may be true, but it's also pretty obvious at this point that if this bullshit with Adam hadn't happened, I would've had plenty of downtime. I should've called. But the truth is, Tyler never even crossed my mind until I needed something from him, which makes me feel supremely shitty.

"Still. I should've reached out sooner." I should have reached out a long, long time ago.

But again, Tyler waves this off, because he is too nice.

"How've you been?" Something about the way he tips his head tells me he already knows the answer.

It's a relief, not having to pretend everything is perfect for once. Not that my friends and family back home wouldn't support me if they knew I've been struggling. They would. My sister would gently suggest I take some time off to "complete my healing journey." My mom would offer to let me come home for a little while, just until I get my feet back under me.

But I've given them no indication that I'm going through a hard time. In fact, I've put all of my effort into convincing everyone I'm living my best life.

Given the circumstances, I don't think I could pull that off right now, even if I had the energy to try.

"I've been better." I swallow and reach for my water glass, even though there's only melting ice left. I fidget with the straw. "Things were okay for a while, after Griffin. I went to work for a different label, and I like it there a lot. But I might get fired soon? So that's a bummer."

I've always hated seeing Tyler frown. He's such a mellow guy, it just doesn't look right on his face. "What makes you think you might get fired?"

I let go of my straw and cross my arms. "My boss sat me down a couple of months ago and gave me a list of things I needed to work on before the end of the fiscal year—which is in like two weeks. I've tried, but . . ." I shrug.

Tyler makes a considering noise. "Well, what about life outside of work?"

I can't help it. I laugh. "Uh, things aren't going much better in that regard."

The food was cleared from our table while I was in the

restroom. Tyler rests his hand right where Adam's plate was, fingers tap-tap-tapping while he stares at me, and I know he's not a prosecutor, but it feels like some kind of intimidation tactic. Like he's waiting for me to spill my guts.

"Ever since the Griffin thing, I've tried *so hard* to make sure everyone thinks I'm thriving. Especially Iris and my mom. And the more time passes and the worse things get, the harder it is to admit that I'm broke, and that work—the part of my life I've prioritized above all my personal relationships and made all these sacrifices for—has been going downhill. So instead I keep faking it, and doing stupid shit like buying my sister the designer wedding gown she had her heart set on, that my mother couldn't afford."

It didn't matter that I couldn't afford it either. What mattered was that she believed the lie I've been cultivating for years now—that I'm successful and that I don't need anyone's help.

Across the table, Tyler lets out a slow exhale. "I wish I'd known you were having such a rough go. I feel bad I haven't been there for you."

"Well. That's hardly your fault, is it?"

I have never, not once in all the years I've known him, felt judged by Tyler. Not when I went through my phase of refusing to wear a coat out to parties, even when it was in the single digits or blizzarding in the part of Michigan where we attended college. Not even at the height of my social media addiction sophomore year, when I attempted to go viral with a video of me looking like an absolute fool doing a choreographed dance to a song I wouldn't be caught dead listening to now. He was probably silently judging me, to be fair. But he never made me *feel* judged, and that's what counts.

All that said, it was very clear he never approved of Griffin. And, like, I get it. In hindsight, I also do not approve of my decision to get involved with the man. I've invested a lot of time and money in therapy trying to figure out whether I would've been better off if I'd never met Griffin, or at least if I'd never slept with him. I'm still not sure of the answer.

But Tyler visited LA when I was in the thick of it. Right when things were turning bad, but not yet so bad that I was ready to leave. It was sunk-cost fallacy at work.

Unlike me, Tyler was considerate enough to reach out ahead of time so we could make plans while he was in town. I wound up inviting him over to Griffin's house. I'd been spending a lot of time there, because Griffin wanted me to, and because it was a literal mansion in the Hills, whereas I lived in a run-down one-bedroom apartment in Studio City.

We were hanging out by the pool when Griffin came home. I can still picture his smile while he shook Tyler's hand, can feel the kiss he pressed to the crown of my head as he draped his arms over the back of my chair. I remember how red his face got a little while later, when I told him I couldn't come to the dinner he'd sprung on me because I'd made plans with Tyler—plans he *knew* about. But we were standing in his kitchen, on his turf, which somehow made it seem like he had a right to tell me I had to cancel, because this was his biggest client, and he wanted me there, needed me there—*This is a huge opportunity for you, Eleanor; you'd be an idiot to pass it up.*

Holding my ground would only lead to an even bigger fight later, and the prospect of dealing with Griffin when he was that angry had my anxiety spiking. So I backed down, and I let Griffin walk me outside, to where Tyler was waiting by the pool. I couldn't tell how much of our argument Tyler had heard, whether he saw it coming when I made my excuses and bailed on our plans. He didn't get mad, or try to change my mind. He simply told me that we'd catch up again soon.

But then, of course, we didn't.

It makes me cringe, thinking about how long it took for me to finally accept Griffin was an irredeemable bastard. And cringe harder, being confronted with another lasting impact he's had on my life.

Shame sits heavy on my shoulders. I shift in my seat, trying to shake it off. "I'm glad we're getting the chance to reconnect now."

"Me too," Tyler says, folding both arms on the table. "Speaking of which, are you ever going to tell me the rest of the story from last night?"

"What are you talking about?"

"Let's start with the sex and then work our way back. Was it good? Adam's built like a runner; I bet he has great stamina."

"Holy shit, we did not have sex." I glance around, flustered by the abrupt change in topic, but no one within earshot seems to care about us. Obviously, we are not the main attraction at this venue. "Nothing happened."

My gaze drops to my bag. I resist the urge to peek at the photo from the chapel. That kiss doesn't count.

"You two really aren't a thing?"

I snort. "God, no."

"Well, as your wingman—"

"Pretty sure you stopped being my wingman like six years ago."

"—I feel obligated to point out that if you *were* interested in him, this is kind of the perfect opportunity to hook up. I don't know if you've heard, but what happens in Vegas stays in Vegas." He wags his eyebrows ludicrously.

"I'm sorry, have you forgotten why I'm here? I'm still actively trying to fix the mistakes I've already made."

Tyler holds a palm up. "My point exactly. You already messed up, so what's the harm in having some fun with it?"

I sputter for a moment, then latch on to the first argument that comes to mind. "Wouldn't fucking Adam make it so we couldn't get an annulment anyway?"

"Bah." Tyler waves his hand. "I can do a workaround."

"Okay, well. It's moot, because I'm not into him. In case you haven't noticed, he's an asshole. And I've sworn off assholes. I feel like you of all people should be supporting me on this."

Tyler shifts again, propping his chin in the L of his hand. He never was capable of sitting still unless he was stoned. "I'm not saying you have to marry the guy."

"Oh, ha ha." I fish an ice cube out of my glass and throw it at him. He dodges it gleefully.

"You're really going to tell me you're not even a little bit interested?"

"I'm not."

Tyler's got his shit-eating grin on again. "You want to climb him like a tree."

Everything I say, Tyler is just going to twist around. I cross my arms and give him a flat look.

"All I'm saying is I picked up on some tension there." Tyler holds his hands up in surrender. "And you know as well as I do how much fun a hate fuck can be. Remember my roommate sophomore year?"

"Oh god, Bobby. He was so obnoxious."

Tyler laughs. "He was. And yet, I seem to remember the two of you sexiling me for an entire night that one time."

I roll my eyes skyward and briefly consider firing Tyler and finding another attorney to handle this. I bite my straw and suck down the little bit of melted ice at the bottom of my glass while Tyler mercifully changes the subject to what he might get from the buffet. My phone buzzes on the table. It's a text from Adam, asking me to meet him outside.

I relay the message to Tyler, and when we both stand up he draws me in for a full-body hug.

I can't fathom why he seems so invested in the prospect of Adam and me fucking. But I have to admit, I missed this—the casualness of a friendship that goes back years. Having enough history with someone that you can joke with them, say what you want without running every thought through a filter first. Without worrying what it will make you sound like. I feel unburdened in a way I never would have predicted when I walked into this strip club.

"Missed you, buddy," I tell him as I step back.

"Missed you too. Don't disappear on me again."

"Promise." I blame the hangover, but I find myself getting weirdly emotional at the prospect of saying goodbye to Tyler, even though we'll be in touch soon enough about the annulment. I shake my head and quickly press fingers under my lashes. "Okay. Time to go."

"Go ride Adam's cock into the sunset?"

Jesus.

"Enjoy your lunch," I say as I start to back away. "Don't choke on any congealed mac 'n cheese."

"Enjoy your hate sex. Don't choke on Adam's—"

Despite the fact he is clearly immune to my wrath, I shoot Tyler the middle finger. He cuts off with a giggle, and I'm left stumbling toward the exit, scrambling to think about literally anything other than Adam's dick.

It's a jarring transition, stepping out of the club and back into the light of day. I wince and raise my hand to shield my eyes from the glare as I walk over to Adam, who is hovering a few yards away from the entrance.

I tell myself to compartmentalize. Tuck the conversation I had with Tyler away to think about later. "Any luck?"

"Yeah. I looked through my pictures from last night like you suggested. We were holding microphones in a few of them, so I called around and found my ID at a karaoke bar across town. I already ordered an Uber."

"Excellent." I dig through my purse until I find my sunglasses, which I shove onto my face before asking: "Why don't you look happier?"

A car pulls into the parking lot and Adam gestures for me to follow. We slide into the back seat and he greets the driver and confirms our destination before turning back to me.

"There's an unrelated issue." He frowns and hands me his phone. Which is cued up with a picture of us feeding each other bites of cake. The three-tier monstrosity is blurry in the background. A wedding cake.

The most disturbing part is not that one of my fingers appears to be in Adam's mouth, but that this picture is posted to the events account of the hotel Adam's staying at.

"I've already untagged myself so it's off my feed—"

"They *tagged* us in it?"

My anxiety has been on the rise all morning. Sometimes it's like my own heartbeat—always there, but easy to ignore until something sets it off, and then suddenly I'm hyper-aware of it pulsing through my body. I've been ignoring it for hours now, focused on dealing with the annulment. Maybe because that's handled and I let my guard down with Tyler, or maybe because I drank tap water from a strip club and am now probably going to get norovirus—whatever the reason, I can't ignore it anymore. My chest is tightening and my lungs won't fill all the way anymore, no matter how deeply I try to breathe.

"It was posted less than an hour ago," Adam says. "I highly doubt anyone has seen it. But you need to untag yourself before they do."

I reach into my bag for my own phone, then freeze. "I can't."

"Uh, why the hell not?"

I cover my eyes with both hands. "I deleted all my social apps from my phone. And I don't have any of my passwords memorized."

"Can't you do a password reset?"

"Theoretically, yes. But . . . my personal email isn't syncing to my phone right now. I've been meaning to fix that."

"So your phone is basically a brick," Adam says, exasperated.

"It's a *phone*. I just need it to make calls."

"You sound like my grandmother, oh my god." He drags both hands down his face. "Who deletes social media?" he mutters, mostly to himself I think.

"It was supposed to be beneficial for my mental health!"

My therapist recommended it. The idea was that less

screen time would help me sleep better, and that cutting out socials would help me focus on my own goals rather than making comparisons to strangers on the internet. It would also prevent me from lurking on Griffin's socials, which I have, at my lowest points, been known to do. We all collectively know that social media is terrible, so dropping it seemed like a great idea at the time. I was actually proud of myself for following through. And this morning, it had seemed like a saving grace. One less thing to worry about, because god only knows what kind of nonsense my drunk ass would've posted last night if I'd had access.

He takes his phone back to glare at the photo some more. I watch as he sends the account a DM asking them to remove the photo.

"What is that even from? Did we have a reception?"

"How would that even be possible?" Adam shakes his head, wearing an adorably confused expression that scrunches his nose. ". . . I do vaguely remember licking an ice sculpture, though."

"Okay, I don't know what to do with that information," I tell him as I pull out my own phone. I may not be able to untag myself, but I can certainly track down the social media manager for the resort and make sure they delete the post.

I've managed to navigate my way through the hotel's website to the phone number I need when an alert pops up that I have a new message from Josie. I tap over to it and my stomach pitches as I scan through it.

Hey E—
Nora relayed your message, but if you have a moment before the show, I'd love to hear how last night's dinner

went. I'm sure you'll let me know as soon as you have any updates, or if you need anything from me in the meantime.
—J

The phrasing is gentle enough, but I know how to read between the lines with Josie by now. She's irritated with me, and I can't pretend I don't understand why. Increased transparency and communication came up in my last performance evaluation.

A small voice in the back of my head—one that sounds suspiciously like my therapist's—is whispering that this might qualify as another side effect of the two years I spent under Griffin's thumb. The urge to hide my failures. To fix things on my own. It's nothing new. But I'm not avoiding Josie. I *am* going to call her. I just want to have good news when I do.

By the time I realize what a supremely bad idea it is to spend the entire cab ride staring at my phone screen, it's too late.

Nausea hits me all at once, my mouth flooding with saliva and a cold sweat climbing up my spine. I drop my phone into my bag and hastily roll down my window. My gaze snags on the ring on my finger, which somehow I'd forgotten about for a minute, and I tug ruthlessly at it, but still can't get it over my knuckle.

We're stuck in stop-and-go traffic, and the stagnant air carries a smell of exhaust that only makes it harder to breathe. We turn and traffic lets up, finally affording more of a breeze through the window. But by the time we pull up to the curb in front of the bar, I'm breathing through my mouth and have the strap of my bag in a choke hold. I scramble out of the back seat as quickly as possible while Adam thanks the driver.

Instead of going inside the bar, which likely smells like stale beer and liquor, I press my back against the brick wall of the building. My hands shake as I paw through my purse for my emergency stash of antiemetics. I never go on a trip without Zofran. Especially not one involving a plane ride. I know I packed some. Except I have looked in every single interior pocket of this fucking bag, and it isn't here. I find hand sanitizer and three different lip balms and a Tide To Go stick and a tampon, but not the one thing I goddamn need.

I'm practically dumping the entire contents of my bag out onto the concrete sidewalk when I sense Adam hovering over me.

"Uh . . . everything okay?"

"I'm fine," I insist. I haven't thrown up in years. I have white-knuckled my way through the flu and two separate stomach bugs. A hangover and a social media post will not be my undoing. I am *fine*.

My breath is coming faster—too fast—and my eyes are starting to burn with the press of tears, but finally I find the Zofran packet, inexplicably tucked inside my sunglasses case. I hurry to punch out a tab and stick it under my tongue. I'm crouched on the sidewalk, palms over my closed eyes as I swish my tongue back and forth and wait for it to dissolve.

When I open my eyes again, Adam is right there. Crouched beside me with his hands clasped between his spread knees and this expression on his face like he's a little afraid to approach me.

Which makes sense, because I probably resemble a feral raccoon. I'm still too keyed up to even feel embarrassed about that, though I suspect the humiliation will come later, once the anxiety recedes. For now, I focus on evening out my breath.

"Do you want me to get you some water?" Adam asks in a gentle voice. "Or call someone? My mom is a nurse, actually; she usually knows what to—"

"No, just. Shut up." I squeeze my eyes shut.

The only person I want to talk to right now is Iris. She always knows exactly what to say to bring me down from a panic attack, and I try to summon her voice in my head, pretend she's here with me. I could call her, and given how much she's been texting today, she'd probably pick up. But then I'd have to explain why I'm having a panic attack in the middle of a Las Vegas sidewalk, and as soon as I knock down one domino, the rest will fall, and I'll have to tell her not only about Adam but about work and bills, and then she'll feel like shit for borrowing money even though it was my idea to give it to her.

Adam shifts. He's quiet for all of ten seconds before he says, "So, should I go?"

"No!" I shout, the idea of being left alone abhorrent to me right now.

"Okay," he says, sounding a bit panicked himself. "I don't know what to do."

"Stay there. Don't talk."

Adam does exactly that, sitting down on the dirty sidewalk next to me. He leaves a couple of inches of space between us, careful not to touch me, but close enough that even with my eyes closed I can feel his presence.

My hands are still trembling when I grab my earbuds and phone, pulling up my calming playlist and hitting play on my safe song I always listen to during attacks. The second time through, I'm able to breathe a bit deeper again. I'm stable enough that when Adam speaks—offering again to get me a glass of ice water from inside the bar—I nod.

His hotel slippers shuffle back into view before the track ends. He crouches in front of me and carefully passes over the glass. I take a few sips, the cold condensation against my palms distracting me enough I manage to even out my breathing. I catch an ice cube between my teeth and suck on it, focusing on that sensation and nothing else.

I crunch the melting ice between my back molars and pull out one earbud. "I'm okay now," I tell him. "You can go inside."

He hesitates, his eyes tightening in the corners, like he still expects me to pass out or something.

"I'll be right there," I say before he has a chance to ask if I'm sure. "I'm just going to call the resort and get ahold of that social media manager."

My tone leaves no room for arguing, and so Adam nods once and stands up. His hands slip into the pockets of his shorts. "All right. See you inside, then."

Once I'm alone, I tip my head back against the brick facade and blow out another long breath. I'm exhausted, craving a nap the way I always do after an episode like this. The only upside is that I'm too worn out to care that Adam keeps seeing me at my worst.

In fact, I realize it doesn't bother me as much as I'd expect, that Adam was here to witness my panic attack. Maybe it's the fact that we got into this mess together, or the fact that he's still wearing those horrendous slippers. But in this moment, more than anything else, I'm grateful he was here.

CHAPTER EIGHT

ADAM

I'm reluctant to leave Eleanor alone while she's still recovering from her anxiety attack, or whatever that just was, but I like to think I've become somewhat adept at interpreting body language over the years, and hers is reading loud and clear as *back the fuck off, thanks.*

I get it. I'm not exactly her favorite person. Makes sense she wouldn't want to be vulnerable in front of me. At least not any more than she has to be, given the circumstances. Anyway, she's fierce to the point of it being borderline scary. She can take care of herself. So I glance back at her only once more before pulling open the door and stepping into the bar.

I had hoped returning to the karaoke bar might jog my memory. But as I take in the curved booths lining one side, the glass-walled private rooms in the back, all I get are flashes. Eleanor with a microphone in one hand, the other high in the air as she belts out a Britney Spears song from fifteen years ago. Me, serenading her with a Chappell Roan banger, and thinking that on my knees in front of Eleanor wasn't a bad place to be.

It's funny. I remember us being good. Amazing, even. In reality we probably sounded like a couple of stray cats screaming in a back alley somewhere. Can't speak for Eleanor, but I'm not the strongest vocalist even on my best day. I can carry a tune all right, at least when I'm sober. But that drunk? I likely couldn't have found the right pitch with a map.

I knuckle my glasses up the bridge of my nose and shuffle over to the bar. The bartender looks up as I approach and I give him a nod. "Hey. I called earlier, about leaving my license here?"

He wipes his hands on the bar rag over his shoulder. "What was your name again?"

"Adam Shaw."

He turns and plucks my ID and a receipt from a tumbler by the register. Fucking finally, something is going my way.

He keeps hold of the ID and slides the paper over to me. I hold up the receipt and nearly have a stroke. It says we racked up a bill of over two thousand dollars. "This is a joke, right?"

"Do I look like I'm joking?" the bartender replies in a flat voice. And yeah, no. I'm not convinced this guy has ever cracked a joke in his life.

I huff a sigh, and then pull out my wallet. I'm too out of sorts to negotiate with this surly motherfucker. I just want to get my ID so I can get my annulment and focus on more important things, like doing my job. I pass him my credit card and try not to question every choice in my life that's led me to this point while he rings it up.

It's not until the machine beeps angrily that I remember. The card is frozen.

"Shit," I say, as the bartender holds the card out between his middle and index fingers. I take it and he crosses his arms, a look on his face like I'm trying to scam him on purpose. "Uh. Let me make a call real quick."

I pull out my phone and call my credit card company. I navigate the automatic menu and am put through to a customer service rep named Peter, who I'm pretty sure is actually a bot. Peter the bot tells me a purchase at a pawnshop last night was flagged as suspicious—fair enough—and that they sent me an automated text message alert asking me to confirm whether I had made the transaction. Evidently, I replied indicating they should cancel the card instead.

"That was a mistake. Uncancel," I say. Then, louder: "Un-fucking-cancel, *Peter*."

"Uh . . ."

My spine straightens, a hot flush rushing up the back of my neck.

"Sorry, Mr. Shaw, there's not really anything we can do once the card has been deactivated."

"No, yeah, that's—I get that." I squeeze my eyes shut and pinch the bridge of my nose. "I apologize for being so rude. I . . . thought you were AI."

". . . nope. I'm a man." Another awkward silence stretches out between us. "So we've sent a new card to the address on file, and it should arrive in five to seven business days."

"Fantastic," I grumble.

"Is there anything else I can do for you today?"

I'm still wondering what I could have possibly bought at a pawnshop last night, and am about to ask if Peter can provide any more information on that, when it hits me: the rings. “No,” I say with a sigh. “Nothing else.”

“Okay. Thank you for calling, have a great day.”

The line goes dead. I nod and slowly lower the phone. After a deep breath, which does not diminish the urge to find a wall to punch, I turn back to the bartender. Who, judging by the unimpressed look he’s giving me, heard enough from my side of that conversation to understand the situation.

Before I can come up with something to sway him, Eleanor comes striding in. My gaze sweeps over her, clocking her stiff posture and the way her skin still looks a bit too pale. But she lifts her chin and sidles up next to me, shooting me a steady look that almost reads as a dare. Like she’s waiting for me to coddle her, so she can go ahead and bite my head off for it. The worst possible thing I can do right now is give Eleanor the impression I pity her. Which I don’t. I just . . . didn’t love seeing her like that. The way she curled her knees into her chest, made herself small. The way her hands shook. It was so backward from her usual confidence, like seeing a seasoned musician suddenly develop stage fright.

In the end, I settle on a gruff: “You good?”

The relief is easy to read in her expression, and she nods once in response as she sets her empty water glass on the bar. “All set here?”

“Not exactly.” I make a pained face. “You want the good news or the bad news first?”

Her expression turns to stone. “You’re kidding me.”

“Sadly, no. I’ve solved the mystery of where that bottle of Lagavulin came from.”

She takes a measured breath. Her hand is fisted on top of the bar, and I get the sense she’s barely restraining herself from turning around and flipping a table. "Okay. And the bad news?"

"Turns out we didn't pay for it." I straighten and slide the tab over for her to see.

"Fuckkk."

"And I sorta need you to take care of the bill." When Eleanor's head whips up, I tack on: "Please."

Despite my use of the magic word, this does not appear to go over well.

She laughs a bit incredulously. "Excuse me?"

"Look, I'll reimburse you for my half—"

"Your *half*? Why should I pay any of it?"

"Pretty sure I didn't drink an entire bottle by myself, Eleanor." This, she doesn't argue. I'm not in the mood to argue either. "Look, I can reimburse you for all of it, but not until we get home. My credit card is still frozen, and the company said I have to wait for my new one to come in the mail. He won't give me back my ID until we settle the tab."

Eleanor's gaze sinks back to the receipt. I fully expect her to cave at this point, because there's no real alternative, but she taps her painted nails against the bar and shakes her head.

She doesn't quite look me in the eye when she speaks again. "I can't pay it."

I'm ready for another round of the blame game, but her tone throws me off. She's not being belligerent. And I realize: she isn't saying she won't pay it. She's saying she *can't*.

"Oh."

"I've been traveling a lot for work, and I haven't submitted all my reimbursements yet," she goes on. "So I only have about a hundred dollars in my debit account right now. And the other night when I was on Ambien, I sleep-shopped and bought like three pairs of shorts from Bergdorf's. I returned them, obviously, because no one needs one pair of sequined hot pants, let alone *three*, but they haven't credited me for that yet either. Plus, my sister's wedding is coming up, and I'm the maid of honor, so there have been a lot of expenses this past month, and . . . long story short, my credit card is maxed out."

All of this is said with an edge of defensiveness, like Eleanor fully expects me criticize her for not turning in her expense reports on time. Or maybe she thinks I can't relate—that because my dad is who he is, I've always had money. But the biggest issue Mom had with my dad postdivorce was that he was inconsistent at best when it came to paying child support. I know what it's like to be strapped for cash.

"Can we use your debit card?" she asks.

"It's not in my wallet."

"I thought you said you'd only lost your ID?"

"No—I left my debit card at home. I haven't used it in forever. I'm not sure I even remember my PIN."

Eleanor holds a hand up. "Wait, I'm sorry. You gave me shit for not knowing my social media passwords, and you don't even know your own PIN number?"

My jaw twitches. "It's PIN, not PIN number."

The look she sends me in reply is so scathing, I instinctively draw back a half step. "Point is, I only ever use it at ATMs, but I rarely need cash. Usually, I Venmo people."

"So then Venmo me," she grinds out.

I clear my throat. "Can't do that either. There's a weekly limit to how much they let you transfer, and since I pay my rent through Venmo, I've already hit that. . . ."

Eleanor's lips are pressed so tight together, I get the sense it's all she can do to hold in a scream. Relatable.

The bartender seems to have reached the end of his patience with us and ambles over, saving me from having to say anything at all. "You figure something out?"

"We're still working on it," I tell him.

"What's your name?" Eleanor asks as she leans her forearms on the bar.

"Mark."

"Mark," she repeats, "maybe you could help me out." She smiles and bites her bottom lip. Somehow she manages to make her eyes look Bambi-big. Right now there is zero evidence that she just had a panic attack. It would seem Eleanor is a master at compartmentalizing.

"My friend and I have been having the worst day," she goes on. "You can't even imagine."

I look from her to the bartender, to see if any of this is working on him. He appears remarkably unswayed.

"Is there any way you could give us a discount? Or maybe you could copy down his address, so you know where to bill him?"

The bartender coughs a laugh. "Nice try."

Eleanor straightens and her eyes go back to normal, if not a bit more narrowed than usual.

"You're not getting your ID until you shore up. If you need cash, there's a pawnshop down the block." Mark gestures to where my wrist rests on the bar top. I cover my watch protectively with my opposite hand.

Over my dead body am I pawning this watch. It belonged to my dad. It's pretty much the only thing I have of his. Mom got rid of most of his stuff after he split, and all of his guitars and other memorabilia got sold at auction after he died.

I drag a hand over my mouth. "Excuse us for a minute."

Mark rolls his eyes and goes back to stacking glasses while I drag Eleanor across the bar.

"Is there someone you could ask to loan you the money? What about your sister?"

Eleanor crosses her arms. "Iris is getting married in a week. She will lose her mind if she finds out about this."

"Okay . . . but couldn't you just not tell her the reason?"

"Look. You don't have any siblings, right?"

That I know of. And probably if there were any half-siblings out there to know about, they would've come out of the woodwork by now. I shake my head.

"Well, I don't know if it's a sister thing, or an Iris thing. Maybe it's because we shared a room for sixteen years. Whatever the reason, I cannot keep a secret from her. Like, I physically cannot. The only way to keep a secret from Iris is to avoid her altogether, but if I reach out to ask for a loan, she will ask questions, and she will keep asking until I crack."

I'm not sure if she intended to make her sister sound terrifying, but she has.

"Besides," Eleanor goes on, "she doesn't have this kind of money either. Things are tight with the wedding. How about *you* ask someone?"

The only people I can think of are Billy and my mom. Billy is no stranger to a bender, so it's not like he'd necessarily judge me for letting things get out of hand last night. But this nonsense has nothing to do with the band, and therefore has nothing to do with Billy. I'd like to keep it that way. As for my mother? I'm twenty-eight; I'm supposed to be making her life easier at this point, not running to her with my problems like I did when I was a kid. Aside from that, she's nosy as fuck. If Eleanor thinks Iris would wheedle the story out of her, my mother would do it faster. And then she'd either have a heart attack or insist I bring Eleanor with me when I go over to her house for dinner Sunday night.

"Unless you want to get roped into meeting your mother-in-law, I think it's best not to involve my family."

I glance down at my watch again, and then cut my gaze over to Eleanor's hand.

"We need to get that fucking ring off."

We wind up in one of the gender-neutral bathrooms together, in an attempt to have some semblance of privacy. When the door snicks shut behind us, Eleanor steps up to the mirror. I watch as she runs a finger under her lashes to wipe away smudged mascara.

I have the urge to tell her she looks good—that she always looks good—but Eleanor likely doesn't need or want my approval, so I bite it back and wait for her to turn around again.

She runs her hand under the sink and tries to twist her ring off under the tap, her sharp elbow aimed at me as she lets out a frustrated huff.

"Let me try." I step closer, and Eleanor turns and leans back against the porcelain edge of the sink. She holds her hand out between our bodies, slides it into my waiting palm.

A charge zings up my arm, and I realize this is the first time we've actually touched since this morning, when Eleanor kicked me out of bed. Which brings to mind a fact that I've been steadfastly ignoring ever since: that we slept in the same bed. Which means Eleanor *invited me* to sleep in her bed. Sure, nothing more happened, but it makes me wonder, if we'd been more sober, whether something could have. Whether that was or ever would be on the table.

I blink hard and adjust my glasses before touching the ring. I give it an experimental tug.

"Ow. Fucking *ow*."

"Sorry!" I let go immediately, but apparently it still wasn't fast enough, because Eleanor swats my arm with her opposite hand.

"That hurt."

"Sorry," I repeat again, a bit softer.

Eleanor deflates a bit, shoulders rounding in defeat. "Can't we go to a fire station or something and have them cut it off?"

"We're not going to cut a platinum band. We'll get nothing for it if we do."

She holds her hand up to inspect the ring. "How do you know what kind of metal it is?"

I give her a look like, *please*. "I wouldn't buy anything but platinum."

Her nose wrinkles, and she mumbles something under her breath that sounds a lot like *pretentious*. "Well, we might have to. It's clearly not coming off."

My hands rest on my hips. "How is it stuck? The ring obviously fit fine twelve hours ago."

"Well, now I'm bloated. I ate god knows how many fried things last night and it's hot outside. My fingers are swollen. I don't know what you want me to tell you."

"Do you have any lube?"

She blinks at me. "Why the fuck would I be carrying around lube?"

". . . Preparedness?"

"Jesus." She turns and shakes her head, almost like she's looking into an invisible camera somewhere. "No, Adam, I do not have any lube."

I gesture to her giant tote bag. "You've got to have something useful in there."

She rifles around and comes up with a tube of sunscreen. "It's not lube, but . . . this is the best I can do."

Worth a try. I gesture with two fingers for her to hand me the bottle, which she does, before hopping up to perch on the edge of the porcelain sink. She holds her left hand out for me to take and braces her right hand behind her. I step closer, so I'm slotted between her knees. I squeeze out a bit of the lotion onto her knuckle, careful not to let it drip onto her clothes. I dab it around a bit with the pads of my fingers.

"Tell me if this hurts, okay?"

She nods, which is somewhat unnecessary, because she made it quite clear last time that she has no problem speaking up when it hurts.

I twist the ring around her finger a few times before I pull. I keep my gaze fixed on her face, searching for any sign of discomfort. Because regardless of what I said before, she's right. We can always go get the damn thing cut off. It's not worth hurting her over.

Eleanor lifts her head and we're face-to-face. It's a ridiculous situation—locked in the bathroom of a bar together while an old Tom Petty song plays over the tinny speakers, trying to remove a wedding band she never should have been wearing in the first place. But for a moment, the details go hazy, swept toward the back of my mind. My focus has narrowed to the tiny freckle on Eleanor's top lip, barely noticeable unless you're standing close enough to kiss it.

The ring slips over her knuckle.

I drop my gaze, nearly fumbling the slippery metal. I catch it and hold it between my thumb and forefinger. "Got it."

Eleanor sucks in a breath and I step back. She wipes her hand against her thigh, getting rid of the sunscreen—the last bit of evidence that she ever wore a ring on that finger.

The nearest pawnshop happens to be one specializing in jewelry. I'm wholly unsurprised when they offer us half of what my credit card record shows we paid last night. Eleanor all but elbows me out of the way to haggle with the guy, which seems like a waste of breath to me—the shop has case after case of rings on display. I doubt he's going to budge on price.

I leave Eleanor to it and wander down the counter a ways, taking in all the random stuff they have for sale. There are a few nice guitars hanging up behind the counter—a Gibson and a couple of Fender Stratocasters. I linger in front of one of the Strats, a three-color Sunburst with a maple fingerboard. My dad played one just like it early on in his career, before he upgraded to the Les Paul that became his signature instrument. Sometimes I wonder what happened to that first guitar, the one he made it big playing on. When a bunch of his memorabilia went up for auction, I kept an eye out for that particular guitar. I figured it wasn't worth nearly as much as his others, and if I lived off Top Ramen for a while and maybe sold a couple of my more valuable records, I might be able to afford to buy it. But it wasn't included in his estate. Most likely, he gifted it to someone along the way. That or he played it into the ground. Still, I see one that looks so similar, even though this Strat is in too good of condition to possibly be his, and I'm always tempted.

What I told Eleanor back at the club was the truth—I never wanted to follow in his footsteps, exactly. I don't want to be my dad, or really anything like him.

My mother wasn't one to offer up stories about the version of him she knew, before he hit it big—not the kind of stories I wanted to hear, anyway. They were mostly together before the digital age, and while I'm sure photos of them do exist—or did, once—Mom didn't keep any evidence of him around the house. Which meant the only way I could try to know him was the same way as the rest of the English-speaking world: through his music.

So no, I didn't want to follow his path. But there's no denying he was a big part of why I got into music.

I turn my wrist, just to feel the metal watchband shift against my skin, and drag myself away from the display.

When I finish a loop around the cramped store, Eleanor has reached an agreement with the owner. Fifty whole dollars above his original offer. She looks extremely satisfied at having worn him down, even if it still leaves us about a thousand dollars below what we need to pay off the bar tab.

"How do you propose we pay for the rest?" I ask once we've collected our money.

"What about your company card?"

"I don't think—"

"You were the one who said you're only in Vegas for business. And we both know Exeter has deep pockets. Just expense it."

"No way. Cab fare and coffee is one thing. But an expense that big, dated today, is going to raise red flags." The kinds of red flags the label is actively looking for, these days. Over the past year they've proven they have no problem firing anyone who garners a bad reputation. Look at Griffin Hastings—he was executive level, had been with the label for the better part of two decades, and primarily because of his relationship with Eleanor (and a couple of other workplace indiscretions that cropped up in the aftermath) he was ousted. They've been cleaning house, getting rid of anyone who demonstrates any moral ambiguity, as they should. I don't want to work with fuckers like Griffin. I certainly don't want to be someone HR has to keep an eye on. "The dead last thing I want is for anyone to find out about this and think you and I are involved."

I'm made aware of how dickish that sounded when I catch Eleanor flinch. A tiny crease between her eyebrows, a downward pull of her mouth. She blinks and that quietly stunned expression is wiped clean away.

"Shit, I didn't mean—"

"No, I get it." Eleanor shrugs. She is radiating indifference, to the point where I start to wonder if I imagined the wounded look she wore a moment ago. "I don't want anyone thinking we're together either."

I wince hearing it repeated back to me. I open my mouth to explain that it wasn't about her, or her reputation, but before I can parse the right words, Eleanor is spinning on her heel and walking away.

"Let's just get this picture taken offline, yeah? We'll figure out the rest later."

My throat tightens around everything I can't figure out how to say. In the end, the only thing I can do is trail after her.

CHAPTER NINE

ELEANOR

Griffin and I slept together for the first time on a Monday night. Which meant the morning after, I couldn't lounge in his luxurious Cal king bed, or even hole up in my own apartment to obsess over every detail from the night before. We both had to go to the office.

Griffin had gotten up before me, so I helped myself to a quick shower and borrowed some of his toothpaste before dressing for my walk of shame. I found Griffin in the kitchen, sipping coffee and scrolling through his email on his phone. I was fully braced for him to give me a whole song and dance about how he'd had fun, but no one at the label could find out, and maybe it would be better if this was a onetime thing. Instead, when I tried to preempt him by ordering an Uber, Griffin had frowned.

"I'll drive you to work."

"Oh. Aren't you worried about people seeing us?"

He tipped his head. "Are you?"

My lips parted, and when I didn't answer right away, Griffin nodded in understanding.

"We can wait," he said, gentle. "However you want to handle it is fine by me."

Some of my nerves began to settle. He wasn't treating me like a dirty little secret. In fact, he didn't seem remotely concerned about being seen with me. Even so . . . I glanced down at my wrinkled clothes. I couldn't very well show up to the office on a random Tuesday morning with Griffin, in the same outfit I'd worn the day before. "I don't want to make you late, and I still have to head home and change."

"Where do you live?"

"Studio City." The exact opposite direction from the office.

"Hmm. Might be faster to buy you a new outfit."

I laughed, thinking it was a joke, but then he added: "Rodeo Drive is on the way."

". . . You want to take me shopping on Rodeo Drive. Like in *Pretty Woman*?"

Griffin's lips twitched. "Is there somewhere else you'd rather shop?"

"No, that's not . . ." I licked my lips. What was even happening? ". . . You really don't have to."

"But I want to," Griffin said easily. He picked up his coffee and took one more sip before pocketing his phone and keys and gesturing with two fingers for me to follow him. "Let's go."

Twenty minutes later, he was parking his Tesla outside a bougie store that wasn't even open yet. This did not deter Griffin. He walked straight up to the glass double doors and knocked to get the attention of an employee who was carefully folding knitwear. She smiled tightly and came over, probably to tell us to come back later, but Griffin slipped her his business card and while she read its contents, he asked if she wouldn't mind making an exception.

It was that easy. *Everything* was that easy for Griffin. People bent over backward for him, and problems evaporated, and I'm not proud to admit that sometimes I miss that part of being with him. Just . . . having things handled for me.

Especially in moments like this.

Given the trajectory of this entire trip, I guess I shouldn't be surprised that getting the picture taken down isn't as easy or straightforward as I expect it to be.

Calling the resort accomplished precisely nothing, so Adam and I go to the hotel to speak to someone in person. We hit the information desk first, where the employee gives me a deer-in-headlights look when I explain the situation. They call their manager, who tells me the person I need to speak to is the social media manager, Mae. Fifteen minutes later, no one has been able to track her down. Eventually, they take my number and assure me they'll pass along my request and reach out as soon as it's taken care of.

Which would be great, if I actually believed it would happen. Unfortunately, from what I've gleaned, Mae is perhaps not the most reliable employee.

I check my phone, half expecting there to be another message from Josie, since it's already quarter to three, hours past when I should have replied to her last email. Instead, the only message I find is an automated text from my credit card company, reminding me I have a payment due. In case I weren't already painfully aware of how dire my financial situation has become. I take a slow, steadying breath.

The truth is, I don't actually want someone like Griffin handling things for me. What I want is to be the person who can make things happen for themselves, easy as snapping their fingers.

"Come on," I say to Adam, cutting across the marble floor toward the elevator bank.

I jab the up button with my knuckle and glare at my phone screen while I wait for the elevator to arrive. The last story the social media manager posted was a half hour ago at this point, but it looked like an elaborate event setup near one of the pools. This hotel has five different pools, but they all seem to be located in the same rooftop area, so I figure if she's still up there, it won't be too difficult to track Mae down myself. Aside from the fact that I don't actually know what she looks like. But the last of my dignity was drained back at the bar, and I am not afraid to wander around calling out her name until someone answers.

"You sure we should be doing this?" Adam asks behind me. I roll my eyes up to the screen above the elevator, the numbers ticking down as it approaches.

"You're free to wait in the lobby," I tell him evenly.

He makes this put-out little noise, but when the elevator arrives and empties, he's quick to follow me inside. I repeatedly punch the button marked for the pools until the doors close again. We start to move and make it all of two floors before Adam opens his mouth again.

"Just seems like we might be wasting our time."

My jaw clenches. The walls in here are mirrored, so I don't bother turning around, but flick my gaze up to Adam's reflection. "If waiting around for the hotel staff to get their shit together seems like a better option to you, then by all means . . ." I lean forward and smack the button for the next floor. "You can leave."

The elevator stops quickly enough to make my stomach swoop. The doors open, revealing an empty hall. Adam holds my stare in the mirror for a moment, then reaches around me and hits the button to close the doors.

"Sorry. You're stuck with me."

"As long as it's not until death parts us, right?" It comes out sounding bitter, even to my own ears.

It goes without saying that neither of us want rumors to start spreading. This whole situation is a veritable shit show. But Adam made it sound like being associated with me in any capacity is the worst thing that could ever happen to him. It hurt my fucking feelings, and I hate that he is apparently capable of doing such a thing.

The doors finally slide closed. "You sure you don't want to at least ride in separate elevator cars? Or one of us could take the stairs." I snap my fingers. "Maybe you should put on a disguise."

"What are you talking about?"

"You're obviously concerned about us being seen together."

The elevator is moving again, though it feels like a painfully slow climb. Especially when we stop again on the next floor to let a middle-aged man on. The guy taps the button for the floor he wants, then goes back to looking at his phone.

Adam frowns in my direction. "I knew you were upset about that."

"I'm not upset." I don't miss the way the random guy next to us lifts his eyebrows, like even *he* doesn't believe this statement. "I just wouldn't want to tarnish your pristine reputation. Though, honestly? It's sort of funny you're so worried about your image, yet for all your discerning taste you still jump to defend Billy Draper."

I may not know Billy like Adam does, but I know him well enough. We met once, at one of the exclusive country clubs Griffin belonged to. It was the sort of place that charged a six-figure initiation fee, a club rich people joined either because they were serious about golf, or serious about networking with other West Coast elite. Griffin may have been a bit of both, and while I was neither, I sometimes tagged along to sip cucumber water in the spa, or get an overpriced pedicure and charge it to Griffin's account.

Billy was one of Griffin's regular golf partners, and we were introduced after they'd already played eighteen holes and imbibed god knows how many cocktails out on the course. They were in the clubhouse having another drink, and I walked up to their table in time to catch the tail end of Billy's rant.

". . . how many hours I put into building her career. I made her. Then she drops me for some unproven chump who gets to benefit from my hard work. Ungrateful bitch."

Griffin coughed a laugh into his beer. I watched as he swallowed his drink and tipped his head. "Good riddance."

At that point, I considered turning tail and texting Griffin to meet me when he was done, but it was too late. Griffin had noticed me.

"How was the spa, darling?"

Billy turned to follow Griffin's gaze as I closed the remaining distance.

"It was great." I stopped at Griffin's side and smiled tightly across the table. "You must be Billy."

"I am." Billy stood, slightly unsteady on his feet, and reached across the table to shake my hand. "Nice to finally meet you." He sank back into his chair and picked up his glass, using it to gesture at Griffin. "This guy brags about you all the time."

I lifted a brow and looked down at Griffin. "Is that right?"

Griffin shrugged and wound an arm around my hips, tugging me off-balance until I had no choice but to perch on the wooden arm of his dining chair. "Of course. Billy could never land a girl like you. It's fun to make him jealous."

A flush rose up my neck. Not the pleasant kind, accompanied with a fluttery stomach and a hit of dopamine. This one prickled. Griffin had a habit of speaking about me like I was a prize he'd won. It became less flattering each time.

"Yeah, yeah." Billy's gaze cut to me and he smirked. "Maybe if I were a little higher up on the payroll, right, Eleanor?"

I sucked in a breath, momentarily shocked into silence by Billy's boldness, if not by the sentiment itself.

"Ignore him; he's an asshole," Griffin said with mirth.

That much was abundantly clear. Griffin's hand trailed down my back, and perhaps he'd clocked how stiff my spine had gotten, how over this encounter I was, because he dropped a kiss on my shoulder and began wrapping things up.

From that point on I always made sure to ask who Griffin's golf partner was before agreeing to come with him to the club.

The elevator jolts to a stop, jolting me out of the memory in turn, and the man in front of us scoots out, hoofing it down the hall like he can't get away from Adam and me fast enough.

As the doors slide closed, Adam huffs behind me. "I've known Billy practically my whole life. It's different."

I cut Adam a look over my shoulder. "It's literally not? He's a sleazy guy. You think I'm a sleazy woman—"

"I never said that."

"Okay, well." I shake my head and face forward again, though I avoid his eye in the mirror this time. "How about your buddy JJ Sinclair?"

Another guy with a list of alleged misconduct the length of a CVS receipt. He's produced more than one of Adam's artists' biggest hits.

"Fuck that guy," Adam says sharply, drawing my gaze back to his reflection. "He's been fired. And we are not *buddies.*"

"I've seen pictures of you two looking tight at parties—"

"Are you friends with everyone you've ever been in proximity with at some fucking industry event?"

"So, you've been friendly enough with JJ to be photographed together at events, but I should instinctively know that you aren't actually friends with him? And what, you get a pass for your connection to Billy because he's always been nice to you? Meanwhile, I used to date someone I worked with, which is something loads of people do, but because he turned out to be a toxic piece of shit, I need to publicly atone for the rest of my life."

The elevator doors open—we've reached the rooftop. I step out into the fresh air and Adam catches my elbow, stilling me. "That isn't fair—"

"You're right, it's not." My voice has started to shake—from anger, definitely *not* the urge to cry—and I take a deep breath. "I'm so sick of constantly trying to prove I'm more than the mistake I made when I was twenty-two."

Adam's jaw works, his hand on my arm just firm enough

to keep me in place. I know I could pull away if I really wanted to, but a bigger part of me wants to hear what he has to say for himself.

Unfortunately—or possibly in the first bit of good fortune I've had all day—he doesn't get the chance.

"Oh my god, you guys came!"

We look over at the same time to find a petite woman wearing five-inch heels and purple lipstick rapidly approaching us with her arms wide open. She pulls both of us in for a fierce group hug, and Adam's hand falls away from me in the process.

I hazard a guess as she pulls back: "Mae?"

She beams in response. "Seriously, I'm *so* glad you guys decided to come." She lowers her voice as she pivots and loops an arm around each of ours, steering us into the courtyard, where a small stage is set up. "This whole show has been a bit of a nightmare. Only two other couples signed up."

"Uh," Adam says smoothly. "What show?"

Mae guides us forward a few more steps before releasing us with a cock of her head. "The newlywed game."

Adam and I blink at each other, then turn back to Mae.

"The one I told you about last night?"

"Right," I say. "Last night. That's actually why we're here. We need you to take down that picture of us you posted."

"Oh." She pulls her phone out of her back pocket. "Why? It's so cute!"

"Yeah, no, it's adorable. But . . . we haven't really told anyone about getting married yet. And we want to keep it that way."

"Oh my god, I'm so sorry." Her fingers swipe the phone

open. "I knew you guys eloped, but you didn't mention it was a whole clandestine thing."

"We were a bit out of it," Adam offers, which probably didn't need to be stated, if Mae spent any more than a few passing moments with us last night.

"No worries. I'll take it down and get you guys registered for the game."

"I don't think we'll be doing that," I tell her.

Adam cuts me a sharp look, which baffles me until I see Mae lower her phone screen and lock it again. She smiles sweetly at me. "That's a shame. It would really help me out. And since you need *me* to help *you* out . . . maybe you could reconsider?"

". . . Are you blackmailing me right now?"

"I mean, that feels a bit dramatic." Mae's nose wrinkles as she laughs. "But kind of, I guess. I'll take down the post if you do this event."

Unreal. Un-*fucking*-real. I open my mouth to light into Mae, but she rolls her eyes and beats me to the punch.

"It's seriously not that big of a deal. It'll take half an hour, tops. And the grand prize is twenty-five hundred, so it's really a win-win situation."

That gives me pause. "Twenty-five hundred dollars?"

She nods pleasantly. "You two are, like, relationship goals. You'll probably win."

I decide to ignore that comment, because it's bonkers. Instead, I turn to face Adam, who is frowning in a way that suggests he is as baffled and resigned as I am.

"Still a few hours before the show," I hedge, despite the anxiety building in my stomach. In an ideal world, I'd already be back at my hotel. I'd be showering and maybe squeezing in a nap because a few hours is barely enough time to get my head in the right place for tonight.

Adam checks his phone, like he doesn't trust my ability to tell time. "Probably the best chance at getting the money without having to explain ourselves to anyone."

Without anyone potentially learning we got married, is what he means. Which, again, is a goal he and I share. Even if I'm less inclined to constantly comment on how humiliating it would be if people found out.

I turn back to Mae. "So . . . I guess we're doing this."

"Yay!" She grins broadly at me, as though she didn't have to twist my arm to get me to agree. She leads us around the first pool and through a row of cabanas, until we reach an open space near one of the bars. There's a small stage set up, in view of two of the pool areas.

"We'll be getting started in about twenty. Feel free to grab a drink on the house while you wait, okay?"

How generous. Too bad I'm never touching alcohol again.

She points to the stage. "The Ryan Seacrest look-alike testing the mic onstage is Jonathan, our MC. He'll be over in a bit to give all of you guys a rundown of the rules and explain how the game is going to work." She glances at the borderline-deserted patio area in front of the stage and purses her lips. "Meanwhile, I'm going to go wrangle up more of a crowd."

Adam and I stand side by side, wearing twin frowns as we take in the group of people standing next to the stage, who I can only assume are the other contestants. They're all dressed in resort wear, the men in board shorts and linen button-downs. Everyone is wearing some form of swimwear, come to think of it, which makes sense given we're standing on a pool deck. I tug the hem of my cutoff shorts and feel too grungy for this scene.

Mae starts to step away, then hesitates, her purple lips scrunched to one side.

"Okay, I know I kind of roped you guys into this, but the idea is we want people excited to get married here. So can you at least pretend to be having fun? You're newlyweds! Give us some PDA!"

While I watch Mae leave, Adam watches me. I feel his sidelong stare like a caress, starting at my neck and traveling all the way down my torso. I stand stock-still as he slides a stiff arm around me. His hand flutters over the curve of my waist for a moment before balling into a fist, which he rests featherlight against my hip bone, like he's trying to minimize points of contact as much as possible.

"Jesus, if it's that painful for you to touch me then forget it," I snap, nudging his hand away from me.

It's not like I'm thrilled with the prospect of getting on-stage and pretending to be in love with Adam either. But given that the only alternative involves begging our loved ones to bail us out, I would think he could suck it up for an hour and quit acting like I have cooties.

He should be so lucky to land someone like me in real life. I'm a better-than-average cook, a tidy roommate, I don't snore when I sleep. I'm like an LA eight and a Midwest ten. So contrary to what Adam seems to think, I am top-shelf wife material.

Adam shifts to stand behind me. His hands find my hips, and my breath hitches when he tugs me closer, so my back is flush against his chest. One of his hands shifts to splay across my stomach. My abs tense. He dips his head so his lips skim the shell of my ear.

"I'm sorry for earlier. What I said about people thinking we're involved."

I shrug and try to relax my shoulders. "No big deal."

Super not a big deal. I am, in fact, completely unfazed by anything Adam has ever said to or about me, and also by the span of his palm against my stomach. I let one hand come to rest atop Adam's forearm to prove it, and lift the other to examine my nails.

"I didn't mean it as a slight against you," he continues. His thumb sweeps softly back and forth against my shirt, and my stomach clenches again in response. "I'm not usually one to bend the rules. The idea of using the company card for something I'm not supposed to and getting caught freaks me out. But let me be perfectly clear: the idea that someone might assume we're together is not the issue. Not a single thing about you is embarrassing." He considers this for a moment, and then adds: "Aside from the fact that you like Justin Bieber."

My elbow needles into Adam's side, and he huffs a warm laugh against my neck. I suppress a shiver and duck my chin. "Understood."

We've caught the attention of the other couples waiting for the game to begin, and before I know it, a woman who barely looks eighteen is pulling her equally baby-faced husband over to us.

"Hey, y'all! You're here for the newlywed game too?"

"We are," I say, unable to stop myself from eyeballing her. She's the kind of pretty that you'd think I'd be numb to, after living in LA for so long—perfect teeth and a youthful glow, long legs and a narrow waist emphasized by the fact that she's wearing only a bikini, sheer cover-up dress, and espadrilles. Maybe it's *because* I live in LA that my brain automatically catalogues all of her features that way, as if searching through my mental Rolodex to determine if she's someone borderline famous that I should recognize. But no, in this case she's just a girl from Texas, which she tells us immediately.

"We're from Dallas. Well, not actually Dallas—a suburb outside Dallas. You probably haven't heard of it. We were on the news last year because we got this really freaky snowstorm? But I'm not sure if it was on the news everywhere, or if it was only big news in Texas because we don't usually get much snow, and we lost power for like two weeks. I was walking around in every sweater I own—it was crazy."

Beside her, the husband chews gum and nods slowly.

"I'm Tess, by the way," she goes on. She hip-bumps her partner and beams up at him. "This is Danny."

She looks back at us expectantly, waiting for us to introduce ourselves. This shouldn't present a challenge, but my palms are sweating, and despite the fact that we're outside, I'm feeling a bit claustrophobic.

"This is Eleanor," Adam volunteers. "I'm Adam."

"How long have you two been married?"

"Twelve hours," Adam answers, and I can't see his expression from our position, but his tone suggests they've been the longest hours of his life. "Give or take."

Tess's face lights up. "A Vegas wedding? Us too!"

We're joined by the third couple, who introduce themselves as Chris and Harvey.

"They're from California," Tess informs us dutifully.

"The Bay Area," Chris adds, to which Tess nods excitedly. "What about y'all?"

"LA." I brace for an enthusiastic response from Tess, and am not disappointed. She bounces on the balls of her feet and claps her hands, and I get the distinct impression this woman has been a cheerleader at some point in her life.

"Oh my god, what a small world!"

Despite the urge to point out that LA and San Francisco are six hours apart, or that it really isn't that big of a coincidence so many of us are from California, I find myself reluctantly charmed by Tess and bite my tongue. It's her relentless positivity—it reminds me a bit of Iris.

"So did the two of you elope?" Adam asks, and naturally, Tess is the one to answer.

"Yes! We were high school sweethearts. Our parents are actually pretty supportive, but we didn't want to spend money on a big wedding when we still have college to pay for. Well—I do, at least. Danny has a football scholarship."

She loops her arms around his waist and gazes up at him adoringly. One corner of Danny's mouth tugs up, almost sheepish, and he drops a kiss on her forehead. The whole exchange is unaffected and sweet and reinforces how in love they actually are.

Chris volunteers that he and Harvey met back in college and have lived together for nearly twenty years, but only got married last month. "We have a big trip to Europe planned this summer—"

"A cruise," Harvey adds with a bit of an eye roll.

Chris scoffs. "It's a luxury ship with stops in the Greek Isles. Don't act like you're not excited."

Tess bites her lip. "I went on a Disney cruise once when I was in middle school!"

Harvey blinks at her. "I'm sure that was lovely."

"Anyway," Chris cuts in, presumably before Harvey can say anything snarky. "We're just here for a quick mini-moon."

No one says anything for a long moment, and in spite of the awkwardness, the bit that I'm still hung up on is the fact that they've been together *two decades*. I begin to cast my gaze around for Mae, or the Ryan Seacrest guy. This is going to be excruciating, and likely humiliating, and I want it over with.

When Adam speaks behind me, the soft rumble of his voice against my back reminds me that he is still, for some reason, holding me close to his body.

"We're planning our honeymoon," he says.

I turn my head to look at him, baffled. He shoots me a wink. I whip my head to face forward again and his hands tighten around my waist. My breath hitches. His pinkie slides down and catches on the waistband of my shorts. I cross my legs and refuse to be turned on right now, even if Mae did ask us to sell it.

"I want to travel through Asia." He gives me a little squeeze and adds, "But this one isn't a huge fan of flying, so maybe we'll go somewhere a bit closer, like Hawaii."

How does Adam know I don't like to fly? I can't remember if this is something I mentioned at some point, or if he's just making shit up and happened to stumble upon something true.

I clear my throat. All I can think to say is: "Hawaii?"

"You know I'd go anywhere with you, baby."

My nails dig into Adam's forearm, hard enough to leave little half-moons behind. It's not that I have strong feelings one way or the other about that particular pet name. But the husky quality of Adam's voice has my gut turning molten. I blame Tyler for how easy it is to imagine Adam using that voice in bed, lips against my neck as he talks me through an orgasm. My skin flares hot enough to broadcast how much he's affecting me, and I risk a glance over my shoulder. I can only watch helplessly as Adam's brows pucker, and then slowly—so slowly—understanding dawns and his lips curve into a smug smile.

We're already playing a game, Adam and I. It's my turn to make a move, to say something flirty and push the boundary a bit more, but my brain is having trouble keeping up. The heat of his gaze feels too real.

I have not gotten this far in life without learning how to tell if someone wants to kiss me. Adam thought about it, back at the bar. Call it a moment of weakness, but I would've let him.

I'm abruptly aware of the fact that I didn't have time to shower this morning, and that the powdery scent of my deodorant is nowhere near as nice-smelling as Adam's cologne. I'm also very aware of the fact that if I turned my head another couple of inches, the stubble along his jaw would scrape against my lips.

Which makes me think about how his stubble would feel in other, more sensitive places.

"Have you been together a long time?" Tess asks.

"No, we actually got together pretty recently," Adam answers. "We've known each other for years, though."

"Oh, really? How'd you start dating?"

"Do you want to tell the story, babe, or should I?"

The spark in Adam's eye does not help my nervous system settle down.

"Actually, can you excuse us?" I blurt out, grabbing Adam's

hand. I drag him away without waiting for a response. Once we're on the other side of the stage and out of earshot, I release his hand and cross my arms.

"So, I think we have a problem," I tell him.

Adam's lingering smile slips. "What do you mean?"

"These people are real couples," I say, gesturing vaguely behind me to where Tess and the others are standing. "They have histories and inside jokes. And as good as you are at spinning bullshit, there is no way we can compete with that."

"It's not like we're strangers."

"Sure. Fine. But we're not *together*." Regardless of how surprisingly good Adam was at pretending.

Adam's mouth tightens. He steps fully in front of me, and then both hands are on my shoulders. Adam dips his head so we're eye to eye, and then just . . . maintains eye contact while saying nothing. It is highly unnerving.

"What is happening right now?"

"We're getting on the same wavelength," Adam says without blinking.

I stare back into his hazel eyes, noticing every speck of color in his irises and the tiny freckle on his right eyelid—details I should probably never be close enough to notice—and for a few seconds, it almost feels like it's working. Like we're connecting on some deep, intimate level. But then, of course, I realize that's ridiculous. This is just some bizarre pregame ritual of Adam's. A way for him to hype himself up and get in the zone, and we are not connected in any way besides circumstance, no matter how much we might have seemed like "relationship goals" to Mae last night.

I break eye contact and swat his hands away. "Okay, stop. I feel like you're trying to hypnotize me or something. It's creepy."

Adam frowns like I'm the weird one, but he straightens and gets out of my personal space all the same. "Don't stress out about this. We know each other well enough to fake it."

"Yeah? What's my favorite color?"

". . . Green?"

"Blue. What pizza toppings do I like?"

"I really don't think they're going to ask about—"

"See? We're screwed."

Adam draws in a breath, a serious set to his brows. "Do you want to bail?"

I shake my head. "We can't bail."

Mae made it clear she wouldn't take down the post unless we played along, and she strikes me as mildly unhinged, so I wouldn't put it past her to promote it even more if we piss her off.

So really, there's only one solution.

"We have ten minutes to learn everything important about each other."

CHAPTER TEN

ADAM

"So, we met at work," Eleanor says matter-of-factly. "Where was our first date?"

We find a couple of free lounge chairs across the pool from the stage, and I open the bag of pretzels I snagged from the snack bar on the way over and hand them to Eleanor. She needs to eat something, and I figured these would be a safe choice, since they're packaged and bland.

I make myself comfortable, legs stretched out and one of the complimentary towels tucked under my neck like a pillow, while Eleanor sits with her legs crisscrossed on the chair next to mine, pretzels cradled between her palms and her back ramrod straight. She is taking this extremely seriously. Which is hard for me to wrap my head around, to be honest, because she's right—we have zero chance of winning. None whatsoever. Despite the fact that Eleanor seems to know this, it's obvious part of her is still hoping.

Maybe it's a side effect of seeing her suffer through a

panic attack earlier, but I am not equipped to crush that hope. So I play along.

"Where's your favorite date spot?" I ask her.

"I don't know. Just pick somewhere." When I take too long thinking, she huffs and says: "How about Bestia?"

My nose wrinkles automatically. "A dinner date? That's so boring."

"It's not boring, it's classic."

"I think the word you're looking for is *cliché*." I'm aware that this conversation is going off the rails a bit. That none of this is particularly important, in the grand scheme of things. But Eleanor's nostrils flare when she gets indignant. It's cute and I can't help myself. "What about the zoo?"

"Was this a date or a fourth-grade field trip?"

I snort a laugh, and Eleanor's lips twitch with the urge to smile in response. "Oh, or the botanical gardens!"

". . . Sure. Fine. You took me to the botanical gardens." She shakes her head and shoves a pretzel into her mouth.

I turn my face toward the sun and grin. "And since it's right there, we took a stroll through the zoo after, so you could see the sloths."

This actually does sound like fun. I'd go on this date. Not with Eleanor, necessarily. Though it takes surprisingly little effort to picture the two of us strolling through the gardens, one arm slung across Eleanor's shoulders to keep her close.

"How'd you know I like sloths?"

"You had that calendar on your desk," I say, feeling some mixture of caught out and smug. "One of the months had a photo of sloths, and after the month was over you tore out the page so you could hang that picture up."

Her eyebrows hike up toward her hairline. "I forgot about that."

The unspoken addendum is that she can't believe I remembered. Which admittedly is kind of weird. It's not like I remember every little interaction we've ever had. But we started at Exeter together, and then she became a bit notorious in our shared circles, and then the whole thing with Maya happened. So yeah, it's fair to say Eleanor has always been on my radar.

I clear my throat. "So, next question. Biggest pet peeve?"

"Um . . ." Eleanor blinks hard and refocuses her gaze on the nearest shimmering pool. "I guess when someone listens to something on their phone without headphones in public. What's yours?"

"Wet socks." I shudder at the thought, and don't miss the twitch at the corner of Eleanor's mouth.

"How is that a pet peeve?"

"Oh my god, have you never been walking through your kitchen and stepped in a puddle you didn't see? It is the worst sensation in the world."

"Why are there puddles all over your kitchen floor?"

"There aren't usually. But, you know, it happens."

". . . How, though?"

"I don't know. Spills from cooking. Or watering plants."

I do not actually own any houseplants. My mom gave me a succulent when I first moved into my apartment, but it died, like, immediately, and I haven't replaced it.

Eleanor's smirk stretches wider, and I get the feeling she's picturing me getting my socks wet and having a meltdown over it.

"How about your favorite album?" I ask.

"Like, at the moment? Or of all time?"

"Both."

She blows out a breath. "I've been listening to a lot of Teddy Swims and Arctic Monkeys lately. But of all time . . . probably *Nevermind*."

I huff a small laugh.

"What?" she asks. "Is that too trite?"

"No, not at all. That's actually my favorite album too."

She beams. "Really?"

"Yeah. Nirvana was my favorite band as a teenager. I come back to that album all the time. My mom actually saw them live once."

Eleanor's eyes go wide. "No shit?"

"Unfortunately, she didn't get any merch to pass down to me," I say with a nod to her Bowie shirt. "But yeah. She was really into the live music scene before my dad kind of . . . soured her on it all." I snort. "I think he was always weirdly jealous of some of the acts she saw before they got together. Like he wanted to be the sole music aficionado in the relationship."

"Well. She sounds pretty cool in her own right."

I nod. "She's the best."

Eleanor bites her lip and looks down at her pretzels. She stuffs one in her mouth and avoids my gaze while she chews. Once she's swallowed, she keeps her gaze locked on her fingers, still picking at the bag of pretzels as she prompts: "What song would we have had our first dance to?"

"Um . . ." I think about Eleanor's comment at the chapel this morning, about missing out on an Elvis impersonator. "'Can't Help Falling in Love'?"

"That's a good one." Her smile softens, and she dips her chin as if to hide it. "Your turn."

"What's your dream job?"

Eleanor gives me a funny look. "A&R manager."

"Oh. You don't want to become an executive down the road?"

She shrugs. "Not particularly. I mean, I wouldn't hate getting promoted to director one day, but I definitely want to stay in artists and repertoire."

This surprises me, mostly because Eleanor is ambitious. I'd assumed she had the same ambitions as me—to rise through the ranks and gain enough experience to run a record company one day. Then again, her indie label is much smaller than mine. Not as many executive positions in the first place, and those that do exist probably stretch a person that much thinner.

"I'd like to have an impact at the label," she goes on, "and help Josie develop a strategy for the future. But discovering new artists and supporting their careers is what I love to do. I have no interest in taking on a bigger role in finance or business aspects." She gives a self-deprecating laugh. "And in case it wasn't obvious, fiscal responsibility is not my strong suit."

"Sure," I tell her, a bit distractedly. The thing is, as much as I hate to admit it, there's another reason I assumed Eleanor wanted to be an executive. It makes my skin itch and feel too tight for my frame, to think about the things people have said about Eleanor. To acknowledge how much of it I readily believed.

Eleanor wasn't the only intern people gossiped about—me being Atlas's son was certainly a topic when we started, and everyone liked to rag on another kid whose uncle was a producer. Nepotism runs rampant in this business, something that's ridiculed by bitter peers at the same time it's accepted as the norm. So it's hard to pinpoint exactly when Eleanor went from being one of us, almost an underdog considering she had no industry connections, to the person all the other interns collectively decided didn't belong.

If I had to choose one moment that turned the tides against her, it'd probably be the day she brought everyone band merch. Which sounds ridiculous, because it was ridiculous, that a bunch of underpaid interns who were always psyched to score free stuff reacted with anything but gratitude. The problem was, the swag came from a marketing meeting with Exeter's biggest artist of the year. A meeting Eleanor had no real business attending as a lowly A&R intern.

We were all eating lunch in the kitchen area when Eleanor came in and dropped the armful of T-shirts and stickers and other swag right in the middle of our cramped table.

"Oh, sweet," said this kid Sanjay, immediately lunging for a branded baseball cap.

"Whoa, hang on, were you at the Reagan Marquette meeting?" This came from Dana, the only other girl out of a half-dozen interns.

"Yeah. Mr. Hastings asked me to sit in."

Dana was sitting across the table from me, so I was the one she made eye contact with. Her brow quirked, and it read to me as *that's some bullshit, am I right?*

I dropped my gaze back down to my lunch. I didn't even look up when someone finally broke the dead silence that had settled over the group with a mumbled "Of course he did."

It hadn't escaped any of our notice that Griffin had taken a special interest in Eleanor. And it hadn't taken long for jealousy to turn into speculation, about what kinds of things happened in their closed-door meetings, about whether it was a coincidence that they came in on the same elevator some mornings.

Eleanor cleared her throat. "They had samples of all this stuff sitting around, so I figured you guys might want some of it."

"How thoughtful," Dana said as she viciously stabbed at her salad.

It was beyond clear that Dana did not read this gesture as thoughtful. She—all of us, maybe—had read it as calculated. Like Eleanor only brought us that stuff so she'd have an excuse to brag about meeting Reagan.

That's how it went from then on. Every time Eleanor tried to defuse the tension and offer an olive branch to the other interns, it blew up in her face. I was an asshole, and a sheep, so I never defended her. I didn't even tell Billy to knock it off when he dragged her after I closed Maya's contract earlier this year, or when he said that stuff about her and Griffin on the phone this morning.

At some point I matured enough to understand how unethical Griffin's actions were, yet I still bought into the idea that Eleanor is a social climber. Or that she was trying to skip ahead like her career was a game of Chutes and Ladders.

Meanwhile, I'm the one who is never satisfied with my position in life. I'm the one who is never successful enough, who is always shifting my own goalposts, always looking for the next win. And taking backdoor deals along the way.

The reality is, Eleanor never bragged about opportunities

she got from Griffin. If anything, she tried her hardest to downplay the relationship, for as long as she could get away with it.

I feel like I understand Eleanor so much better, after today. Yet there's still one thing nagging at me. I turn to sit facing her, feet planted on the cement ground. "Hey, can I ask you a personal question?"

Eleanor eyes me for a moment. "Okay," she says, putting a false-positive inflection on the word that tells me she's not really sure at all.

"It's relevant to the game," I add quickly. "Sort of. In the sense that it's about your dating history. Or—well, your taste in men, I guess. . . . You don't have to answer."

"Spit it out, Shaw."

"What did you see in Griffin? Like . . . how did you two even get together in the first place?"

She laughs at this, which I suppose is a better reaction than her telling me to mind my own business. But it makes me nervous all the same, and I start to regret asking before she's even given her answer.

"You've seen him, right?"

"I have." And I'm willing to acknowledge he's not a crusty old man or anything. He's in good shape for his age, and still has all of his hair. That's about as generous as I can be. "I've also spoken to him. Guy's an asshole."

Eleanor rolls her eyes. "Yeah, but he's a total daddy."

Nope. I do not like hearing that. I don't know what kind of answer I expected, or whether *any* answer would have landed better than this one, frankly. But this insight into their dynamic has my baser instincts surfacing fast.

". . . Ah," I manage.

Eleanor seems to be relishing my discomfort. She shrugs and offers me a grin. "It's true. That's his entire draw, pretty much."

"If you say so," I grumble. It's possible I'm still fixated on the term *daddy* and what it meant in the context of this relationship. I am from a generation that grew up with easy access to the internet, which is a polite way of saying I have watched my fair share of porn. I understand the daddy kink. At least in the abstract. But this sliver of information is a curse, really, because it brings up more questions that are all way too invasive to actually ask.

Like whether Eleanor ever actually *called* Griffin "Daddy." Or whether she has a submissive streak. Or whether she's only attracted to older guys.

"So you were into the age gap?" I manage to ask, while my fingernail pick-pick-picks at a snag in the upholstered cushion underneath me.

"I wouldn't say I was *into* it. It didn't bother me, at the time."

At the time. My brain latches on to that last bit. The implication that it does bother her now. And I'm curious when her opinion changed. Whether it was as soon as they broke up, or even *why* they broke up.

It wasn't until Griffin was fired that my own perspective shifted. Before that, yeah, I thought he was a dick. But when Eleanor left Exeter, my first thought wasn't that she might be trying to get away from a coercive relationship. I sort of figured she was done riding his coattails. That she saw a way to leverage her recent promotion and jumped at the chance. Not something I'm proud to admit. But then when Griffin got canned, and some other women had come forward to report inappropriate behavior, and people started talking about his thing with Eleanor again, it was like, holy shit. How did I not see this before? Like, would I ever date an intern? Absolutely fucking not, and I'm much closer in age to the interns now than he was. He was a creep, and it pisses me off Exeter didn't get rid of him sooner.

Eleanor tips her face toward the sun and sighs. "The truth is he's one of those guys who pulls a bait and switch. I mean, I like to think I went into the relationship with my eyes wide open. I knew there was a power imbalance. I knew he was kind of an asshole. I was fine with all of that, because we both agreed we were going to keep it casual. But it got messy, fast. I'm not sure Griffin is capable of doing anything casual. He's too possessive."

"He wanted something more serious?"

Her brow creases and she turns her face back to me. "I guess? But probably not in the way you're imagining. He just . . . wanted to be in control. And initially I was on board with that, because it was fun."

I guess that answers my question about her submissive streak.

"Until it wasn't," she adds.

This has my hackles up. "What'd he do?"

Eleanor purses her lips. "He promoted me."

" . . . Which was a bad thing?"

That was the general consensus, at least among the other interns. But as established, that was jealousy speaking. None of us had promotions on the horizon. We knew we'd be lucky to stay on as A&R reps once our internships ran their course, never mind be offered a position so quickly. Watching her meteoric rise was bound to breed resentment.

"What people say is true, in the most abstract sense. Griffin absolutely did promote me because we were sleeping together. But it wasn't like, *Oh, I'm fucking this person so I'll play favorites and give them a leg up*. It was more, *I've taken an interest in Eleanor so I'm going to try to control as many aspects of her life as possible, including making it so she reports directly to me*."

". . . Huh. I definitely never thought about it that way."

She waves this off. "Yeah, no one did. It just sort of sucked. Like, we were not in love. I know that now. I think I even knew it then. But I did genuinely like him, at first. Then he became this . . . black hole, almost. And my anxiety was through the roof, always bracing for Griffin to get irritated with me about some stupid thing. I realized it was unhealthy and that I wanted out, so I got out, and then people hated me for that too."

"No one hated you," I say immediately.

Her eyes have a challenge in them, and I have to concede. "Well, *I* never did." I tap my fingers against my thigh, knowing I should let it drop, but too curious for my own good. "Do you still see Sanjay around? Or anyone else from Exeter?"

Eleanor's mouth pinches. "Not so much. After I fell out with everyone I sort of . . . stopped trying to be friends with people from work." She huffs a dry laugh. "And since all I really *do* is work, my entire social circle is composed of my sister and her friends."

Awareness of our surroundings filters back in, the low thrum of background noise becoming louder and more obnoxious. The crease between Eleanor's brows is still there—she's still stressed, and I suck in a breath and say the first thing I think of to lighten the mood.

"Dogs or cats?"

"Dogs," she answers without hesitation. I nod my appreciation, and she takes her turn: "Any tattoos I should know about?"

"No." I side-eye her. "You saw pretty much my entire body this morning."

"First of all, I wasn't looking," she says, and not to sound arrogant, but that's definitely a lie. "Second of all, you were wearing underwear."

"I do not have a tattoo on my ass."

She makes her eyes all big and doe-like and lethal. "And now I know that."

I look away and run a finger over my lips to smooth out my smile. "What about you? Any tattoos?"

To my surprise, she nods. "A hummingbird on my left shoulder blade. My second-biggest drunken mistake."

"Aw, does that make me number one?"

"Sure does."

I put a hand to my heart. "I'm honored."

A dude by the stage catches my eye and waves us over—the newlywed game is about to begin. Eleanor sees him, too, and puts a hand on my chest to keep me from moving.

"One last question." Eleanor's eyes flicker between mine. "Who told you about my meeting?"

I didn't expect her to let this go. If anything, I'm surprised it took her this long to ask again. I should've been ready for it, should have some coy, snarky answer all teed up.

In spite of all this, the question lands like a gut punch. Unlike this morning, evasiveness no longer comes naturally—I'm more inclined to tell her and offer up an apology. But I already know what her reaction would be. I know it would only remind her that a handful of hours ago she didn't trust me at all, didn't want anything to do with me.

I should tell her anyway. But I'm stubbornly unwilling to lose the ground I've gained.

Her eyes narrow, and I can see in her expression that she doesn't actually expect an honest answer to come. So I take the out.

"Nice try." My voice is hoarse, and I cover it with a smirk that feels foreign on my lips. "Come on. Let's go win this thing."

CHAPTER ELEVEN

ELEANOR

The Ryan Seacrest comparison Mae made is not off base, but as I get a closer look at the MC, I decide he reminds me more of the Ken doll Iris and I had when we were little. Jonathan's hair has so much product in it, it looks like a hard shell, and he's wearing a periwinkle suit jacket made of some kind of fabric that glitters in the afternoon sun.

"You must be Eleanor and Adam," he says when we join the group. We shake hands, and he immediately launches into the setup of the game, distributing cue cards and a black marker to each of us.

The rules are all pretty straightforward, so I mostly focus on taking deep breaths and blocking out the sidelong glances Adam keeps sending me. I can't tell if he's nervous, or if he just knows I am. Either way, his constant attention isn't helping.

Six deck chairs are situated on the stage. Jonathan directs Adam and me to the pair on the far right, tucked close to each other but angled in a way that will make it near impossible to see what's written on each other's answer cards. I sit down and fiddle with the Sharpie I was given, flicking it back and forth between my fingers.

"You all right?" Adam asks in a low voice.

I still my hand and nod. "Yeah. It's like a game of trivia, right? I'm great at trivia."

Granted, usually the trivia I participate in is more focused on pop culture than Adam Shaw's personal life. But my competitive streak is surfacing all the same.

I find myself thinking of Iris, my trivia partner of choice. I wonder how well she and her fiancé, Eric, would fare in this game. They're the sort of couple who immediately switched to "we" statements, who keep no secrets from each other and share to the point of it being sort of gross—like, I would not be shocked to find out they use the same toothbrush—so chances are, they'd do pretty well.

Adam reaches over and rests his hand on the back of my neck. I'm surprised by how not-annoying I find the gesture. How much I like the grounding weight of his palm. I stifle a little whine when he withdraws his touch a moment later.

Everything would be so much easier if Adam were consistently an asshole. Instead, he's a part-time asshole, and then he sneaks in these moments of wit and insight and thoughtfulness. What am I supposed to do with that?

On the one hand, he's sworn that coming to Vegas and going after Dempsey isn't personal, and I'm inclined to believe him. We've established he's just as competitive as I am, and it is, after all, a cutthroat industry. I'll even admit my anger toward him about Maya was misplaced. Blaming him was an understandable if knee-jerk reaction, but I'm the one who let her walk.

The thing is, though, why won't he tell me who tipped him off about last night's dinner? It's not like there are all that many possibilities. Why can't he fess up already so we can move past it?

Adam catches me looking at him, and I shift my gaze straight ahead, picking out details of the so-called audience, which amounts to a handful of people who are being subjected to this farce while they try to enjoy the pool. One woman in particular catches my eye because she is wearing the most complicated, gravity-defying swimsuit I've ever seen in real life. It's mostly composed of straps, and I can't make sense of how she got into it, never mind how it's staying put while she swims. Then there's a man with a waxed chest who is applying some kind of oil all over himself, and I'd be willing to bet the entirety of my admittedly sparse bank account that he will be leaving here today with a nasty sunburn. Maybe it makes me a bad person, but I'm mildly comforted by the knowledge that I won't be the only one coming away from a trip to Vegas worse for wear.

Finally, Jonathan grabs a microphone, which—good lord—is bedazzled with crystals that glimmer when the light catches it, and welcomes everyone to the game. After a quick introduction of each couple, he poses the first question:

"Okay, this one is for Harvey, Danny, and Adam. Please write down your most prized possession."

Adam thinks for a moment, then scribbles down his answer. And I have . . . no earthly idea what it could be. Jonathan starts on the other end of the stage, which at least gives me a moment to think. Absurdly, I keep hoping Adam will meet my gaze so he can prove his little wavelength plan worked, and telepathically tell me his answer.

I don't hear Harvey's answer, or whether Chris gets it right. I'm vaguely aware of Tess correctly guessing that Danny's prized possession is his state football championship ring—which feels so on the nose it's no wonder she got it right. And then it's my turn.

"Uh . . ." Beside me, Adam is clutching his answer card close to his chest. My gaze lingers on his wrist—or rather, the watch wrapped around it. It certainly seemed important to him earlier. "His watch?"

Adam's face breaks into a gigantic grin, and he turns his cue card around to reveal the answer.

"Well done!" Jonathan says, and I get a little rush of adrenaline and find myself sitting up straighter, leaning forward while I wait for the next question. "Who said 'I love you' first?"

I scribble Adam's name down immediately. I mean, come on.

Jonathan waits for Tess and Chris to finish writing their answers, and then turns back to me, switching up the order. "Okay, Adam, Eleanor has jotted down her answer . . . Who said those three little words first?"

Adam fixes me with this put-out look, and I curl my lips in to keep from smiling. "I suppose that would be me."

I flip my card around to reveal Adam's name and give him a sweet smile. "Obviously."

Next up are Danny and Tess, and of course they get it right, too—they've probably whipped out the story of Danny sweeping Tess into his arms after he won the big game countless times to all their friends—hell, considering they were in high school, their friends were probably all there to witness it.

Last up, Harvey answers he said it first, and Chris is immediately outraged.

"You absolutely did not!" Chris bursts, without even bothering to turn his card around.

Harvey frowns. "Yes, I did. Our first Christmas together, I—"

"You said, and I quote, 'I love spending time with you.' I remember, because I didn't think anyone actually used that line in real life, but I figured maybe you were *close* to saying it, so I waited, and then *three months* went by and you still hadn't said it, so on your birthday *I* said it to *you*, and you said it back."

Harvey purses his lips. "That's not how I remember it."

"Shocking," Chris mutters, loud enough for me to hear but probably not the rest of the spectators. He tosses his card aside and stares resolutely ahead until Jonathan clears his throat and moves on to the next question, which is about our partners' guilty pleasures.

Again, I draw a complete blank. I think about how pretentious Adam can be sometimes and guess K-dramas, because it seems like the kind of thing Adam would be embarrassed to admit he likes. But when I offer up that answer, Adam gives me a bewildered look and flips his card, which reads: *strip club meat.*

I let out an appallingly loud snort-laugh, and cover my mouth with both hands. Jonathan doesn't seem to know what to do with this response, so he moves on without comment. I put all of my energy into not laughing, which proves impossible the moment I meet Adam's eye again. I look away as a fresh bout of giggles bubble up, biting the inside of my cheek and thinking about decidedly not-funny things, like . . . waking up in Vegas married to an almost-stranger, for example.

I've managed to get a handle on myself by the time Jonathan comes back to us with the next question—what my partner finds most attractive about me.

My gaze is drawn back to Adam, who meets my eye for a long, intense beat. He looks away first, and nudges his glasses up his nose in a gesture that makes me imagine what he was like when he was younger. What it would've been like to know him in high school, during his awkward stage, assuming he ever had one.

I'm not entirely sure when I started to find the glasses endearing, but the realization is unsettling.

It would've been uncomfortable to offer up something about Adam I find attractive, but the inverse is somehow even worse. Despite my certainty that Adam wanted to kiss me earlier, I have no clue what his answer will be. I've never caught him staring at my mouth or my tits. He doesn't strike me as the sort of person to obsess over any particular body part. In the end, I have to choose *something*, so I scribble down the feature I like best about myself.

"Her eyes," Adam answers easily when it's his turn.

My cheeks go hot as I turn the card around to show my matching response. Not that I'm reading anything into it—eyes are a safe, non-objectifying answer. Finding them attractive doesn't necessarily mean he's *attracted* to me, if he even meant it in the first place.

The questions keep coming, and Adam and I keep getting them right. By the time we reach the final round, it's clear that by some miracle we actually do have a shot at winning. So of course, that's when Jonathan asks the most obnoxious question of the day.

"Eleanor, what are you most likely to nag Adam about?"

Beside me, Adam immediately starts scribbling his answer. I clench my jaw and try to move past the fact that he needed absolutely no time to think this one over.

I'm probably expected to offer an answer that's demure and funny and relatable, but my nails are digging into my palm and I can't stop myself from blurting out: "That actually feels like a really sexist question."

Jonathan is taken aback. He glances at the other contestants, as if he's hoping they'll bail him out, but they're all staring at me, most of them with a mixture of amusement and respect, although Danny has more of an *oh, shit* look on his face, so I'm guessing his answer isn't going to go over well with Tess.

"It's meant to be hypothetical," Jonathan says, in the same tone men use when they say something inappropriate at the office and then follow it up with, *lighten up, it was a joke*. A tone that implies it's my fault for not having a sense of humor, and oh, buddy, I am so not in the mood for that kind of fuckery.

"Yeah, well, I'm not going to answer it."

Jonathan huffs a humorless laugh. "No answer. All right—you'd better hope your husband shares your thoughts on this. Adam?"

Adam smirks without making eye contact with anyone and flips his card over. It reads: "That's pretty sexist, dude."

Now, does Adam seem a touch too proud of himself for something that should be common sense to anyone who respects women? Yes. Do I find myself feeling incredibly fond of him regardless? Also yes. It's possible I just fell the tiniest bit in love with him. Which is a testament to my untapped acting skills. I've committed to the role of Besotted Newlywed, and am, frankly, impressed with myself.

Jonathan seems less impressed.

"Is that what your wife wanted to hear, or are you as like-minded as your answer suggests?"

Adam shrugs and casts his answer card aside. "Both."

He shoots me another wink, and I bite down on my grin. The idea that Iris would approve of Adam comes to me unbidden. His answers don't seem like ones a person who has said disparaging things behind your back would give. I want to believe that. I want to believe I've been projecting onto Adam all this time, and that he never spread any of the gossip about me, never listened to a word of it. I want that to be true so badly.

I've lost track of everyone's score. I'm pretty sure we're neck and neck with Chris and Harvey, who are responding now. And of course their answers match up as well. My foot *tap-tap-taps* against the stage and I sit ramrod straight on the edge of my seat as Jonathan wraps things up and turns back to the audience.

"All right, let's give all our contestants a round of applause!" Jonathan says. I give a few half-hearted claps, my body moving on autopilot. A hand finds mine, Adam finally giving in to the urge to touch, or maybe the instinct to soothe my nerves. I lace our fingers together and grip hard. "They all did a fantastic job, but let's see what the final tally looks like."

Someone from the front row of the audience stands up and passes Jonathan a piece of paper. He stares at it for a moment and then folds the paper back up. "With a total of eight correct answers, our top scoring team—and grand prize winners—are . . ."

Jonathan has proven he has a flair for the dramatic, but it feels like he draws the pause out for an eternity, and I am about three seconds away from launching at him and screaming, *FUCKING TELL US ALREADY*.

The longer Jonathan unnecessarily drags this out, the harder I squeeze the life out of Adam's hand.

"Adam and Eleanor!" He turns toward us and claps some more, his hand meeting his bedazzled microphone. "Let's hear it for our winners!"

"Holy shit," Adam says beside me.

The sentiment echoes in my head, and then I'm moving. On my feet, then jumping into Adam's arms. He straightens to his full height and my toes lift off the ground. His astonished laughter fills my ear and his warm breath huffs down my neck. I loosen my hold on him enough to lean back and look him in the eye.

His smile slips into something more serious, hazel eyes growing heated as his gaze flickers down to my mouth. Jonathan's mic'd voice and the smattering of applause filter away, until all that remains is Adam. His strong arms holding me up and his soft hair brushing against the back of my wrist and his lips—full and slightly chapped—meeting mine in an adrenaline-fueled, celebratory kiss.

CHAPTER TWELVE

ADAM

Eleanor seems to process what we're doing first. I'm still wrapped up in the moment, one hand lifting to thread my fingers through her hair, to tilt her head and deepen the kiss. She tastes like honey somehow, though I haven't seen her consume any today. I want that flavor on my tongue, always. My hand tightens around a fistful of hair and my other arm is securely wrapped around her middle as I gently lower her back down. Her feet touch the floor and just like that, the moment's over. Eleanor breaks the kiss as abruptly as she started it.

She shuffles backward a step, her fingertips tracing her lips briefly before dropping back to her side in a loose fist. I'm left off-kilter, like those few seconds were all it took to get used to her weight against me, and now I have to relearn how to stand without it.

"Wow, so—yeah. Cool. We won. Cool, cool, cool." All of this is said without Eleanor making eye contact. She seems restless, looking out at the audience, crossing her arms only to uncross them a beat later.

It's surreal, remembering that we are in a public place. Standing outside, some twenty stories up, surrounded by swimsuit-clad strangers sipping cocktails. Sharp laughter carries across the nearby pool, but I can't look away from the woman in front of me.

"Yeah." I lick my lips. My brain isn't fully back online yet. All I can think is that I want to still be kissing her. I have a caveman urge to drag her offstage and into one of the private cabanas lining the pool so we can continue this without an audience.

It wasn't intentional, the way I memorized every detail of that kiss, but they're etched in my brain now, right alongside the image of Eleanor wearing only a loose shirt and lacy black underwear this morning.

The other contestants come up to congratulate us and I barely manage to acknowledge them. Jonathan tells us Mae will be over with the prize, and Eleanor nods her understanding, and I stare at the side of Eleanor's face.

I know how to act casual, I swear I do, so I force myself to look elsewhere while I try to figure out some super-chill way to ask whether Eleanor would like to do that again sometime.

"Do we need to clear the air at all?" she asks. "After that kiss, I mean."

On the one hand, I suppose it's reassuring that Eleanor also felt compelled to say something. Maybe I'm not the only one who still feels the ghost of it on their lips. Only, *clear the air* seems like a very deliberate choice of words. That's the phrasing you use when something is one-sided, when you feel obligated to let someone down gently.

I'm convinced that's what's happening here, right up until she catches her bottom lip between her teeth and eyes my biceps like she'd rather be biting me. It's only for a second, and then her eyes snap back up to mine, but it's long enough to bolster my confidence.

"No, I think we're on the same page," I say, unable to suppress my smile as color floods her cheeks. "We were both keyed up from the game."

Eleanor nods along with a tight purse to her lips. This could be wishful thinking. I could be reading the signals all wrong. But if I am—if Eleanor already regrets the kiss, if she never wants it to happen again—then I have nothing to lose. Perfect time to take a gamble.

"Plus, you've been thinking about it for so long, it was bound to happen eventually," I add.

She nods once more, then frowns. "Wait, what?"

"Kissing me." It's easy enough to slip on a cocky grin and pretend I already know the answer. I've had plenty of practice, though it's a strategy I'm more accustomed to using with industry blowhards than as a form of flirting. "You've thought about it, right?"

"Excuse me?" The annoyed edge to Eleanor's voice is somewhat undermined by the way she can't stop fidgeting.

I step closer, knuckles barely grazing the curve of her waist. She looks up at me through her lashes and her lips part. The air between us grows heavier, thrumming with tension.

"Tell me I'm wrong." My voice drops basement low, turns the statement into a something like a dare.

She doesn't tell me I'm wrong. For a long-drawn-out moment, she doesn't say anything at all. She stares up at me and it feels like that moment before a live show, when the lights go down and the crowd goes quiet, breath held while you wait for the first chord to strike.

"'Cause I have," I admit. "I've thought about it." Eleanor's tongue darts out to lick her lips, and she gets that tiny crease back between her brows, and I'm holding my breath again, still, almost dizzy with anticipation.

I'm so completely wrapped up in this moment, in Eleanor, that I have a full-body jump scare when Mae pops up right in front of us again.

"See! What did I tell you!" She squeals at us, oblivious to the way Eleanor and I startle apart. "Total relationship goals."

Mae presents us with an envelope stamped with the hotel's insignia. When neither of us takes it, she gives it a little shake. Chips rattle around inside. I grab the envelope and nod my thanks.

"As promised, I've deleted the post," she adds. I pull out my phone and open the app to double-check. Sure enough, the post has been taken down. "I really am sorry about all of this. You guys helped so much by staying in the game, though. We actually had one couple sign up for a tour of the venue."

I turn my attention to the chips, opening the envelope and counting them, if only to distract myself from the dull sting under my rib cage when Eleanor refuses to meet my gaze.

It takes a moment for the chip in my palm to fully come into focus. "Wait, what is this?" I hold it between two fingers and raise a brow at Mae. "Nonnegotiable chips?"

Mae's brow puckers slightly, as if to ask what the issue is. "That's right."

"Nonnegotiable?" I repeat, sounding much more exasperated this time.

"What's the problem?" Eleanor looks from me to Mae. "You said the prize was twenty-five hundred, right?"

"That's right," Mae says calmly. "You can use them in any one of the hotel's casinos," she goes on, as if this is a selling point.

"You mean . . . we can't cash them in?"

"Jesus." My fingers curl around the chip, squeezing hard enough my knuckles blanch. My fist drops to my side, defeated. "We can only gamble with them."

"Have fun, okay?" Mae says with a smile. "You guys are still in town another night, right? Hit me up if you want to get a drink tonight!"

With that last delusion, Mae moves away from us. We both stare blankly in her wake, until finally Eleanor turns to face me.

"It's fine," she says. "We can just . . . we can find someone to buy these chips from us, right?"

"Why would anyone want to do that?"

She massages her temples. "I don't know."

The feeling of failure settles over me with the weight of a familiar, well-worn blanket. It's ridiculous, because I never expected to win in the first place. But getting announced the winner, and the kiss that followed, and the fact that Eleanor is now standing several feet away with her arms crossed—it's given me whiplash.

I heave a sigh. "I'll call in a favor."

"Oh, suddenly you have a favor to call in? Why wasn't that on the table earlier?"

"Because now we're out of time."

Dempsey will have loaded in and finished sound check by now. They're probably already on their way to the brewery.

Eleanor eyes me suspiciously. "Who are you going to call?"

The urge to answer, *Ghostbusters*, is strong, especially because I know she won't be any more appreciative of my actual answer. "Look, I know you don't like him, but Billy will—"

Her expression ices over. "Absolutely not."

Slowly, I let out an exhale. My hands settle on my hips and I squint at the sun reflecting off nearby pool water as I try to draft a convincing response in my head. Eleanor is better at arguing than me, or she's at least more stubborn than I am, but she has to know we're out of options.

"Don't you want this over with?"

"Yes. Obviously. But I'm not going to be beholden to that guy."

"I won't mention your name. He doesn't have to know you're involved."

"That's not—it's the principle of the thing. And you expect me to believe he won't needle you for details?"

Honestly? It's difficult to say. If I told him I needed money, no questions asked, he'd probably respect that. Then again, I could just as easily picture him badgering me for details, assuming there's some salacious story he'd feel entitled to in return.

"I wouldn't tell him anything."

The crease between Eleanor's brows deepens. It's more than irritation there—she seems genuinely upset about Billy getting involved. "You know he's friendly with Griffin, right?"

"What?" That cannot be true—at least not in the way Eleanor's implying. I'm sure they know each other, the way anyone who has been in the industry for long enough knows each other. But Billy has hardly ever mentioned Griffin's name, at least not outside of the context of Griffin's involvement with Eleanor.

"They have a standing golf date," she says. "Like, every month or two."

I almost ask where she heard that, but the answer readily supplies itself. She was with Griffin for over a year. And if he was as involved in her life as she says, it makes sense she would've gotten to know his schedule pretty well in return.

"If Billy did find out about this, then so would Griffin. And I'd really like for that not to happen."

I grit my teeth against the ugly, possessive feeling rising in me. I'm not sure what bothers me more, the implication that Eleanor still cares what her shitty ex thinks, or the idea that Billy and Griffin get together and talk about her. I want to call Billy up and warn him to keep Eleanor's name out of his mouth. But that would be counterproductive. So. Instead, I just stand here, irritated and impotent, wishing I could magic all of Eleanor's problems away.

"Can we at least try the casino first? We can see if anyone wants to buy the chips off us, or we can play a round of blackjack. Can we try that? Please?"

I rake my teeth over my bottom lip, completely helpless in the wake of that one word from Eleanor. And really, she's right. Billy doesn't need to be involved in this.

It's something I have struggled with, in the past—knowing where to draw the line with Billy between the personal and the professional. Knowing how to draw a line in the first place.

The closest I've come was about a year ago, right before Billy got sober. We'd gone to a show in Silver Lake together, to see an up-and-coming band that was getting a lot of buzz. We weren't the only industry people in the audience that night, and after the first set I made my way over to the bar where Billy was camped out, drinking and networking.

He was quick to introduce me to a producer, someone he'd worked with before, albeit with an artist Billy no longer repped.

"Adam, do you know Rob Grimmer?"

"No, I don't think we've met." I stuck out my hand. "Adam Shaw."

"Adam is my old protégé. He's over at Exeter now, killing it."

We shook hands and Rob nodded. "Nice to meet you."

"Same. You enjoying the show?"

"For sure." Rob glanced away as the bartender set three bottles down by his elbow. He passed over a few bills before turning back to me. "I've been following them for a while, but it's nice when a band holds up live."

"They're something special," Billy said with a decisive nod, and I had to suppress an eye roll because he spent the first few songs complaining to me about how overrated they were before I abandoned him at the bar so I could actually *hear* them play.

"Anyway, I should get these to my friends," Rob said before gathering all three bottles in one hand. "But I'm glad I ran into you guys."

"We'll see you around," Billy told him.

"Bet." Rob clasped each of our hands once more before heading over to his group.

"Sorry about that," Billy said as soon as Rob was out of earshot. "Guy is a fucking hack."

I frowned. "Thought you worked with him more than once."

Billy shrugged at this. "He used to be decent, I guess. Now he's a has-been, lurking around clubs like this trying to drum up business."

I took a long swig of beer and swallowed back the comment my mind supplied: *Sort of like you?*

It had started to bug the hell out of me, how underhanded Billy could be—he talked more shit than anyone I'd ever met, but never had a bad word to say to anyone's face.

Being my mentor, Billy had introduced me to countless people. Many of whom he genuinely liked and respected—he'd helped me make some really incredible connections when I was starting out. He'd always been pathologically complimentary about me, seemingly unable to resist singing my praises or calling out a recent accomplishment, to the point it was sometimes embarrassing. But looking across the crowd at Rob, I grew uneasy for an entirely different reason. I couldn't help but wonder what happened when I was the one to walk away first. Whether Billy had ever turned to his contact and immediately started backpedaling about me, telling them I was Atlas Shaw's kid, that he'd taken me under his wing out of pity, that truth be told he didn't *really* recommend working with me.

I went home after the show and couldn't wind down, kept replaying past encounters from events I'd attended with Billy, looking for some clue I might've missed that he wasn't always on my side. I hated that I was even questioning it, but once the seed was planted, I couldn't get it out of my head. By morning I'd made a decision. I needed to take a step back from Billy—stop attending anything industry-related with him, at the very least. Just until I felt more established in my own career. Until I'd solidified my own reputation. I hoped it could be a subtle shift in our relationship, because frankly I had no idea how I'd ever tell him.

Then the accident happened. And clients and friends started dropping him in droves, and I couldn't pile on, I couldn't abandon him like everyone else. And I knew that no matter how gently I tried to distance myself, even if it was only on a professional level, he'd take it that way.

He's been better, since then. Sober, and generally less two-faced and prickly as a result. So I've continued to push it to the back of my mind. But I know it's probably still in my best interest to establish some boundaries between our personal and professional lives.

"Okay," I tell Eleanor. "Yeah, we can try the casino. I won't call Billy."

I glance at my watch. One hour until I'm meant to be at the brewery, and I still have to pick up my ID. Whatever is going on between Eleanor and me, eventually we're going to have to deal with the actual reason we both came to Vegas. I should be focused on work. *She* should be focused on work. Running around a casino and losing more money is not going to help anyone.

But it's what Eleanor wants to do. And somewhere along the line, giving her what she wants became irresistible to me.

CHAPTER THIRTEEN

ELEANOR

Walking onto the casino floor feels like entering a labyrinth. Not only is the floor a literal maze of card tables and banks of slot machines and electronic games, but it's evident how easy it would be to lose sense of time and space in here. There are no windows, no way to track the sun. No clocks either. The music playing overhead is nondescript—no lyrics to sing along to and no breaks between tracks.

Plus, smoking is permitted, so it feels weirdly like entering a time warp. I literally cannot remember the last time I was inside a nonresidential building where cigarettes were allowed, prior to this weekend. My clothes and hair are going to reek, which should probably be the least of my concerns right now, but I'm fixated on it because I don't know if I'll have time to shower before the show.

I follow Adam past a poker table where the dealer is the only one who appears sober. One of the gruff-looking men seated in front of him drains a whiskey glass as I watch. He has a five-o'clock shadow and deep purple bruises under his eyes. I get the distinct impression he's been here all night. And from the modest stack of chips in front of him, I don't think he stayed all that time because he's on a winning streak. The pit in my stomach deepens. Adam is right—this is going to go poorly. And then we'll be back where we started, and I won't be able to stop him from involving Billy Draper.

Today's events aside, I don't think about Griffin anymore. Hardly ever. I don't care how he's doing, or what he's doing, or whether he ever thinks about me. But I can't be blamed for wanting to keep this escapade off his radar. I'd be embarrassed for any ex to hear about it, never mind one with as many industry contacts as Griffin.

As much as I detest reminding anyone how close Griffin and I once were, it was worthwhile if it reinforced Adam's resolve to keep me out of the story, if and when he does talk to Billy.

Now Adam stands beside me, shoulder to shoulder, his gaze warming the side of my face.

"Let's hit the blackjack tables first," I say, "then poker. If neither of those work, we can loop back to the slots."

Adam remains silent, and when I cave and side-eye him, I find him frowning. "No judgment . . . but is this the real reason you're at your credit limit? Do you have a gambling problem?" I can tell by his tone he's dead serious, trying his best to ask delicately. "Because you're not alone. My neighbor struggled with a gambling addiction a while back. There are hotlines you can call—"

"Oh my god." I close my eyes and try not to fixate on what it is about me that made Adam jump so quickly to *gambling addict*. I take a long breath before looking at him head-on.

"No, Adam. While I very much appreciate your concern, I do not have a gambling problem."

He purses his lips. "That's exactly what someone with a gambling problem would say," he mutters. "Well, should we try different tables?"

"Yes," I say immediately. Splitting up is definitely a good idea. Not only because both of us sitting at the same table would mean we were playing against each other, but also because Adam is giving me whiplash.

First he accuses me of wanting him, and then he admits to wanting me back, and now it's like he's forgotten about the teasing and the kiss and all of it. Meanwhile, ever since we left that stage I've felt like I'm trying to inhale underwater. I need space. Need to catch my breath and figure out how I lost the upper hand here, and how the *hell* Adam could tell I'd thought about kissing him.

A seat opens up at the blackjack table Adam's been eyeing, and I hand over half the chips. "We'll meet back here in half an hour."

Adam gives me one last lingering look before he steps away. Mercifully, he does not glance back to catch me watching until he takes a seat. I really wish it were clearer whether he was flirting because he genuinely wants to continue what we started, or if it was just another way for him to get a rise out of me. I sigh and snap myself out of it, turning to weave through the tables and banks of slot machines, scoping out my prospects.

I hadn't noticed until now how loud it is in here. All these people, all the electronics, the sound effects. It's like being stuck inside a dozen different video games at once, and I can't think over all the noise. Interrupting someone sitting at a table seems like a bad idea. But people at slot machines aren't typically betting big money, so I suspect they'd be less likely to make a trade.

My first thought, possibly fueled by the last remaining threads of denial over my feelings for Adam, is to approach one of the single men I see throwing their money around. I could flirt my way into their good graces, maybe have a drink with them and then play the damsel-in-distress card. Men eat that shit up, especially if they suspect they'll get a reward for being the Good Guy who helps you out.

But I've dealt with enough skeevy, ego-tripping men to last a lifetime. Sometimes it feels like they find me, no matter how hard I'm trying to put out an unapproachable vibe. I certainly don't need to go initiating conversations, making them feel like I owe them.

Just—no.

So I narrow my focus to a middle-aged couple standing over by one of the craps tables. They're dressed casually, the man in a polo and khakis, and the woman in a sundress. They look like they're probably my mother's age, maybe a couple of years younger. And most importantly, the woman is wearing a massive diamond on her ring finger.

"Hi," I say when I'm infringing on their personal space enough that they look up. "I'm Eleanor. I was wondering if you could help me out." At this point, it occurs to me that I really should have thought through what I wanted to say ahead of time.

Adrenaline and self-consciousness have me talking fast. "See, I have these promotional chips. My friend and I won them in this newlywed game—it's a long story. We're not really married. I mean, technically we are. But we're not in love or anything. I only realized I might actually have feelings for him like an hour ago, but that's . . . well, that's beside the point."

The two of them exchange a look, like they're both unsure how stable I am. My throat feels tight. I'm no longer sure how stable I am either.

I swallow and shake my head, waving my hand like I can swat my emotions away. "Oh my god, sorry. I truly don't even like Adam that much. This has been a really long, confusing day. And we won these chips, but we can't cash them in, and we *need* to cash them so Adam can get his ID back—"

The man raises his hand, palm facing me, and reaches into his pocket. I drag in a breath and ignore the way my throat is still aching like I'm about to cry—it's the air in here, smoke-tinged and stifling—and preemptively start thanking him when I see a stack of chips in his hand.

"Thank you. Seriously, you have no idea how grateful I am."

He tosses me a chip—literally *tosses* it at me, and I somehow manage to catch it, nearly fumbling all of my own chips in the process. When I lift my head, his back is turned and he's steering his wife to another table.

I look down at the chip he gave me. It's worth ten dollars. It occurs to me that he only gave it to me to get me to stop talking. Which . . . I guess isn't the worst response to a stranger all but accosting you out of nowhere.

My lips pinch and my breath catches and I'm once again struck by the urge to call Iris. This is humiliating, and it's hard to say whether it'd be more or less humiliating to confess everything to my sister and beg her for help.

"Oh, honey . . ."

I look up to find a woman who bears a striking resemblance to Betty White in her later years standing a few feet away. She clucks her tongue and looks me over, head to toe. Then she beckons me toward her group of friends—three women well into their eighties, all wearing bright lipstick and embellished athleisure suits. They look like a band of mall walkers from North Jersey.

I shuffle over to where they're occupying a nearby bank of slot machines, uncertain of what they want from me, but strangely compelled to do what this lady asks, if only because of the Betty White thing.

"I couldn't help but overhear you talking to that couple," she tells me as she gives the jumbo plastic cup in her hand a little shake. "What do you need?"

". . . Sorry, what?"

She's picking chips out of her cup, but pauses to glance at me, over the top of her glasses. Something about that look has me standing up straighter. "You want to trade your promo chips, right? We may not look like high rollers, but we do all right on the electronic poker machines. Don't we, girls?"

The other women nod their agreement, and one of them leans forward to tell me: "Angie is on a winning streak."

Angie—the Betty doppelgänger—is wearing big gold earrings that look painfully heavy, stretching the lobes of her ears, and an honest-to-god visor. She touches two fingers gently to my wrist and leans forward. "What's your name, honey?"

I tell her, and she introduces herself, the other three women—Helen, Maryellen, and Isabella.

"Not that it's any of my business," she says next, "but where's this man you were talking about before?"

"Adam," I say. "He's around. At one of the blackjack tables."

Helen's lipstick has feathered slightly around her mouth, which is made all the more noticeable when she purses her lips in distaste. Beside her, Maryellen tuts. Clearly, these women are not feeling generous toward men at the moment.

"Typical," Angie says, and then grabs the big plastic cup that contains all of her chips and coins. "So, what do you need, sweetie?"

I look down at my handful of chips. "Um. I have twelve hundred and fifty worth of chips. But anything you could do would be really great."

"Sure thing. We've got you covered."

She and her friends each dig out a handful of chips from their respective stashes, and Angie holds them out to me, just like that. I hesitate, unable to believe it's really this easy, then reach to trade the chips with her. "Thank you. Really."

She waves her hand while she divvies the chips up among the group again. "No problem. Like Isabella said, I've had a good weekend. Besides, we're celebrating."

I slide my chips into my pocket, terrified of losing them. "Oh yeah? Is it your birthday?"

"Heck no, I've stopped acknowledging those."

"According to her, she's sixty-five," Helen says with a cackle.

A smile tugs at my lips and Angie rolls her eyes. "I got divorced," she tells me.

"Oh. Well . . . congratulations?"

"Hear, hear," says Maryellen, raising her wineglass. All of them scramble to find their own drinks, and then they clink and down the contents.

"Should've done it years ago, but in families like ours . . . there's usually only one way out of marriage." She gives a shrug, and I'm left to interpret what kind exactly she means by that. Religious families? . . . Italian families?

"Not sure which way is messier," Helen says in a voice so low, I'm not sure I'm meant to hear. I smile and nod, even as my stomach grows slightly unsettled. She almost makes it sound like her husband . . . didn't die of natural causes?

As soon as the thought crosses my mind, I realize how ludicrous it is. These sweet old ladies are harmless. They may be tough, but they're not out here offing their husbands and subtly bragging about it.

"Anyway, son of a bitch used to come to Vegas all the time," Angie goes on. "He was a piss-poor gambler too. But got lucky often enough that the hotel gave him a handful of vouchers." She smiles. "I made sure to get those and his airline miles in the divorce. Paid for our girls' weekend. I'm gonna put the pictures up on Facebook so he can see how much fun we had with his money."

My smile grows wider as I picture this sweet old lady trolling her ex-husband on Facebook.

"Serves him right," Helen chimes in. "He always underestimated you."

These ladies get it. They talk as though their lives are infinitely better without the presence of men. I can definitely see the value of that mindset.

Isabella is mostly fixated on her cocktail, poking her straw at the ice in the bottom of her glass, but she offers a grunt of agreement.

"He sure did," Angie says with a smirk. She leans a bit closer again, her voice going low and conspiratorial. "That was his undoing in the end. He had no idea, but I'd been saving up for years. A little here, a little there. I hired the best attorney in town."

Maryellen grins. "Made all of our husbands nervous."

"If only we'd met your lawyer while Vincent were still alive," Helen says. She turns to me. "I got my due in the will, but if I'd tried to leave him, he would've fought tooth and nail for every dime. If I could've, I would've hired that lawyer, and Vincent never would've seen it coming."

"They never do," Maryellen says before draining the last of her wine. "Despite how they run their business. Not like they're strangers to skimming off the top. But the idea we keep any money they don't know about, make any *plans* they don't know about . . . They can't fathom it."

More and more, their lives are sounding like an episode of *The Sopranos*. I'm dying to ask what kind of shady business these men are involved in, but I'm also slightly afraid to hear the answer. Even though it's ludicrous, and they obviously aren't *actual* mob wives. That's my exhaustion talking.

I wish I could spend the entire day with this coven of old ladies. Aside from the *I'm not like a regular grandma, I'm a cool grandma* vibe they all give off, they also seem content to blame men for everything, which is a sentiment I can really get behind.

A waitress stops by and the ladies all order another round of drinks. The waitress turns to me, but I decline. I don't plan to drink any more for a long while, and I don't have time to sit around anyway.

"I should probably go track Adam down now," I say when the waitress leaves, and Maryellen does not look impressed.

"Let him come to you," Angie says, and the other women

nod their agreement. "I want to hear more about this situation of yours."

Despite the fact that I've spent all day wanting this experience to be over, it occurs to me that I am never going to see these women again. They don't know me. We have no connections out in the real world. I'm not going to get a better opportunity to vent about Adam and the past twenty-four hours.

Which is how I find myself rehashing the entire story.

"So, let me get this straight," Maryellen says when I've finished, manicured finger tapping against her new gimlet glass. "You shared a bed last night, but he didn't make any sort of move?"

"Right. Nothing happened last night."

"Maybe you can work it out," Isabella interjects sweetly, and the other three women groan. I've learned Isabella is the only one of them that's happily married, so it stands to reason that the others shoot down her optimism on sight.

"All I'm saying," she continues doggedly, "is that he sounds decent. It means something that he spent the night with you."

"Yeah, it meant he was too drunk to navigate to his own room," Maryellen says, echoing my own thoughts. "Eleanor's too young to set the bar so low."

Isabella shoots her a look, then turns back to me. "Have you asked him?"

"Asked him what?"

"If it meant anything to him? Last night, or the kiss?"

"Not exactly." Technically, I did ask about the kiss. My phrasing could've been a bit more straightforward, though.

"If you want to stop playing games, sometimes you've got

to fold first," Isabella concludes, and catches her straw to suck down the last, rattling gulp of her Long Island iced tea.

"Or you could put a hit out on him," Angie says.

For a beat I'm frozen, unsure whether she's joking or not. Because on the one hand . . . at first glance she seems so sweet and harmless, and she was so generous with her help. But on the other, I'm now like eighty percent certain these ladies have some Mafia ties back in Jersey.

And then all four of them start cackling. "Your face!" Maryellen exclaims, wiping tears from under her glasses. "Oh, sweetie, you're priceless."

I join in their laughter, but it comes out sounding a bit stilted and forced. It falters more when Angie asks to see my phone, and programs in a number under the contact name: *Brando—Trash Collector*. "In case your lawyer friend needs reinforcements," she says with a wink.

"Uh. Thanks." I lock my phone screen, and when I glance up I spot Adam a few yards away. He's standing with his hands in his pockets and a bemused smile on his lips as he takes in my company. He gives me a little wave, and it hits me all over again—that swell in my chest and the shaky swoop of my stomach. Not because he's a selfish prick I want nothing to do with. The opposite.

"Um . . . I have to go."

Helen follows my gaze and purses her lips again. "That him?"

The other ladies all rubberneck, and of course Isabella immediately starts cooing. "Look at that jawline! Oh, honey, you know how to pick them."

"What the hell kind of shoes are those?" Maryellen mutters to Helen.

I slide off the stool I was occupying and tap my pocket to make sure the chips are all there. "Thank you again for your help," I say. "You ladies are amazing, and I hope you win millions."

"You take care of yourself," Maryellen says, and the women all wave me off, a couple of them glaring at Adam for a beat before turning around and resuming their video poker.

As I approach Adam, he drags a hand through his hair, gaze dropping to the floor until I'm right in front of him. It's not the face of someone who won big.

"That went about as well as I expected," he says with a grimace.

"No worries," I tell him. "Those women traded chips with me."

"Seriously?" Adam looks over my shoulder, and I turn and follow his gaze to find all four women eyeing him as they sip their drinks.

"Uh . . . yeah. They were really nice. . . . A tiny bit scary. But anyway, between this and the money from the rings, we should have enough. Let's get these cashed."

We head over to the wall of cashiers and turn in our chips. I watch, hawklike, as the teller counts out the cash and Adam carefully tucks the stack of bills away in his wallet. I'm still basking in the sense of relief at finally having this problem solved when someone yells behind us.

"Hey you!" Adam and I both instinctively turn toward the voice, and I barely have enough time to process the fact that the silver-haired man who spoke is rushing directly at us before he winds his arm back and decks Adam.

I jump out of the way, hands covering my mouth as I watch Adam stumble to the floor. A whooping laugh, followed by a smoker's cough that could only belong to Helen, can be heard over the commotion.

"Oh god, they did it. They hired a hit man."

"What?" Adam says from the ground, one hand cupping his cheek where he took the hit.

I don't have time to answer, because the next moment, security is on us.

A guard grabs the stocky man who punched Adam, who is yelling again, calling Adam a son of a bitch and demanding to be let go. And then a blonde woman—maybe a couple of years younger than me—is scrambling forward, eyes darting back and forth between Adam and the man.

"Daddy, oh my god," she shrieks.

"That's the guy who crashed your wedding!"

"So you *hit him*?" another woman screeches. She's blonde as well—though in her case it definitely comes from a bottle. Judging from her protective hold on the younger woman and their similar traits, I'd say she's the mother of the bride.

It's becoming clear this man was not hired to kill Adam. And also, that the cake we were eating in Mae's photo can be added to the list of things we did not pay for last night.

On the floor, Adam seems stunned. He sits with both hands in his lap, looking up at everyone hovered around him with this baffled expression on his face until another security guard kneels next to him. He helps Adam to his feet, and Adam touches his face once more, checking for blood. His cheekbone is red and his eye already seems a bit swollen, but the punch didn't break the skin at least.

"I'm so sorry," the older woman is saying, frantic as she grabs her purse from the chair she was occupying a moment ago at the blackjack table.

"Mr. Caruso, you need to come with us," one of the guards says.

For the first time, I notice another guy in their group. He's hanging back a few feet, looking resigned to the proceedings. He's well over six foot, but stands with his hands in his pockets and his shoulders rounded, like he's trying to avoid drawing any attention to himself. The tearful bride barrels into him for a hug as Mr. Caruso is led off the floor.

"You two. Come with me," the remaining security officer says.

My gaze falls to the security tag clipped to his lapel. Muscles bulge beneath the suit sleeves. He looks like a bodybuilder dressed for a job interview. Like he probably moonlights as a professional wrestler called The Boulder.

He is not the sort of person you argue with.

"I think there's been a misunderstanding," I say, even as I fall into step beside him and Adam.

"We'll discuss this off the floor." The guard keeps walking, brooking no room for argument. My heart races—I knew things could still get worse. They're going to take our winnings back. Or make us give them to that Mr. Caruso guy. Or—god—call the actual police to sort this thing out, and then we'll miss the show, and Josie will see the police report—

I am fully spiraling by the time we reach a nondescript door along the back wall of the casino. The security guard tugs on his ID, which is connected by one of those pulley strings, and touches it to a black electronic keypad. The light turns green as the automatic lock opens. He holds the door open for us, and I hesitate a moment before stepping through. I'm trying to recall Tyler's number from memory as the heavy door clicks shut behind us.

CHAPTER FOURTEEN

ADAM

We're led down a fluorescent-lit hall to a windowless room that seems straight out of the movies—the kind of place they hold people who cheat at cards while giant men like our security guard friend toss them around to send a message.

That kind of thing probably doesn't happen in real life.

The guard gestures toward the metal table and four chairs. "Have a seat," he says.

Eleanor sits first, tucking her hands under the table and glancing around the room. I wonder if she finds it as vaguely threatening as I do. I slide the second seat closer to hers before I sit, and have to consciously stop myself from draping my arm protectively across the back of her chair. It's possible I'm still stuck in fight-or-flight mode. Doesn't help that she looks a little worse for wear at this point. Her hair's a bit frizzy and tangled again, like it was first thing this morning, and her mascara has started to smudge under her eyes. Though I have no room to talk. My clothes are rumpled, and the slippers have turned a disgusting shade of gray around the bottoms, and my feet have been sweating in them for hours. I am very ready to get my hands on some new shoes.

The guard stays by the door while we get situated. "Would either of you like a bottle of water?"

"Yes, please," Eleanor says. Her voice trembles a bit, and it has my hackles up. She's scared, and it's that Caruso guy's fault.

She tips her head toward me. "One for him too."

Then the guard is gone, shutting us alone in the room that may or may not be locked from the outside. The room is small and exceedingly bright from the fluorescents overhead and four white walls that feel like they're closing in on us. Despite no evidence of a two-way mirror or anything of the sort, I'm fairly certain somewhere in this room is a microphone, and the casino can hear whatever we say to each other. Which is why I probably shouldn't say anything to Eleanor, at least until we figure out whether we're in some kind of trouble. Evidently, Eleanor has no such reservations.

"You okay?"

"Me? Yeah." I grimace and touch my eye again. "I'll live."

"You fully got punched in the face back there."

"I did," I say with a slow nod.

The concern doesn't leave her eyes. "You're sure you're okay?"

I suck my cheeks in, ignoring the way it sends another twinge of pain across one side of my face. It's hard to feel anything other than pleased, at the moment. "Aw, you care."

Eleanor immediately leans back and crosses her arms, all traces of distress vanishing. "About your face? I mean sure, it's a nice face."

I grin. "Is it?"

She scoffs, trying and failing to look irritated. "Oh, whatever. You know you have a pretty face."

"Not as pretty as yours."

Speaking of pretty, her cheeks are rosy now, eyes bright. She squirms in her chair and huffs again. Oh, she wants so badly to seem flippant. "Obviously."

My grin gets wider—wide enough it kind of stings my bruised cheekbone. "Obviously," I echo, soft and earnest.

We hold each other's gaze for a long-drawn-out moment. It feels like an unspoken dare. Like we're both waiting for the other one to look away first, or to say something cutting to balance out the compliments. Or maybe to lean in and close the remaining distance between us.

Once again I wonder if this room has a hidden camera. If somewhere else in the building, someone is eating popcorn and watching this all play out on a security feed like we're their new favorite reality TV show, waiting for one of us to break the silence.

After a few beats, the drive to win fades to the background, and I duck my head with a small laugh. "I've never been hit like that before. It kind of sucks."

"You were very brave." Eleanor's voice is teasing again. It might even be considered fond-adjacent.

"Granted, my ears were ringing a bit from that punch, but did I hear you accuse that guy of being a hit man?"

"Ha, no," she says, too quickly. "That would be absurd."

The door pops open, and the giant security officer from before lumbers in carrying a tablet in one bear paw of a hand, and two bottles of water in the other. He sets them down on the table and Eleanor thanks him before passing one to me.

While she unscrews the cap and sips hers, I lift my own

and press the chilled plastic to my bruised face. It really does hurt like a bitch.

"No problem," the man says without looking up from his tablet. I squint and read the name off his badge. Malcolm.

"I'm sure you know why I brought you two in here."

Eleanor and I exchange a glance. She must've heard what the guy said about me ruining his daughter's wedding. So yeah, I have a hunch.

"I assume it has something to do with that asshole cold-cocking me," I say.

"Well, yes. Mr. Caruso is being held down the hall. It's up to you whether you'd like to press assault charges. He's still pretty adamant you pay for the ice sculpture—"

"The what?" Eleanor interjects.

Malcolm hesitates, taking in my confused look. "Last night, you two were uninvited guests at the Caruso-Vitale wedding and knocked over their ice sculpture. Mr. Caruso is seeking compensation in the amount of seven hundred dollars."

"For an ice sculpture?" I burst out.

"This is normal ice we're talking about, right?" Eleanor asks. "The kind that melts after a couple hours anyway?"

"Are we sure it was actually broken?" Like I told Eleanor, I vaguely remember a swan carved from ice, but I definitely do *not* remember causing a whole fucking scene.

Malcolm heaves a sigh like he is not paid enough to deal with this kind of drama. He taps away at the tablet, then spins it around so we can watch the security footage he's cued up.

As the video starts playing, I lean forward, desperate for any scraps that will help fill in the remaining gaps of last night.

It becomes immediately apparent that it's really us on the tape, and that we did in fact sneak into a private event being held here last night. From the time stamp of 3:20 a.m., it was likely an hour or so after we left the karaoke bar and right before we called it a night and headed back to Eleanor's hotel.

Eleanor's leg jiggles under the table as the video continues, and for a moment I lose track of the events I'm supposed to be paying attention to—the room that's elaborately decorated with florals and, yes, an ice sculpture of a swan—and my focus fixates on Eleanor and myself on-screen.

I watch as past-Eleanor rubs her arms as if she's cold. Past-me takes note of this, and immediately shifts closer, pulling Eleanor's back to my front. Then my arms wind around her and my chin hooks over her shoulder.

Mae called us "relationship goals" earlier. I was dying to ask what she meant by that. What she saw and heard last night, when she met us. Apparently, whatever interaction we had with her was enough to convince her we were not only a real couple, but head over heels in love with each other.

I've always been cool with PDA in relationships. And I get extra tactile when I'm drunk. So it's not altogether surprising to see myself on this screen, reaching for Eleanor like I have permission to do so.

What *is* surprising is that she reaches back. Even from this limited camera angle, I can see Eleanor put her arms over mine, see her melt into the embrace. As though my touch was something she craved.

I can't look away from the screen. I want to pause it and rewind. It feels like I'm watching some other couple, one who has been together for ages. One who is effortlessly comfortable with each other.

Past-Eleanor tips her head back onto my shoulder, and past-me straightens enough to graze my lips across the top of her head, my arm still wrapped around her and my thumb rubbing a small pattern against her bare arm.

And then we shift a little closer to the ice statue looming behind us, and I see myself pull out my phone, hold it out for a selfie, only to fumble it a moment later.

In my effort to catch the phone, I lose my balance and knock into the sculpture, and the next moment it's shattered on the ground. Everything in the video goes eerily still for a moment, and then past-Eleanor grabs my hand and runs.

Malcolm pauses the video. "This jog your memory at all?"

I finally tear my gaze away from the tablet to glance sidelong at Eleanor. Her head is tipped toward mine, but she won't meet my eye. The space between us feels charged. Magnetic. Like I could reach out and she'd mirror my movement.

I've spent a significant portion of the day wishing last night never happened. Right now I'd give almost anything to go back—not to change what happened, but to relive it and actually remember this time.

Eleanor clears her throat and the tension between us snaps. Her poker face is back. "That was clearly an accident."

Malcolm lifts one hand in a concession, and then there's a knock on the door. He gets up slowly—seems like everything Malcolm does is at half speed, which makes sense. It probably takes a lot of effort to move all those muscles around. He steps into the hall to speak with another security guard, leaving the door cracked open behind him.

A moment later, Malcolm steps back into the room, trailed by the younger woman I saw out on the casino floor. The bride. She offers us a nervous wave.

"Hey, guys," she says, twisting the diamond rings on her finger around and around, like she's not used to wearing them yet. "Um. I'm Andrea. We didn't really get a chance to meet last night."

I palm my face and immediately drop my hand, because *ow.*

"Are you hurt?"

This is directed toward me, and it's not like *she* decked me, so I smile tightly. "I'm all right."

"Listen, I talked to my dad. You totally don't have to worry about the ice sculpture."

Eleanor and I exchange another quick glance. "Oh . . . that's great. Thank you," she says.

"No problem. And I would so super appreciate it if you didn't press charges against him for the whole . . ." Her diamonds glitter as she does a little shadowboxing, finishing with a wince.

I nod. "Yeah. If you're good, I'm good."

Her face floods with relief. "Thank you. I've never seen him get angry like that. He's really embarrassed about it now. As he should be."

"Weddings are stressful," Eleanor says carefully. "I get it—he wanted yours to be perfect."

My gaze cuts over to Eleanor. Hearing the melancholy in her voice, I'm suddenly swarmed with guilt. I've been so focused on the inconvenience of last night, and the fallout. But for the first time, it occurs to me that we didn't just get married last night. We had a wedding. A shitty, unplanned, drunken ceremony that was probably nothing like the one Eleanor has dreamed about. Followed by scraps of cake at a reception that wasn't even ours.

One day she might get married again. And next time, she

can get a beautiful dress, and flowers, and have her sister there, and I hope if that's what she chooses down the road, it's everything she wants it to be. Because she deserves it, and I took that away from her. Feels like shit.

"I'm really sorry about all this," Andrea says.

"Hey, we're sorry we crashed your reception," I tell her. "I really hope we didn't ruin anything . . . besides the ice sculpture."

"Oh no. Honestly I didn't even notice you guys until the sculpture fell. But it was late; the party was totally winding down anyway." She grins broadly and gives us another wave before stepping back into the hall and letting the door fall shut behind her.

"Guess that's settled, then," Malcolm says, already gathering his tablet and pushing his chair in. "Thanks for your time."

Eleanor and I get up before he changes his mind, and together we file out into the too-bright hallway. He leads us back to the door and leaves us on the casino floor.

Once we're alone, we both hesitate, as if waiting for the other shoe to drop. Which is somewhat absurd, because this is nowhere near the first bad thing to happen to us in the past twenty-four hours.

"Let's get out of here," I say finally. Eleanor is still clutching her half-empty water bottle, the weak plastic crinkling between her palms.

We walk out of the casino and through the lobby in silence, not stopping until we reach a stone pillar a dozen yards away from the entrance. Outside, the sun is hanging lower in the sky than I expected, making all the artificial lights shine brighter. It's nearly five p.m.—we spent too long in the casino. The band probably doesn't have much downtime left. If

I don't leave right now, I'll miss my chance to see them at the brewery.

Eleanor leans against the pillar, watching as new guests arrive and bellhops move forward to help them unload their bags from the car. My gaze slips down to her tan legs, stretched out long and crossed at the ankle.

She meets my eye and smiles, so radiant it puts the city's neon lights to shame. She pushes herself upright when I come to stand in front of her, and I shove my hands into my pockets so I don't do something regrettable, like reach out to hug her.

I match her smile. "What a totally normal and relaxing day, huh?"

Eleanor snorts a laugh that turns into a groan partway through. She laces her hands together on top of her head, elbows pointing out. "At least we managed not to get arrested?"

"Yeah. I'll take that win." I bite my lip. This feels like the last day of summer camp, like we're gearing up for some great big goodbye. Which is beyond ridiculous, because we'll see each other at the show later tonight. Still, it feels heavy, this moment. Not because Eleanor owes me anything, but because maybe I owe her.

"You know, I haven't really apologized. You were right, this morning. Not about everything . . ." Eleanor was awfully quick to blame me for what happened last night, and to be fair, it's not like I forced her into any of it. But she had a point. I came here and fucked with her meeting, and I did it on purpose. "I was telling the truth when I told you I didn't know who the band was having dinner with. But only because I didn't care enough to ask. I was chasing a lead; that's all I cared about. I'm . . . not sure that makes it any better. So yeah, I'm sorry."

Eleanor breathes in, slow and deep. She nods once. "I'm sorry too. For giving you such a hard time earlier."

I wave her apology away, not sure how necessary it is in the first place. We both gave each other a hard time—we're even. Almost.

If I had my priorities straight, I'd tell Eleanor to head over to her hotel now. I don't need her help anymore. We've got the money—I can get my ID back, then go to the brewery to meet the band, like I'm supposed to. But apparently my instincts are all fucked up, because they're telling me we should stick together. Which is absurd. We've spent the *entire day* together. We should be sick of each other by now. Instead, I feel sick at the prospect of parting ways and going back to how things were before.

It's possible my crush isn't quite as dormant as I originally thought.

"Listen . . . I know you probably want to go decompress," I tell her, "but I was actually about to head out to meet up with the band."

It's jarring, how quickly Eleanor's expression shutters in the face of this information. "Oh."

"You should come," I say before she can get pissed all over again.

She shifts her weight and looks away from me.

"Seriously. It's a casual thing at a brewery across town." I tilt my head and bend my knees, trying to snag her gaze again. When she looks my way, I offer a grin. "What do you say?"

"Why are you even telling me about this? It's your chance

to win them over. That's the whole point of you being in Vegas, isn't it?"

I shrug. "More fun winning if we play fair."

This earns me an eye roll and a bitten-down smile. She rocks forward, until we're standing toe to toe. For one irrational, hopeful moment, I get the idea she's going to kiss me. Instead, she reaches up and taps my uninjured cheek with her palm—too gentle to be called a slap, too rough to be a caress. Just enough to stoke the desire that's been burning through me all day long. "Cute that you think you still stand a chance."

CHAPTER FIFTEEN

ELEANOR

After a day of wild stress combined with desert heat, my skin is past the point of what any reasonable person would consider dewy. In the back seat of a cab on our way to the bar to pay off our tab and pick up Adam's ID, I rifle through my bag in search of a tissue or napkin—anything I can use to blot my face. When I come up empty I swipe the back of my hand over my forehead in an effort to control the shine.

I'm not the only one concerned about my appearance. I keep catching Adam tenderly touching his face. When he resorts to pulling out his phone and turning his camera to selfie mode, I take pity on him.

"It's really not that bad."

He lowers his phone and rolls his head against the headrest to look at me. "It's not great, though."

"No, it's . . . very rock 'n roll." I maintain a straight face for a five whole seconds before we both start laughing. I'm not sure I've ever heard someone earnestly call something *rock 'n roll* in my entire life, so it's no wonder he didn't buy it. "Honestly, I'd be more concerned with your shoes."

"Shit." He looks down at his feet, apparently having forgotten that he is still wearing hotel slippers. It reminds me of our first cab ride this morning, and I don't understand how only a few hours have passed since then. Feels like a lifetime ago.

"I should probably do something about that," Adam muses. We pull up outside the Desert Cowboy and I wait in the car while Adam runs inside to pay the tab and recover his ID. When he slides back in beside me a few minutes later, he hands me some folded cash.

"What's this?" I ask as I unfold them and count six twenty-dollar bills.

"Your half of what was left over." He leans forward and asks the driver if he could reroute us to a shoe store.

"Sure. What one?" the driver asks.

"Doesn't matter. Any shoe store that carries men's shoes."

While the cab pulls away from the curb, I fiddle with the money in my hand. Part of me wonders if we really had that much left over, or if Adam gave me more than half of what was left. But asking means skirting around the fact that Adam now knows I'm flat broke, and I'd rather not get into that yet again, so I pocket the money and say nothing.

The driver chooses a discount shoe store near the brewery called Kinky Boots. I don't even attempt to keep a straight face this time. Based on the pictures taped to the window, it seems like the sort of place the dancers at Deja Vu would buy their footwear.

Adam grimaces at the sign, and apparently can't resist casting a glare my way—which only makes me laugh harder—before paying and getting out of the car.

"Solid choice," I tell the driver.

He meets my eye in the rearview mirror and shrugs, but I catch his grin as he looks away. Despite everything that has gone wrong on this trip, I've truly been blessed with some excellent cabdrivers.

I slide out after Adam and the cab starts to pull away when my phone buzzes. Yet another text from Iris.

Did you get my voicemail??

Shit. She's really freaking out about this. Not that she needs to—I was always going to do whatever I could to make her big day perfect.

"I'll wait out here for you," I tell Adam, who nods and heads into Kinky Boots with the air of a man walking the plank.

I shake my head and turn my attention back to my text chain. Considering how prominently Duchess was featured in my sister's engagement photos, she'll probably be the star of the wedding, anyway. So really, I should be honored. Both that Duchess likes me, and that Iris trusts me to care for her incredibly high-maintenance dog, who she possibly loves more than her future husband. And why shouldn't she trust me with this? I can be responsible. I will get Duchess down that aisle, and we will look fabulous doing it.

Yes

OMG wait I just remembered this is Dempsey day!!!

Ignore me, we'll talk later

Good luck!!!

Iris knows better than anyone how obsessed I am with Dempsey. She listened to me endlessly rave about them when I first discovered their demo, then rant after they slipped through my fingers. It's why she chose their concert as the place to finally confront me about Griffin.

They were touring their debut album, and Iris snatched up tickets the moment they went on sale. Just two.

Sister night, she'd captioned the text when she sent me a screenshot of her ticket confirmation, no boys allowed.

It had been ages since Iris and I had gone to a show together. We did our preshow ritual, hitting the bathrooms before they got busy, the merch line before the good T-shirts sold out, and then grabbing bottles of water before finding the best vantage point. They were playing a popular venue in Echo Park, and Iris and I weaved our way along the side of the balcony until we found a spot right against the railing, close to the stage.

As soon as we were settled in, Iris turned to me. "So. When are you going to dump Griffin?"

My head reared back, and for a moment I could only blink at her. "What the fuck?"

She shrugged and lifted a single brow. She's a few inches shorter than me, but standing there with her feet firmly planted and her arms crossed, she looked immovable. Ready for a fight. "You heard me."

"Where is this coming from? I thought you liked him."

Griffin had made an effort with Iris. He'd taken her with us to fancy, Michelin-starred restaurants on more than one occasion. He'd referred some TV producer he knew from the country club to her for personal training. He'd been nothing but nice to her, because he knew she was the most important person in my life.

Iris sipped her water, finally letting her gaze flick away. She licked her lips and fiddled with the cap before finally speaking in a careful voice I'd never heard from her before. "He can be very charming. And he's good-looking and rich. But, Ellie, come on." She turned to face me again. "He is a complete jackass and he doesn't treat you right. And I feel like you know that?"

My jaw clenched. She was being shitty. It pissed me off that out of nowhere she was springing this on me, calling my long-term boyfriend a *jackass*. But my anger accounted only for a small part of the heat washing over me. Mostly, I was embarrassed.

I stared at the stage, empty aside from the drum kit and sound equipment. We'd gotten here as soon as the doors opened, and the floor was finally starting to fill in. Dempsey would be coming on any minute.

"Have you been thinking this the whole time we've been together?"

She didn't respond, aside from a purse of her lips.

My mind filtered through all the times they'd hung out together, Iris laughing at Griffin's jokes, and I'd known it was forced, could tell her smile was strained, and I'd ignored it.

My hands tightened around my bottle of water, crinkling the plastic. "You could've said something sooner," I snapped.

Iris scoffed, exasperated. "When would I have done that?

At the party my roommates and I threw last month that you didn't come to? Or at Mother's Day brunch, when you brought Griffin for some reason?"

"Well, his own mom is dead—"

"Because he's like a million years old."

"So, what, this is all because you think he's too old for me?"

"No." Iris waved her hands, as if to erase her previous comment. "It's not about his age. I don't care about that. It's—he's your *boss*. It's fucking weird that he pursued you in the first place. But whatever, I'd get over that, too, if I thought he actually deserved you. If I thought he made you happy."

"He—"

"Ellie, don't fucking lie to me. Look me in the eye and tell me you're happy."

My mouth opened. Then snapped shut as a lump formed in my throat. She was right. It would be lying to pretend I was entirely happy. The truth was, I was anxious all the time. Always worried about disappointing Griffin, or saying the wrong thing and having to listen to some condescending lecture about how I should have done better. I hated my job. The job I'd worked so hard for, that I used to love, I now hated, and it was his fault. Because he'd promoted me so he could micromanage all of my projects and now everyone else at work despised me more than ever, thought I didn't deserve to be there. And Iris was right—I'd barely seen or spoken to her for months, because Griffin always needed me to be with him, even if it was just to hang off his arm and listen to people verbally fellate him at some boring party.

The buzz of the crowd grew to a roar as Dempsey took the stage. As luck would have it, they opened with my favorite song: Track five from their debut album—a song about what it's like to lose yourself in someone else, and to feel untethered without them. About how romantic it seems when someone first steals your breath away, until eventually parts of you start to die without oxygen.

I'd always loved the song simply because Sheridan's lyrics are brilliant, but listening to her sing it live, especially right after that conversation with Iris, I connected to it on a whole new level. I was suffocating in my relationship. And it had happened so slowly, I'd barely even noticed until I was in too deep, and I couldn't picture my future without Griffin in it. But as Sheridan sang onstage, I forced myself to picture it. And I liked what I saw.

That night I went home—not to Griffin's place, but to my own apartment I rarely slept in anymore—and applied for a job at Blue Sky. Being with Griffin had impacted my friendships, my relationship with my sister, had made me lose my passion for my work. But Iris had helped me realize I still loved music. I still wanted to work with artists, even if it meant I had to start over somewhere else.

Iris has always, always been there when I need her. To give me a push in the right direction, or to be a shoulder to cry on, or just to listen when it feels like no one else will.

Right now she needs me, and what do I do? Send her to voicemail and ignore her texts. My baby sister is getting married, and I've been so wrapped up in my own shit that I've barely made time for her and have acted like it's some huge chore to listen to her plans.

Iris is away at some yoga retreat this weekend that promises to reset your chakra through an abundance of herbal tea and a lack of Wi-Fi. Probably there's more to it than that, but Iris told me about the itinerary after a very long day of wedding-related errands, so I may have tuned her out. But I'm pretty sure it's the sort of place where phones are frowned upon, so I figure she must really be anxious if she's spending this much time messaging me.

I call her without giving it another thought.

"I'm so sorry," she says as soon as she answers.

"For what?"

"Uh, because this is your shot at Dempsey, and here I've been blowing up your phone with these dumb wedding logistics. I'm the worst."

"You're really not. It's fine. I'm not even seeing the band until later. And anyway, *I'm* sorry for not getting back to you sooner, but yes. Of course I'll take care of Duchess."

"Yeah?" The relief in her voice is palpable. "Thank you, that's a huge help. Every time I think I'm done with wedding stuff, some new problem crops up."

I shuffle across the pavement and sink against the scratchy brick wall of the shoe store while Iris launches into a whole laundry list of instructions that I don't actually need to think about until next weekend. But I close my eyes and do my best to actually *listen*, to make mental notes so I don't fuck anything up on the big day.

Unfortunately, keeping my eyes closed means I miss the moment when Adam walks out of the store.

"Before you say anything about me buying boat shoes—"

My eyes fly open, and I start cutting my hand across my throat in the universal sign for *stop talking*, and naturally, Adam is too busy staring at his new shoes to notice.

"—it was either this or a pair of platform sneakers. Which were actually kind of cool, but I'm not Harry Styles. So."

Iris has gone suspiciously quiet in my ear, and I move my

free hand even more frantically to get his attention, accidentally clipping Adam on the nose in the process.

"*Jesus, Eleanor,*" he hisses, and I wince as I shift to cover the mouthpiece instead. Which is probably what I should have done in the first place, because if Iris realizes I'm with someone right now, that will open up a whole new can of worms. Adam opens his mouth to speak again and instinct takes over. I don't think—I lunge toward Adam, shoving him up against the wall and covering his mouth with my palm before he can say anything more incriminating.

"Are you with someone?" Iris asks.

"No. I'm—I'm outside. On a sidewalk. It's crowded."

I can feel myself acting a little unhinged. It should've been easy to say, *yeah, I'm with a colleague, can I call you Monday?* It wouldn't have even been a lie. Except for the part about me thinking of Adam as a colleague. Because he's not just a random guy I know through work, he's someone I might really be starting to like, and that's the entire issue, because I don't know how to do this anymore. Especially not with someone in the music business. Griffin made me gun-shy. Made it impossible for me to feel this way about someone without worrying it will all blow up in my face one day.

Adam's eyes burn into mine. His mouth has gone slack beneath my touch, but his fingers are curled into fists at his sides, like it's taking all of his restraint to keep from putting his hands on me. A shiver runs down my spine and I find myself tempting fate—pressing more of my weight against him, one of my legs slipping between his. He exhales sharply against my fingertips.

Iris says something I don't quite catch, too distracted by

the heat of Adam's palms as they wrap around my waist and hold me in place.

My fingertips drag across Adam's full bottom lip. He remains passive, allowing me to explore for a suspended moment before his lips twitch beneath my touch and his tongue flicks out to lick the pad of my thumb.

My breath catches and heat flashes low in my belly. I cut Iris off midsentence.

"Hey, Iris? I'm so sorry—now is actually not a great time. Can I call you later?"

"Oh, sure. No problem. Then you can tell me all about how it goes with Dempsey!"

"Yeah. I will. Enjoy the rest of the retreat." I lick my lips. Adam's smile grows wider. With my eyes locked on his and a tremble in my voice, I say: "Love you. Bye."

I hang up the phone with one hand, and for the span of a breath, Adam and I remain locked in place. His eyes lose their teasing edge, become more earnest. He's no longer wearing the cocky grin that always winds me up. The way he looks at me now is without pretense. It's raw, and unfiltered, and has something warm unspooling inside of me.

"That was my sister." My voice comes out hoarse, and I swallow hard. "She wants me to be her dog's date to the wedding. It's a whole thing."

Adam doesn't reply. Just keeps on staring at me, hungry. Belatedly, I come to my senses and shift back to give Adam space. But the moment I pull my hand away from his mouth, Adam catches my wrist and holds me in place.

He moves slowly, giving me every chance to stop him as he leans in. I don't. I let him kiss me, and do nothing except close my eyes. It starts soft, a brush of his lips across mine.

My next exhale comes out shaky, and Adam releases my wrist so he can gently cup my jaw instead. His thumb sweeps across my cheek, soothing, and I find myself melting into his touch. My hands land on his ribs, fingers latching on to the fabric of his shirt. I keep waiting for him to take control and turn the kiss into something deeper or more demanding, but that never happens. Each time we break apart, it's only so his nose can skim mine, or so he can sweetly press his lips to my cheek before catching my mouth with his once more. I lose track of how much time has passed. Of everything except the way Adam feels and tastes.

After one last, lingering kiss, Adam's forehead rests against mine. Our breaths mingle, and I feel lightheaded in a way that's very different from every other hangover-induced moment of the afternoon.

"I really had been thinking about it all day," he says. I nod helplessly against him.

My eyes open, and I don't know what to do with the vulnerability I see written all over his face, or the fact that I suspect it mirrors my own expression.

I step back, and this time Adam lets me. My thumb swipes across my bottom lip, as if to erase the sensation of Adam's kiss. Doesn't work. I don't know where to look. I am not usually this frazzled after a kiss, but that was, like . . . a lot of kisses, and all of them very intimate, and highly enjoyable, and I kind of want to still be doing it? But that is out of the question, because we're standing in the middle of a parking lot outside of an establishment called Kinky Boots, and I am *thisclose* to becoming unemployed, and I did not come to Vegas to make out with Adam Shaw.

"We should . . ." I cast a gaze around the parking lot in an attempt to get my bearings. "We can walk the rest of the way from here, don't you think?"

Adam doesn't answer right away, seems reluctant to move on from the moment we shared. Not that I can blame him. I feel unmoored in the aftermath, teeming with a buzzing energy that no longer has any outlet. But when I turn back to Adam, he swallows hard and nods once. Takes out his phone and pulls up directions.

"Few minutes away," he confirms.

We walk side by side, and I can't stop myself from wondering what it would feel like to hold his hand. The backs of our knuckles brush together, and my stomach pitches, and I tell myself it wouldn't be a big thing, or all that out of the blue considering we kissed moments ago. My fingers twitch and I am about to go for it, but Adam's hands slip into his pockets.

Never mind, then.

We wait at the corner for the Walk sign to come on, and Adam huffs a laugh.

"Just remembered, I got you this." His hand comes out of his pocket holding something.

He tosses it to me and I catch the small object against my chest reflexively. It turns out to be a stress ball shaped like Elvis.

"I figured you can't leave Las Vegas without a souvenir."

"Oh, don't worry, I'll be leaving with plenty of baggage," I quip. I give Elvis a few squeezes and meet his gaze with a grin. "Thank you. It's cute."

"You're welcome."

I don't overthink it this time. As we step onto the crosswalk, I let my hand do what it wants—reaching out and slipping into his, our fingers lacing together easily. I feel Adam's gaze on the side of my face but keep my own dead ahead. Out of my peripheral vision, I think I see his lips curve into a smile.

He holds my hand until the brewery comes into view, our steps instinctively slowing to a stop. We stand still for a long moment, and when I finally allow myself to look up at Adam, it's to find him watching me with an expression that I struggle to describe as anything other than *soft*. Adam looks down at our entwined hands and shifts his hold so the pad of his thumb can trace gently over my knuckles. The ghost of his touch seems to linger on my ring finger after he gives my hand a squeeze and lets go.

Immediately upon entering the brewery, it becomes clear that this is not a casual hang. Or, it *was*, but stops being one the second I enter the equation. Sheridan and Curtis exchange a look when they spot me, and there might as well be a goddamn record scratch underscoring the awkwardness. I want to melt into a puddle, or at least stomp on Adam's foot for putting me in this situation.

If this were happening a few hours ago, I would've assumed he'd done it on purpose—invited me along only to make me look like a desperate hanger-on. But I know him better now, and his body language is enough to chase away any lingering doubts. He's gone stiff beside me and lifts his hand to the small of my back, only to quickly abort the motion when he seems to remember that we're in front of people we know now, and such gestures are no longer appropriate.

Turning tail isn't an option. I can't dodge Josie much longer, and this may be my last chance to garner some good news to share with her. I am no stranger to the fake-it-'til-you-make-it mentality, so I pretend it's not excruciating to follow Adam to the bar and watch as he does the bro-y hand-shake with Freddie.

"Hey, guys," Sheridan says. "I didn't know you'd be joining us."

"Yeah," I say with a bright smile. "I hope you don't mind me crashing."

"No, not at all," she replies, shooting a pointed look at Freddie. "The more the merrier."

Though Freddie ignores her less-than-subtle glares, I zero in on the way Sheridan's knuckles go white around her pint glass. It occurs to me it might not just be my presence that came as a surprise—I'm beginning to think Freddie neglected to tell her he'd invited Adam too. Fiona isn't even here, for one thing. I can't imagine she'd be pleased to know the band was talking to either one of us without her.

"Did you have that shiner last night?" Ralph asks with no small amount of concern.

"Uh, no. That's a more recent development." Adam smirks, the expression practiced and precise. "Long story."

One of the bartenders nods to us. "Can I get you two anything to drink?"

"Nothing for me, thanks." To Freddie, I add: "I'm not staying long."

Besides the unrelenting urge to flee, I cannot fathom drinking anything besides water right now. But apparently the revolting combination of coconut water and strip club meat did its job, because Adam orders a beer.

Once it's in hand, Adam casually moves down the bar to strike up a conversation with Ralph and his wife, Jane, allowing me an opportunity to relocate to the nearest high-top, to speak with Freddie and Sheridan in relative privacy.

"Look, I'm going to be straight with you guys. . . . I don't remember much of what we discussed after dinner last night."

Freddie tips his head in acceptance. "You went after it pretty hard."

"Yes. I did." I shake my head. "The point is, Fiona mentioned you were having some second thoughts—"

Sheridan sits forward, about to say something, but Freddie speaks over her.

"It's kinda funny," he says with this sardonic little smile. "You and Shaw showing up here together, considering."

My mouth opens and closes twice. "Considering . . . ?"

He takes a big gulp of his beer, draining half of it in one go, and then sets the glass down on the table. "You said Adam was the best at what he does. That Exeter is a great label, and that you 'got it' and that if you were in our shoes, you'd sign with Adam too."

My gaze flickers to Sheridan—whose lips are pursed, a tiny crease between her brows—then back to Freddie. "Well. Yikes."

Freddie smirks and picks up his pint glass again. "You can see why we wanted to explore our options."

Over at the bar, Adam is still talking with the others, though I catch him casting looks he probably thinks are stealthy in our direction. I take in his dorky boat shoes, and his bruised face, and I think about the squishy little Elvis tucked safely in my tote bag. I think about his jacket draped over my shoulders last night, and him giving me a piggyback ride for blocks.

My opinion of Adam has evolved, but I wasn't entirely wrong about his motivations for being here. I still think he wants to sign this band mostly because it will help him get ahead. The thing is, I'm no different.

It's easy to drag Adam for wanting to cash in on Dempsey, as though the money isn't a huge factor for me too. Yes, I have always loved this band, and yes, I wanted to sign them even when they were unproven. But the money still matters. It matters a lot right now.

When she signed off on this trip, Josie warned me it would be the last travel expense she'd approve if I didn't come home with a verbal agreement from Dempsey. And she certainly isn't okay with me spending my own money to cover networking costs anymore. I've poured everything I have into my work, emptied my savings account, because somewhere along the way I convinced myself that one big break was all I needed. One wild success story would be enough to wipe out every other rumor about me, enough to shake off the impostor syndrome that has plagued me ever since I started working for Griffin.

I'm trapped in this cycle—constantly fighting tooth and nail yet only ever scraping by. I'm tired. I am so, so tired, and I don't know how to outsell Adam.

"Adam is great," I say with a shrug. I see no point in trying to walk back on that, pretend I meant something different from what I said. Especially since I already admitted I don't remember saying it in the first place. Instead, I focus on putting my personal feelings for Adam aside. Pretend he's still the relative stranger he was when we first got to Vegas. "Dempsey is in an ideal position. You've got a strong sales record, and you're coming off a successful tour. Signing with either one of us would be a solid choice. But I'm the best choice. If I haven't convinced you of that already, after all the preliminary conversations we've had, then I don't know what more I can say at this point." I look to Sheridan and add, "I think you're an incredible songwriter. Just know that I genuinely am a huge fan and would love the opportunity to work with you all."

"All right," Freddie says. "We'll take that under consideration."

His tone is one I've heard too many times before from men in this industry. Placating. Passive. He won't take it under consideration, because his mind is made up. I know it, and from the tense-jawed look on Sheridan's face, she knows it too.

"Great. Well, you know how to get in touch with me."

Freddie sets his glass down and offers me his hand to shake. He taps my arm with his opposite hand and pulls away. He starts stepping backward, away from us. "You're still coming to the show tonight, yeah?"

"Of course. Wouldn't miss it," I tell him, even though the truth is I'd rather take a long bath and go to bed at nine. Or catch an earlier flight home. Or do any number of things, really, besides stand in uncomfortable shoes for three more hours of the day, listening to a band I love and will probably lose out on. Again.

He nods and turns around, walking the rest of the way to the restrooms.

"Nothing is officially decided yet," Sheridan adds once he's disappeared around the corner.

Maybe not. But I'm not sure anything could change Freddie's mind at this point. Where Curtis and Ralph stand is less clear. Frankly, I'm not even sure if their votes carry as much weight as the Dempsey siblings' do. And I have a sinking feeling they're more likely to follow Freddie's lead.

As if she's thinking the same thing, Sheridan heaves a sigh and says: "Sometimes I think I should ditch all the men in my life and start a solo career."

"Call me if it ever comes down to that," I say with a laugh.

She smiles wryly and together we head over to the bar, where I say a quick hi and bye to the rest of the band, as well as Ralph's wife, Jane.

"Taking off already?" Curtis asks.

"Yeah, I've got a few phone calls to make before the show. But I'll see you all tonight."

My eyes land on Adam last, and he takes a sip of his beer. "Tell Iris hi for me."

I hitch my bag higher on my shoulder and turn to leave, but not before I shoot him a look that says, *I loathe you.*

His lips twitch in response: *Do you, though?*

And god help me, but we both know I don't. I'm not sure I ever did.

CHAPTER SIXTEEN

ADAM

Ralph talks a mile a minute while I nurse my beer, a session IPA aptly named Hair of the Dog, which I ordered mostly out of a sense of obligation. I've taken only about three sips, but I am grateful for something to do with my hands as I watch Eleanor walk away. I didn't expect her to go so soon, thought maybe we'd leave together, even though we'd have no reason to do that.

When she's out the door and out of sight, I refocus on the conversation happening over my head, at which point I realize Ralph's wife, Jane, is watching me with a shrewd expression. Mercifully, she sips her beer and goes back to listening to Ralph list off all the places he's looking forward to eating when he's back home in LA.

Jane is a freelance food writer, so she immediately starts throwing out names of restaurants that are on her list to review, some of which she's specifically saved for when Ralph was home from tour.

"Do you have a favorite date spot?" I find myself asking.

"What kind of food? Are you into Peruvian cuisine?"

"Uh, sure. I like pretty much everything."

"That's the great part about living in LA, right? Something for everyone."

Curtis nods along next to her, though I'm not entirely convinced the guy is paying any attention. I'm fairly certain he has a rhythm playing in his head at all times, maybe even when he's asleep, so that could account for the nodding.

Either way, Jane winds up giving me a whole list, which I diligently type into the notes app on my phone.

"Are you seeing someone?" she asks when I've caught up on typing. I tense, keeping my eyes on my phone screen, but Jane does not bring up Eleanor, despite what I have begun to suspect is a super-obvious crush on my part. "If they have a favorite dish I haven't covered, I've got more recs."

"Um . . ." Against my will, my gaze flickers over to the high-top table where Eleanor was talking with Freddie and Sheridan a minute ago. Now it's just the two siblings, who seem to be bickering in Eleanor's absence, albeit in hushed voices that don't carry to me. Sheridan says something through clenched teeth while Freddie pointedly gulps his beer and avoids her stare. She flicks his shoulder to get his attention and he smacks her hand away with a huff. I clear my throat and run my thumb along the side of my glass, collecting condensation. "No. Not seeing anyone."

"Good to be prepared, though, right?"

"Exactly." I match Jane's smile, even if it feels tight.

My phone buzzes and I scramble to pull it out of my pocket, thinking—hoping, maybe—that it's a text from Eleanor. But it's the group chat again, the guys arguing over which bar they should hit for happy hour. I shove my phone away and turn to ask Ralph his opinion on scooped bagels, which has him off to the races again.

Freddie makes his way over, setting his empty glass on the bar top loudly and flagging the bartender down to ask for another. Sheridan remains across the room. She stands with her back to the rest of us, but it's obvious she's fuming from the tense set of her shoulders, the way her hands brace against her hips. She walks out the same door as Eleanor without a word to anyone.

"Everything okay with Sher?" Ralph asks, evidently having been keeping an eye on her as well.

Freddie downs half of his fresh beer before answering. "She's fine. Just being a bitch."

"Come on, man," Curtis says in a disapproving voice. "We told you to cut that shit out."

"Adam, glad you could make it." Freddie claps my shoulder, acting as though he didn't hear Curtis. "We still have a few things to talk about after last night."

"Shouldn't we wait for Sher to come back?" Ralph asks, his attention divided as Jane slips off her barstool.

"You wanna get your head bitten off? By all means, go fetch her." Freddie takes another pull of his beer and then mutters into his glass: "Or should we sit here discussing bread for the rest of the day?"

Curtis rubs his temples like he has a headache brewing. Jane and Ralph have the kind of silent communication that comes with being together as long as they've been, and then Jane heads outside, presumably to speak to Sher, but possibly just to get some distance from Freddie. It's becoming increasingly clear that tensions aren't high only between the Dempsey siblings. Everyone seems to be having trouble handling Freddie today.

To be fair to Freddie, I have been standing here half an hour and have yet to say a word about signing them.

"Man, it was so cool meeting Chris last night," Freddie says next, and for the first time today, his ego seems to slip away.

I hook one foot on the bottom rung of my barstool. "Yeah, he's a good guy."

"You're lucky, growing up around so many of the greats," Ralph says.

This gives me pause. "I wouldn't necessarily put it that way."

Freddie snorts a laugh. "Uh, okay. I get you're biased, or whatever. But Atlas Shaw is objectively one of the greatest musicians of our time. He left behind such a legacy."

All I can manage is a nod. While Freddie waxes poetic about my deadbeat dad, I nod and think about being nine years old and listening to his albums under my covers, headphones on so my mom wouldn't hear, memorizing every lyric and looking for some sign that any of it was about me.

At some point I stopped expecting anything from him. Stopped waiting around on my birthdays in the vain hope Atlas would show up—hell, that he'd send a fucking *text*. I told myself I was done, I didn't care. I wanted that to be true, but the reality is I never stopped seeking his approval. I didn't grow out of it when I graduated from Berklee, or when I started interning at Exeter, or when I signed my first artist. It wasn't enough when someone on my roster won a Grammy, or when I got promoted.

I gave up on my dad, but I didn't really, because I only transferred that shit onto Billy. I thought I wanted his professional approval, when really I wanted fatherly approval. He's been a good mentor to me, but I'm not an inexperienced kid anymore. I don't need him to fill that role.

It's only now that I'm listening to Freddie fanboy over Atlas, and praise me for how plugged in I am in the industry, that I can admit the truth. I've let Billy be my guidepost for too long. I thought I was being objective about Billy, told myself I could separate his good ideas from the bad ones, and that showing my loyalty was more important than agreeing with every little thing he said. I told myself it was enough to acknowledge when he was being inappropriate, without actually having to *do* anything about it. But Eleanor was right. I've let too much slide.

I was going after Dempsey the wrong way, for the wrong reasons. I like Dempsey's music, I really do. But that's not why I'm here. I'm here because Billy told me to be. I'm here, and Eleanor's not.

The beer sours in my stomach. I set my glass down with a shaky hand. Push it across the sticky bar for good measure.

"I've actually got to head out," I say.

The surprise is evident on Freddie's face. "For real? Thought you'd head back to the venue with us."

"Yeah. I'd love to," I lie. "But something's come up."

It's a weak excuse. Transparent as hell. I don't care.

The smell of spilled beer and brewing mash is making me sick. I have to get out of here.

"Tonight," I tell them, already edging closer to the exit.

"We can go over everything at the after-party. Can't wait. You guys are going to kill it. It's going to be a great night."

It's almost an out-of-body experience. Like watching that security video—it feels like some other version of me is the one backing out of the room like a weirdo, blowing potentially the biggest career opportunity I've ever had. I'm in control, and yet I can't believe I'm acting this way, even as I'm *actively* doing it.

Outside, there's no sign of Sheridan or Jane. I start walking without any clear idea of where I am, or which direction I should be heading in, and after a few blocks I finally make myself stop and check a map. I'm a mile and a half from the Strip. The whole walk back, my dad's voice plays in my head—the grizzled voice I've heard in interviews but seldom in real life—telling me that I'm a fuckup, that he's surprised I even managed to get promoted once since I clearly can't do my fucking job, that if it weren't for him I would've been fired by now.

I hear Billy telling me pussy isn't worth tanking a deal over.

Suddenly, I'm livid. At Billy, for speaking the way he did about Eleanor this morning, and at myself for not telling him to shut the fuck up. I'm angry that I've wasted so much time and energy trying to be a person my dad might like and respect even though he never wanted to know me. That I've based my opinions and important life decisions on what these men would do, despite knowing deep down that I don't want to be anything like either of them.

And why the fuck didn't Billy ever mention being friends with Griffin Hastings? It's a random piece of information, and not really any of my business, so I get why he wouldn't tell me out of the blue. But I keep thinking about how the only times Griffin's name has come up in conversation is when it related to Eleanor. When I signed Maya. And when Billy sent me to sign Dempsey.

Billy is a lot of things, not all of them great, but he's not vindictive. Yeah, he's grumbled about the lack of loyalty in this industry. And yes, he's mentioned Eleanor in a less-than-favorable light, before. But he and Eleanor have never personally had problems. As far as I know, they've never even crossed paths. It makes no sense that sending me here would have anything to do with Eleanor, or Griffin. He would never use me that way.

Loyalty. That's what Billy prizes above everything else. And I have his.

I ignore the painful blisters my six-dollar boat shoes have given me. Pieces of the past day and a half skip around like a scratched record in my head.

The moment I walked into that restaurant and saw Eleanor sitting with Freddie and the guys, I remember thinking, *Fuck me.* Partly because, you know, it was less than ideal for the person I was competing with to be one of the best A&R managers I know, never mind that she had a personal vendetta against me. But also because she looked so fucking flawless in the low amber light that I wasn't sure I'd be able to form coherent sentences around her, let alone make a decent pitch.

Finally getting to kiss her again outside the shoe store felt like the kind of moment people more talented than me write songs about. And it might be the last kiss I ever get from her.

The thought settles at the front of my mind with a certainty that suggests it's nothing new, but something my subconscious has known for a while now:

I don't want it to be our last kiss. I don't want to have a last kiss with Eleanor at all.

I'm back on the Strip, close to my hotel but even closer to Eleanor's. I don't overthink it, just let my shitty boat shoes carry me through the lobby of her hotel and into the elevator. I'm disoriented for a moment when I reach her floor, trying to retrace my steps from this morning. I hesitate in front of the door I'm only 90 percent sure is actually Eleanor's.

After a deep breath, I knock.

"Hang on!" Eleanor's voice calls from inside. Relief and nerves battle it out at the confirmation that I'm exactly where I need to be.

After a few moments of waiting, I lean a little closer, turning my ear toward the heavy hotel door. I can hear rustling, and then what I think is a muffled curse, and then footsteps.

"Adam?"

"Yeah." I straighten and stuff my hands in my pockets, waiting for her to open the door. It occurs to me that she's probably watching me through the peephole, and I don't know where I'm supposed to look. My gaze flicks up to the little circle in the door, and I lift a brow.

The door swings open, revealing a wet-haired Eleanor, fresh from the shower. My gaze involuntarily scans her body, noting the way her T-shirt sticks to her damp skin, the way her nipples show through the fabric, and the thought pops into my head unbidden: *No bra.*

I clear my throat and gather my senses, focusing on her face instead of her bare legs.

"Hi." It's the best I can manage.

"Hi," she says, a lilt in her voice that almost turns it into a question: *What are you doing here?*

"I, um." My brows pull together. I'm a fucking idiot, and despite having ample opportunity to do so, I didn't think through what I would say once I was actually standing here in front of her. "I sent a picture of my ID to Tyler, and he said we're all set."

She nods. "Yeah, he texted me too."

Right. Of course he did. "Good. Yeah. I just wanted to make sure you were in the loop."

Oh god. That doesn't even make sense. I could've called for that, could've texted. Could have waited a couple hours and told her in person at the show.

"I sort of figured you'd still be at the brewery," she hedges.

I shake my head. "I bailed pretty soon after you left."

Her expression shifts into one I can't name—somehow calculating and wary and pleased all at once.

"Actually, could I come in for a sec?" I ask before I lose my nerve completely.

"Yeah, sure." Eleanor steps back, holding the door open. It's moderately reassuring that she doesn't hesitate, though I have to swallow thickly when the door snicks shut behind me.

Housekeeping has been through since this morning—the bed is pristine, the floor no longer scattered with discarded clothing.

The ends of Eleanor's hair are still dripping, getting the shoulders of her shirt all wet. "I'm sorry—you were getting ready and I randomly showed up."

She sticks her hands in her back pockets. "That's okay. What's up?"

I drag a hand over my jaw, scratching a bit at the scruff. I drop my hand and shake my head. "Look, I'm really glad we're not going to be married much longer."

Eleanor's brow furrows. "Uh . . . yeah. Me too. That's what you came here to say?"

"No. Hang on, shit." I pinch the bridge of my nose and shuffle a half step closer to Eleanor. "What I'm trying to say is, I'm glad, but I'm also . . . I don't want to go back to LA and pretend it never happened. I don't want us to act like strangers. Or never see each other."

Eleanor considers this for a moment. "You want to see each other?"

"I really liked getting to know you better today," I tell her. "I want . . . more of that. I want to know you. And I hate to be the guy who waits until his fake marriage is over to finally admit how he really feels—"

"Right, everyone hates that fucking guy," Eleanor says faintly.

"—but I kind of can't stop thinking about you."

Eleanor is standing close enough she has to tilt her head back to maintain eye contact with me, which makes her eyes look huge, especially the way her lashes are still wet and clumped together from the shower. Her breath has gone shallow, chest and shoulders rising and falling faster than I've seen all day.

Her mouth twitches into a teasing smile. "Not sick of me yet?"

Slowly, I shake my head. "I missed you the moment you walked away."

My gaze flickers around Eleanor's face, taking in every microscopic shift in expression. I catch the moment her lips part, the flutter of her lashes. I brace myself when she draws in a deeper breath, tongue flashing out to wet her lips like she's gearing up for something.

Still, it catches me by surprise when she swiftly closes the distance between us and presses her lush mouth to mine. She lifts a hand to cup the back of my neck, drawing me closer. One of mine slips into her still-wet hair, while the other finds her waist. The scent of her shampoo surrounds me—floral and intoxicating.

This kiss is more urgent than the others we've shared, and I feel a tug of arousal. Neither of us pulls away, instead we move together, Eleanor stumbling backward until she bumps against the wall. She gasps against my lips and my grip on her waist tightens. My tongue slips into her mouth and finds hers and I drink in the soft sounds she makes on her exhales. We kiss until we're both a bit breathless, until Eleanor tips her head back, giving me an opportunity to drag my lips along the column of her throat and nip gently at the sensitive skin under her jaw. Short nails dig into my back before she turns her head to catch my mouth in another kiss, looping her arms around my shoulders. A groan is punched out of me when she arches her back, pressing her hips firmly against mine. She must like that reaction, because she rubs herself against me again, a bit slower this time, and I lose my goddamn mind.

I grab on to her thighs with both hands and lift her up, which is not a move I've ever pulled off before, or frankly even been bold enough to attempt, but the impulse pays off when Eleanor wraps her legs around my waist and mumbles, "Fuck, that's hot," against my lips.

I voice my agreement with another low groan.

"Can we—" Eleanor cuts off when my teeth graze against her ear. She taps my shoulder, quick and eager. "Bed. Let's go."

"'Kay." I stumble a bit without the wall there to steady us, but reach the bed in a few quick strides and lower her down as gently as I can. She doesn't unwind her legs, keeping me trapped against her, which is a position I am completely okay with.

Her hands snake between our bodies and tug at my shirt, bunching it up my torso until I reach a hand back to yank it overhead. I cast it to the side carelessly and have to suppress an inappropriate laugh at the thought of doing that exact same thing last night, though under very different circumstances. Her hands land on my shoulders, then slide down to grip my biceps while my fingers skim over the soft cotton of her T-shirt. I graze the swell of her breast, then trail down until I reach the waistband of her shorts. I tease the skin there with a featherlight touch, waiting until she lifts her hips in encouragement. I manage to pop open the top button on my first try, something I'd be vaguely proud of if I weren't so distracted by the way Eleanor's abdomen contracts in anticipation. I find the tab of the zipper and pull it down slowly. My hand slips under the denim and I expect to feel more fabric, but encounter none.

With the arm braced next to Eleanor's head, I push my

body up enough to glance down the length of hers. "Are you . . . not wearing underwear?"

Eleanor shrugs one shoulder. "I was naked when you knocked. Got dressed in a hurry."

"Jesus." I close my eyes and make a concerted effort to collect myself. I feel like a fucking teenager right now, about to shoot off from a bit of over-the-pants friction.

"Doing okay?"

I open my eyes again to find Eleanor looking smug. Her lips are kiss-bitten, an even prettier shade of red than that lipstick she had on before.

It's familiar, at this point—the expression Eleanor gets when she thinks she's got me beat. In a way she does. Eleanor could ask me for pretty much anything right now, and I'd give it to her.

If she wants to turn this into another competition, that's fine. I was already determined to make her come first.

I kiss her once more—can't resist—before moving away. Eleanor lifts her head, a confused crease in her brow as she watches me kneel on the floor at the foot of the bed. With my hands behind her knees, I yank her closer, so her ass is at the edge of the mattress and her legs have nowhere to go except over my shoulders. She gasps and lets her head fall back again. I smile against the soft skin of her inner thigh and slide my hands up to curl my fingers under the waistband of her shorts.

Eleanor plants one foot to make it easier for me to tug the denim over her hips. I slide the fabric down her legs slowly, but once it reaches her ankles, Eleanor loses patience and kicks them off. I dodge her leg with a laugh and take the opportunity to ditch my glasses.

Incrementally, Eleanor's limbs relax again as I move back into position and press a kiss to her inner thigh, right above her knee. I work my way up her legs slowly, reveling in the way Eleanor's fingers grip the bedsheets, the way her breath has gone shallow.

I keep one hand curled around her thigh while the other finally slips between her legs to circle my thumb over the most sensitive part of her. Eleanor gives a full-body twitch and holy shit, I am not going to be able to handle it if she's that responsive.

All my plans to tease her with my fingers fly out the window, and I shift forward to flick my tongue against her clit. This earns another sharp inhale, but when I glance up the line of her body I find her eyes screwed shut, bottom lip trapped between her teeth. Holding back.

I grab her left hand from where it's twisting the bedsheets and guide it to my head. Instantly, she grips my short hair instead. I hum my approval against her and redouble my efforts. Every bitten-off sound she makes, every twitch of her body beneath mine, makes me harder. Eventually, I can't take it anymore, have to let go of her thigh to reach down and press my palm against my erection.

The pressure isn't enough, but it's enough for now—enough to let me refocus on Eleanor's pleasure, reading all of her cues and adjusting my technique until she's panting at the ceiling and her thighs are trembling against my shoulders. Until a steady stream of *yes, fuck, Adam* is rolling off her tongue.

Working my hand and mouth in tandem, I don't stop until she shakes apart. Even then, I want to keep going, but Eleanor squeezes her thighs together, too sensitive to let me.

I wipe my mouth on my hand and crawl back up the bed, over Eleanor's languid body. She hums softly as I drop a kiss on her navel before settling on the mattress beside her. We're quiet for a long moment, both of us catching our breath.

I'm the first one to break the silence: "You were right this morning."

She rolls her head to look at me. Her face is flushed, damp with sweat at the temples. Fucking gorgeous. "About what?"

I shoot her a wolfish grin. "Your vagina *is* amazing."

CHAPTER SEVENTEEN

ELEANOR

I could survive for weeks solely on the way Adam is looking at me right now. His gaze licks over my bare skin like a flame, leaving goose bumps in its wake. The intensity has me feeling singular, like he's never wanted anyone this way.

His fingertips tease across my stomach, and my skin is so oversensitized right now I can't control the way I flail—a response Adam seems to enjoy immensely. I swat his hand away and he relents, folding one arm behind his head and appearing wholly satisfied, despite the fact that he's very obviously aroused.

It takes a minute for my body to stop feeling like it's floating, but as soon as I've recovered, I roll over to straddle Adam. Immediately, his hands find my hips to hold me in place.

I bite my lip as my hands roam over his ribs and abs, following the line of his happy trail. Adam is still wearing shorts, and he shouldn't be. I make quick work of undoing his fly. One of his hands lifts to my neck and pulls me in, only to hesitate with a couple of inches between us, as if he's unsure I'll want to kiss him after what we just did. I hover right out of reach, one hand braced on the mattress next to his head while the other slips lower to touch him through his boxer briefs. He's hard against my palm, and heat starts building between my legs again in anticipation of feeling him inside of me.

Adam moans, eyes falling shut and head pressing back into the pillow. I smile and continue to stroke him gently as I close the remaining distance to kiss him. Adam cups my jaw and tilts my face to deepen the kiss.

I'm still throbbing between my legs, so ready for more. I think about him asking whether I have any lube in my purse and laugh against his lips, but it's followed by a mood-killing realization.

"Shit." I pull back. "I don't have any condoms."

"I've got one in my wallet." Adam lifts his hips to reach his back pocket, and the friction has me stifling a moan.

"Remind me later to make fun of you for keeping it in your wallet like a seventeen-year-old," I say, a bit breathless.

He pulls the foil packet out and sets it on the mattress next to him, but instead of quickly shucking the rest of his clothes like I expect him to, he slides a callused palm under the hem of my T-shirt again.

As much as I appreciate his thoroughness, I'm all set on the foreplay. I want more. I grind against him, and I'd be embarrassed about the needy sound I make if not for the way his fingers flex against me in response.

"C'mon." I tug ineffectually at his shorts. "Off."

Adam nods. He rucks my shirt up and overhead, then

flips me onto my back and *finally* sheds the rest of his own clothes. I hand him the condom and he smirks at my eagerness as he tears the foil open. I watch him roll the condom on, then hook my hand around his neck and tug him back to me.

His skin is warm, his body all-encompassing. My legs slide farther apart to accommodate him, knees hitched up toward his hips. He's notched perfectly against me, about to push in, and I freeze.

"Wait," I say, and immediately Adam puts a few inches of space between us. "You haven't been carrying that thing around in your wallet *since* you were seventeen, right?"

Adam's head drops and he lets out this ball-busted laugh. When he lifts his gaze again, his eyes glitter with amusement. "It's new. You gonna ask me if I'm a virgin next?"

". . . Well, now I sort of feel like I should."

He spanks the back of my thigh in retaliation, drawing a sharp gasp out of me. Slowly, he lowers his weight back onto me. His cock is a hard, hot line against the crease of my hip. "No, Eleanor," he says, lips brushing against mine, "I didn't save myself for marriage."

Bold move, mentioning our marriage at this particular juncture. But my comeback is forgotten when he snakes a hand under my back and hitches my body higher up the bed, right where he wants me. My stomach swoops at the display of strength, and my knees tip in to squeeze his hips.

"Any other questions?" His brow arches, and with one hand wrapped around the base of his cock, he drags the tip over my clit.

I shake my head and fist the sheets.

"No?" He smirks, smug as I've ever seen him. "Nothing you want to ask for?"

A frustrated groan climbs up my throat. My hands splay across his back, fruitlessly trying to pull him closer. "Please."

"Please what?" He kisses my collarbone, the swell of my breast. His tongue flicks over a nipple and I whimper softly. He kisses his way back up to my mouth and says: "Ask for what you want, and I'll give it to you."

Adam's assertiveness is irritating as shit when he's trying to sign the same artist as me, but here? It's having a markedly different effect. I groan, frustrated and turned on in equal measure. "I swear to god if you don't start fucking me *right* now—"

His answering grin is beautiful. He slides all the way in with one slow, fluid roll of his hips. My mouth falls open with a low moan, which Adam smothers with a kiss.

"Oh, *fuck*," he says, tipping his forehead against mine. "You're perfect."

I nod, mindless, and hook my heels around him. He cants his hips back and thrusts in again, slow but not gentle.

And then his hand slides between us, fingers deftly finding that bundle of nerves again, and it really is perfect. It's too perfect, too intense, senses heightened to the point it almost aches. He bottoms out and stays there as he continues to draw light circles around my center. My limbs grow tense as the sensations coil hotter. I tilt my hips, wanting to draw him deeper.

"That's it," he murmurs. "Wanna see you come for me again."

It's become glaringly obvious that Adam is the type of man who gets off on seeing his partner get off. I'm already growing hopelessly addicted. Already know that when I go back to LA I'll lie awake in my bed, craving the weight of his body on top of mine, feeling empty without him filling me up.

My eyes close and I focus on the pleasure, building and building but still out of reach.

"Look at me," he says in a low growl.

I force my eyes back open, willing to do whatever he asks as long as he doesn't stop, never stops. I'm pinned beneath the hunger and intensity of his stare as I start to unravel.

"I'm so close," I manage. "I'm—"

Firmer pressure from his fingers, another fluid roll of his hips, and I can't keep my eyes open anymore as one of the most intense climaxes of my life crests over me. I cry out, nails digging into his skin hard enough to leave marks.

"Eleanor," he grinds out. "Fuck—"

The rest becomes white noise, drowned out by the blood rushing in my ears. I feel his rhythm falter, his hips stutter as he finishes. His hand shifts to grip my hip, hard.

Our bodies rock together, both of us trembling as the aftershocks course through us, until gradually we both grow still.

I lick my lips and finally let go of Adam to run a hand through my own hair, pushing it off my feverish brow. He pulls out carefully and rolls onto his back beside me.

That was a far cry from the hate fuck Tyler was talking about. And somehow even better than I'd let myself imagine it could be.

"Holy shit," he says, almost to himself. We lie there panting at the ceiling for a few moments. Adam is the first to move.

He pushes himself out of bed and pads to the bathroom, where he takes care of the condom and quickly washes up at the sink. I know I should get up, too—to pee, if nothing else—but my limbs are lead and the bed is a cloud and moving is simply not feasible right now.

Adam walks into the room again and pulls on his boxer briefs, and I swallow hard as he crawls back onto the bed. Sweat is cooling on my skin, drawing me out of my post-orgasm trance. I shiver, and Adam grabs the duvet and tugs it over us both.

We lie on our sides, facing each other, heads a few inches apart on our pillow. I bite the inside of my cheek, but I know he can tell I'm smiling. He crooks a grin at me and rolls onto his back, arm out in an invitation. I don't hesitate to snuggle into the nook of his shoulder. His arm curves around my back and he lets out a satisfied hum, eyes drifting closed. My nose nuzzles the base of his throat. He smells like sunscreen and sweat and something woodsy and masculine that may be his cologne, or may simply be Adam. I run fingertips over the stubble on his neck and jaw, then across his cheekbone, avoiding the bruised area around his eye. His skin is baby-soft.

"Do you moisturize?" I ask, almost accusingly.

"'Course," Adam murmurs, his eyes still shut.

I consider for a moment. His complexion is *really* nice. "What brand do you use?"

He opens his eyes and tilts his chin down to look at me. "For a.m. or p.m.?"

". . . You have more than one?"

"Well, yeah. Morning one has SPF in it. And for night I actually have a couple, one for when I use retinol—what?"

A slow smile has spread across my face. "No, nothing. You use retinol?"

“Yes.” He’s getting defensive. It’s precious. “Do you not?”

“No, I do,” I tell him. “I just don’t know a lot of guys with a whole skin-care routine.”

He smirks and relaxes back onto his pillow. “Five steps. I’ll send you links if you want.”

I bite down on a smile. “Sure.”

The temptation is strong to stay right here, with Adam’s heartbeat under my ear and his thumb tracing a soothing pattern over my hip. But if I do that, it’s entirely possible I’ll fall asleep. Which would be bad. Because I really don’t want a UTI, and also, we have a concert to get to.

“It’s almost seven,” I say, a bit wistfully. “Doors open soon.”

Adam nods. Neither of us gets up.

“Dempsey won’t go on until around nine,” he hedges.

“ . . . Probably enough time to order room service.”

“Oh, fuck yes,” he says, “that is such a good idea.”

I grin and force myself to sit up. I grab the menu off the Lucite desk across the room and drop it in Adam’s lap. “Order me a waffle?”

“You got it.”

I move toward the en suite, and as I’m closing the bathroom door, I catch Adam unabashedly checking me out. He tosses me a wink, and I feel my entire body flush before I close the door. I turn on the faucet for modesty’s sake and take care of business, then slip on the hotel robe hanging near the shower before washing my hands and face.

Adam is sitting with his back against the headboard when I come out, still wearing only his boxer briefs. I bite my lip and allow myself another lingering look at his chest and abs.

Adam said he doesn't want to go back to LA and pretend this never happened. Which is a relief, because I don't think I could forget if I tried. I want this too much. I want it to be real.

I've been stripped bare for Adam in every conceivable way. Yet despite everything I've revealed to Adam today, I don't think he truly gets how precarious my situation is—that if I don't sign Dempsey, I will lose my job.

Yesterday, I wouldn't have even considered telling him. Being that vulnerable in front of Adam Shaw of all people would have seemed like the worst possible decision. Now I'm not so sure.

Spending all day with Adam has changed my mind about a number of things. Namely, that he's the sort of person who would use information like that against me.

For better or worse, I trust Adam.

"Hey, I want you to know . . . whatever happens with Dempsey, there's no hard feelings."

If I hadn't spent so much of the day studying Adam, learning his every nuanced expression, I might not have caught the subtle way his face tightens at my words. But I do catch it, and that's when I know—if I told Adam how badly I need this, what it will cost me if I don't sign this band, he would bow out.

The problem is, I want to sign Dempsey because I'm the best choice at this stage of their career, not because I guilted my competition into backing off. I want the possibility of having something real with Adam, which can't happen if a choice like that is hanging over our heads.

More than anything, I need to succeed in my career without feeling indebted to another man.

Adam snags the end of my belt and tugs me closer. I let him pull me down onto the bed for another slow, achingly sweet kiss.

He combs his fingers through my hair and offers a tender smile, like he wants to believe it just as badly as I do. "No hard feelings."

CHAPTER EIGHTEEN

ADAM

"*Fuuuck*, that's good."

Eleanor's moans are the greatest soundtrack I've ever heard in my life. Though, admittedly, I like it best when I'm responsible for her pleasure. Right now the credit goes to a room service waffle. I swallow a bite of my burger and watch with rapt attention as she licks a bit of whipped cream off her finger and hums happily.

My cock starts to wake up again, and I adjust myself in my boxer briefs as subtly as I can. Eleanor is too absorbed in her food to notice, and I can't say I blame her. I'm starving, too, and I ate back at the strip club. I'm not sure Eleanor's had anything besides coffee, water, and pretzels all day.

"Should've ordered two," I say before taking another huge bite of my burger.

She nods and shrugs. "Knowing Ralph, there will be good food at the after-party."

Still chewing, I hold out my plate wordlessly. Eleanor

grabs a few fries and immediately shoves them into her mouth.

I grab one of the thick cloth napkins from the room service tray and wipe my hands off. "Speaking of . . ." I swipe the napkin across my mouth, too, and aim for casual when I say, "Jane gave me a few recommendations for restaurants back in LA."

"Oh yeah?" Eleanor glances over briefly before picking up her fork again and dipping another piece of waffle into the maple syrup.

"Yeah. Maybe we could check one out together."

Eleanor stops chewing for a moment. She looks over at me and lifts a hand to cover her mouth. She hurries to swallow, and with her fingers still hovering in front of her lips, she asks: "Like a date?"

The question makes her flush, cute as hell.

"Yeah. You like cliché dinner dates, right?"

Her hand drops to reveal a scowl. *"Classic."*

I grin and pick up a fry. "If you say so."

"You are really bad at asking people out, you know that? You're supposed to flatter me, not make fun of me."

"Huh. Usually, I just name-drop my dad."

Eleanor's eyes widen. "Have you seriously done that?"

I'm quiet a beat too long.

"Oh my *god*."

"No, listen. I haven't. . . . However, well-intentioned friends may have used that line on my behalf once or twice before."

"Did it work?"

"I mean. For a one-night stand, sure."

Eleanor shakes her head in mock disappointment. "Well,

you're going to need to up your game if you want a date with me."

Before she's even finished speaking, I set my plate back on the tray and knee-shuffle over to her side of the bed. "Eleanor. I think you're really smart and cool and fun to be around."

"Thank you," she says primly. And then she lifts a brow, like, *go on.*

Still smiling so hard my cheeks hurt, I ask: "Will you go on a date with me?"

"I don't know . . . I've never dated a divorcé before."

I tip my head in acknowledgment. "First time for everything."

Her eyes flit down to her plate, and back up to me again. "Fine. You can take me to dinner."

I bite my lip and do a slow, celebratory fist pump, which makes Eleanor roll her eyes, but she's smiling, so I count it as a win.

She's still wrapped up in her plush robe, hoarding all the pillows behind her back. Her plate is balanced in her lap, but she sets it aside as she reaches over to snag her phone from the bedside table.

"Shit. I never called my sister back."

I manfully ignore the way her robe has fallen open to reveal her leg all the way up her thigh and scoop my shorts up off the floor. "I can get out of your hair."

"Oh."

I look at Eleanor over my shoulder as I button my fly. "'Oh'?"

She's sitting with her knees curled in now, cheeks gone pink.

"You don't have to go. I don't really have time to call her now anyway. I should start getting ready for the show."

This mention of the show is momentarily jarring. I didn't forget about it, exactly. But I was preoccupied, for obvious reasons. Now I check my watch and realize Eleanor is right—if we want to make it for the actual show, not just the after-party, we need to get moving.

Eleanor catches my frown and stands up, tightening her robe. "I mean, you can go, obviously. I'm realizing you probably want to go back to your room to shower or change."

My fingers drag across the stubble on my jaw. I still need a shave. A fresh shirt wouldn't hurt either. "I don't have to," I echo. "If you want some company while you get ready."

A shy smile tugs at Eleanor's lips. "Cool."

Eleanor goes to pick out the clothes she wants to wear while I find my shirt and tug it back on, smiling to myself at the sense of déjà vu it brings about.

It's mind-boggling that only a few hours ago I was so concerned about anyone finding out about our night together. Still hate that I hurt Eleanor's feelings over that. I glance over at where she's sorting through her suitcase and feel the question bubbling up. I try to swallow it back, but this trip has proven my willpower is shot.

"Do you think you'll ever tell her about us?"

Immediately, I'm mentally cringing over that phrasing. To be fair, I was inside her like an hour ago. And she said yes to dinner. But that doesn't exactly mean there's an *us*.

Eleanor hesitates, and I start talking again, can't stop.

"I get why you don't want her to know before the wedding. But you two seem pretty close. So I wondered if you would tell her eventually, about what happened."

I watch as she hugs her selected outfit to her stomach. “We’re not as close as we used to be,” she says after a moment.

So that’s a no.

I do my best to keep my expression neutral, to not let my disappointment show. I nod and start loading our dishes and napkins onto the room service tray, accepting her answer without further comment.

“I haven’t been a very good sister lately,” she adds after a moment.

When I look up, she’s got her gaze fixed on the bundle of clothes in her arms. “How so?”

“I guess I’ve prioritized work. To the point I’ve become a bit flaky with everything else.” She licks her lips and takes a deep breath. “After leaving Exeter I felt like I had something to prove. Both professionally and personally.”

Her eyes meet mine then, piercing. Gauging. Like she’s making sure I understand without her having to mention his name. It wouldn’t be the first time we talked about Griffin today, but circumstances have changed. Right now, his name’s like Beetlejuice. Nothing good can come from saying it out loud.

“Understandable,” I say softly.

“I’ve had a few setbacks recently,” she continues, and I wince as I think of Maya. I maintain I didn’t do anything wrong by signing her, but I know it was a huge blow to Eleanor’s roster. “But I’ve sort of kept up a front with my friends and family. Things have been tight for my mom and sister, so I’ve been helping out with wedding expenses.” Her maxed-out credit cards come to mind, and I start to get the full picture. Start to see how determined Eleanor is to maintain the image of success she’s cultivated. She seems to struggle with what to say next. Or maybe with how much she wants to tell me. "I just . . . don't want them to know how badly I'm fucking everything up."

Eleanor's brow is furrowed, and I shuffle around the bed to stand right in front of her. "Takes two to make a mistake like this one. This isn't all on you, you know?"

A small smile tugs at her mouth. "I do know. But, regrettably, I've discovered blaming you doesn't actually make me feel better. Besides, I've been screwing up since well before this trip."

Eleanor is her own toughest critic, and that's something I can relate to. But it kills me to hear her beat herself up like this. I tuck a few hairs that have gone rogue behind her ear. "It can't be all that bad, can it?"

She bites her lip, holding my gaze with shrewd eyes like she's reading an answer off my face to some question she didn't even ask. Then she sucks in a breath and straightens her posture.

"I'm going to tell you something," she says, "but first I need you to make me a promise."

I blink and stuff my hands into my pockets. "All right. What is it?"

"Promise you won't do that thing men do where you try to fix it. Just listen, okay?"

"Yeah, of course," I agree immediately. I can listen.

She sits back down on the edge of the bed. "A couple months ago, I had a performance review. Josie told me I needed to make some changes by the end of the quarter or she'd have to let me go."

"What kinds of changes?" I ask, already tense at the implication that she could be fired.

"She said I needed to prove I was a team player," Eleanor says, and I get the sense she's barely suppressing an eye roll. "My financial outlook was a big part of it. I went over budget last quarter, and my travel expenses were too high. . . . One of the sticking points was that I'd gone around Josie to court a band with my own money—"

"Wait, what? You spent your own money trying to sign a band?"

Eleanor crosses her arms. "Yes."

I clamp my mouth shut. She's made it very clear she doesn't want my commentary.

Neither of us speaks for a moment, until Eleanor tips her head back and sighs. "I know, okay? I know it was a terrible idea. I figured it would pay for itself, and then it . . . didn't. But this is how I was trained. Go hard after the acts you want, and don't take no for an answer."

"From what I've heard, that doesn't seem like Blue Sky's typical approach," I say carefully.

"Yeah. It's not."

Which means she learned it from someone else. Doesn't take a genius to figure out who. And again, it strikes me how much I can relate. Billy trained me up in much the same way. Men like him and Griffin have gotten by on bluster and bullshit for years.

"Anyway," Eleanor goes on. "That's why I've been going after Dempsey so hard. It's my last chance to turn things around. Josie is expecting me to call her with an update, and I've been putting it off because at this point, I have nothing good to report."

I sort of wish I'd kept that Elvis stress ball for myself. I could use it right about now. "You could have told me sooner how much you had riding on this."

She casts me a sardonic look. I get it. This is why she made me promise not to try to fix it, because the most obvious solution is for me to pull my offer. Not something I would even consider, if I were up against anyone else. It's Eleanor, though, so yeah, I do want to snap my fingers and fix this.

But I told her I wouldn't, and I don't break my promises.

Besides, I'm not entirely convinced it's the *right* solution. It doesn't add up. If her increased business expenses were part of the problem, then how is spending all this money chasing after Dempsey supposed to save her job?

"You look constipated," Eleanor comments, drawing a snort-laugh out of me. "Say what you want to say."

"Well." I rub the back of my neck. "I don't know Josie personally, but I've always heard good things about her. You like working for her?"

"Yeah. She's supportive, and collaborative, and listens to my ideas. She's great to work for," Eleanor says, sounding almost sad about it. Like she's already resigned herself to getting let go.

"I'm just wondering what she meant, when she said you needed to be more of a team player."

"I mean, my numbers are the worst out of any of the managers."

"Okay, but she was also unhappy with you spending your own money. Seems to me like it was less about the funds, and more about you skirting the rules."

"Well . . . sure, that was part of it—"

"Because you know damn well expense limits exist so we can evaluate profit and loss, not for you to bypass when you feel like it. They help us be objective, and they maintain boundaries, so we don't throw good money after bad leads."

"I didn't tell you so you could lecture me too," Eleanor says hotly.

I hold a hand up, placating. "I get you're passionate about your work and I sincerely respect it. I'm not trying to lecture you. But I think this is what Josie is really trying to get across. You have this whole lone wolf way of operating, and I understand why, after the shit you went through at Exeter. But you said yourself, Josie is supportive and collaborative. So why haven't you called to strategize with her?"

"Because, I told you—things obviously haven't gone according to plan—"

"Did you strategize with her *before* the trip?"

Eleanor's mouth shuts with a click. Which means no, she did not. "You should call her," I say simply. "It can't hurt. But it will at least show her you're open to feedback, and that you value her input."

Eleanor's gaze flicks down to the duvet. She seems to be considering it, at least.

"Maybe leave out the part about marrying the competition," I tack on.

She reaches behind her and grabs a pillow, then whacks me with it before pushing to her feet again. "Thank you."

"For what?" I ask, now hugging the pillow she hit me with.

"You're a good listener."

I preen at this. "So you're going to call her?"

"Yes. But." She glances at the bedside clock and winces. "I need to get ready for the show first." Eleanor takes her clothes into the bathroom, leaving the door open as she heads to the sink to do her makeup. As she rifles through her cosmetic bag she calls out: "You want to put some music on?"

"Sure. What are you in the mood for?"

"You choose."

I pull out my phone. It feels like an honor to be asked to pick what we listen to. Honestly, it's a little bit nerve-racking. I scroll through my playlists looking for something that feels right, and then remember the demo sitting in my inbox.

I glance up at Eleanor, watching as she lifts onto her tiptoes and leans closer to the mirror while she curls her eyelashes. I connect my phone to the speaker on the bedside table and hit play.

While the music plays and Eleanor does her thing, I busy myself by tidying up the room—depositing the room service tray in the hall for housekeeping to pick up, and remaking the bed. Then I'm out of things to do and venture into the bathroom to perch next to Eleanor, who is using her fingers to blend some makeup under her eyes.

"You want some concealer for that shiner?" she asks, and I'm half-certain she's joking, so I shake my head.

"No," I say, and reach for a travel bottle of mouthwash. "But I'll borrow some of this if that's okay."

She nods and moves on to her own dental hygiene. In the middle of brushing her teeth, she pauses to ask: "Who is this?"

I'm still swishing mouthwash, so I spit into the sink and say: "A band one of my reps sent me."

She finishes up and rinses her toothbrush, then wipes her mouth on a towel. "They're really good. Are you going to sign them?"

"I want to." I turn to rest my hip against the marble counter and watch as she considers two shades of lipstick, both of which look identical to me. "But I'm not sure what kind of budget my boss would give me for a band like this. Or whether it's worth signing them if I don't think I can break them out, you know?"

Eleanor puts one of the lipstick tubes back in her bag. "I get that . . . but it's always a risk, isn't it? Sometimes even the bands that get the biggest marketing push don't meet their targets. But if you can figure out a way to break out the band that no one else will take a chance on, that's the sweetest win."

For so long I've been chasing the next big thing, telling myself these high-profile artists are my ticket to a promotion, which will afford me more freedom in who I sign. But I've gotten a promotion, and I still haven't made any changes to the kinds of bands I bring to the label.

Eleanor's right. Seeing a band succeed because of my efforts—not just because the label threw enough money at the album to ensure its success—is what I take the most pride in. The kind of thing that might make someone like Eleanor proud too. And I want that. I want to be worthy of her.

"I think I've been too chickenshit to take that kind of risk."

Eleanor hums. "And you've got a perfect track record going for you. Wouldn't want a flop now."

It's a jab, sure, but she doesn't say it harshly. Besides, she hit the nail on the head.

"Guess I'll have to make sure they don't flop."

Eleanor swipes her lipstick on, turning her mouth crimson. "Cocky," she says, before grabbing a tissue from the box on the counter and blotting her lips.

"If you like them, I'd say they have a pretty good shot."

Her gaze flicks across the mirror to meet mine, and she arches a brow. "I do have an impeccable ear."

I smile and tip my head in acknowledgment. She does.

She starts packing away all of her makeup, and it hits me how different Eleanor is from the idea I had of her before this trip. She's not effortlessly cool, at least not in the superficial ways I'd assumed. She's drawn the curtain back and allowed me to see her fix her makeup and scrape at the rogue drip of maple syrup that's dried on her robe—all these things that make her so fucking real. The fact that she trusts me enough to let me in might be the greatest privilege of my entire life.

She pulls me out of my own head with a loud huff. "I have sex hair."

I stand behind her, smirking as I look her over the mirror. She's not entirely wrong. I reach out and twist an unruly wave around my finger. It blows my mind that she allows it. And that it feels so natural—that all of this does. Brushing teeth together and watching Eleanor get ready, like we're already in that place.

"You look great, baby."

Her cheeks go ruddy, and I *knew* she'd give me a good reaction to that pet name. Makes me wonder what other terms of endearment might make her blush.

She reaches across the sink to plug in a curling iron. "You're obligated to say that. You gave me the sex hair."

I break out into a grin. "I did, didn't I?"

Another huff, and she needles an elbow into my rib cage. "Go away. I have to fix this and we need to get going."

I drop a kiss on her shoulder blade, right over her

hummingbird tattoo, before giving her space. I flop back down onto the bed and grab my phone, opening the email from my rep about this band.

I smile as I imagine how psyched he'll be as I type out my response:

Let's set up a meeting.

CHAPTER NINETEEN

ELEANOR

We arrive at the club right as the opening act finishes their set. With our names on the list, we're granted access to the balcony above the main floor, which is off-limits to anyone with a general admission ticket. It's mostly empty, but I spot Jane standing off to one side and tap Adam's elbow so he'll follow me over.

She's sipping a carbonated drink from a plastic cup, and lifts her brows in greeting before releasing the straw. "Hey, guys."

It's her tone of voice, and the way her gaze flickers back and forth between us, that tells me she's figured out something is going on between Adam and me. Given we keep showing up together . . . I suppose we haven't exactly been subtle. I decide I don't mind her knowing. Jane is cool, and anyway, I agreed to go out on an actual date with Adam. If it goes well, and *keeps* going well, more people will know, eventually.

Movement onstage snares my attention. It's just a couple of stagehands doing some last-minute set up for Dempsey, but it's enough to get the crowd buzzing with anticipation.

The stage empties, and the lighting shifts, and it's like the entire club collectively holds their breath. Freddie Dempsey steps onstage, followed by Sheridan, Ralph, and Curtis.

They hit their marks, Sher and Freddie in front of microphone stands on opposite ends of the stage, each with guitars slung over their shoulders. I catch Adam's eye, and he grins at me, hand finding the small of my back for a moment before slipping into his pocket.

Curtis hits his drumsticks together to count them down, and over the swell of cheers from the audience, they launch into their opener.

The energy in the club is a vibrant, tangible thing. A reminder of why I got into this business in the first place. A reminder of why I didn't quit after Griffin, even when I wanted to run away and start fresh in some industry where no one knew my name. I love music, and I always will.

The band sounds great—if a little stiff. But it's the last stop on a long tour, so I don't think they can be blamed for having lost some of their spontaneity at this point.

The club is packed, and thunderously loud as the song finishes and Sheridan wraps both hands around the microphone stand.

"Hello Las Vegas!" She grins brightly at the responding roar from the audience. One hand drops to rest along the guitar strapped to her shoulder. "Ooh, we've got a fantastic crowd tonight. I can feel it." More whistles and cheers. "Playing shows like this is a privilege, and we only get to do it because of you. Because you guys show the fuck up, and stream our music, and we want to thank you for that."

Her gaze sweeps over the club slowly, like she's straining to see each and every person's face past the glare of the stage lights. I've seen Dempsey live a handful of times now, between the gigs they played before signing with a label and then their last tour. Sheridan is incredible at crowd work for exactly this reason—because it isn't fake. She isn't just vamping. She isn't a jaded musician reading from the same script night after night. She cares.

Curtis is smirking behind his kit, his eyes locked on Sheridan's back. Ralph is taking the opportunity to quietly retune his bass. Freddie steps back from his own mic to say something to Curtis. It draws Sheridan's attention, too, and before the rest of the band seems to be ready, Freddie is strumming the opening chords of their next song.

The others are quick to jump in, seasoned enough they don't miss a beat. Freddie has lead vocals on this song, so Sheridan takes her time returning to her side of the stage. When she does hit the mic for backup vocals, she looks sideways at her brother. Her expression is not pleased.

The tension onstage is palpable, but they make it through the next two songs without incident. Then Sheridan lets go of her guitar and takes her microphone off the stand, ready to address the crowd again. She barely gets three words out when Freddie starts playing over her.

My head rears back, hardly able to believe what I just saw. I cast my gaze around the room, trying to get a sense of whether the general audience even noticed, but of course it's impossible to tell from up here. Jane definitely noticed, though. Beside me she's pursing her lips and avoiding my gaze, but I catch her give a pissed-off little shake of her head.

Onstage, Sheridan sets the mic back on the stand and scrambles to jump in on vocals, only to step away again when they reach the bridge. Freddie glares at her and jerks his head toward her mic. She stares resolutely back while Curtis and Ralph continue to vamp. After a drawn-out moment, Sheridan bends down to snag a water bottle from the base of her mic stand. She takes a couple of long gulps, then sets it back down and jumps back in on rhythm guitar.

My gaze stays locked on Sheridan for the rest of the song. The band finds the pocket again, and Sheridan's vocals are pitch-perfect, but there's no passion in her voice. She's singing like she's numb.

The song wraps and while Freddie's last guitar riff is still ringing out, Sheridan shouts into her microphone, "You guys have been great, thank you so much!"

She whips her guitar strap overhead and walks offstage.

A beat later Curtis follows, both drumsticks fisted in one hand. But Ralph and Freddie both look like deer caught in the headlights.

I glance over my shoulder at Adam, who leans forward with a frown. "That wasn't their full set."

It's Jane who responds first. "No, they had twelve songs on their set list."

Freddie hesitates another moment before he and Ralph exit the stage as well. A low murmur rolls through the crowd.

". . . Do we think they're coming back?" Adam asks, eyes locked onto the side stage, even though there isn't any movement.

"I don't know." I give a sidelong glance at Jane. "Sher didn't look too happy."

Jane presses her tongue to her upper teeth. "Let's give it a few minutes."

Five minutes pass, and they still haven't come back onstage. Club music starts playing overhead, and some of the crowd closest to the stage starts getting restless, a slow stream of them heading toward the exit.

"I'm going to head backstage," Jane says. "You guys want to come?"

The backstage area of a club like this is probably pretty small. It's not like they're playing a sold-out arena—that's where I'd like to take them, after we put out another album. But here and now, I'm unlikely to go unnoticed if I use my backstage pass earlier than planned.

Then again, if they're really not going to come out and finish their set, I guess it's not technically *early*. And if they *do* sign with me, I won't be out of place at all.

Adam defers to me, and I nod. "Yeah. Let's go."

Doubt settles low in my stomach, even as Adam agrees to come backstage with me. It grows heavier, when we give our names to the security guard at the stage door, who checks his list and lets us through. Solidifies when we round the corner and find Sheridan and Freddie Dempsey at each other's throats.

Ralph squeezes between them, facing Freddie as he lifts both hands and tries to defuse the situation, while Curtis has one arm raised protectively in front of Sheridan, like he knows better than to fully hold her back, but is itching to take her place instead.

"—selfish prick, you know that?" Sheridan is yelling at her brother.

Fiona hovers in the background, her phone gripped tight in one hand while the other pinches the bridge of her nose.

"Oh, fuck off, Sher. You're the one acting like a goddamn diva."

Sheridan launches forward, only to have Curtis lift her off her feet and spin her around. Once he sets her down, his hands hover over her shoulders and he speaks to her in a low, steady voice. I can't make out what he's saying to her—or what Freddie says next—but it's clear as day when Curtis spins around to face Freddie and shouts:

"Man, shut the fuck up. You think we don't know you've been talking to other managers without us?"

My gaze darts over to Fiona. Her arms are crossed and her lips are pursed as she coolly observes the infighting. She doesn't look surprised by this revelation, but then again, Dempsey already dropped their label and their publicist. She'd be smart to wonder if she was next on the chopping block.

"I'm not gonna apologize for exploring every option for my band—"

Ralph huffs, looking flushed and furious, puppy-dog eyes nowhere to be found as finally he speaks up: "When did you decide this was *your* band?"

"He's always thought that," Sheridan yells over Curtis's shoulder. "He just used to be better at hiding it."

"Think what you want," Curtis says next. "But I'm never signing on with Billy Draper."

I feel Adam stiffen beside me, feel him watching me. His gaze itches across my skin, but I don't give in to the urge to scratch.

Billy Draper. Freddie reached out to Billy Draper.

The band is still slinging insults at one another, but I've heard enough. I grab Adam's arm and drag him away from the group, skirting past them right as Sheridan pulls one of Curtis's drumsticks out of his back pocket and throws it at Freddie's head. It misses, and the whole display of sibling rivalry might even be funny in some other context. But right now, I'm not laughing. Right now, the pieces are clicking into place and the only thought in my mind is that Adam could have made this so much easier on both of us.

I don't know where I'm going. I turn down a hallway, and the bright lights are jarring compared to the darkness backstage. There's a greenroom on my right, and I pull Adam inside.

I let go of Adam's arm and round on him. He fidgets with his glasses, a nervous tic I've noticed throughout the day. Silence stretches out between us, and I'm tempted to force him to speak first, if only to see what he comes up with.

But in the end, I'm too angry to stay quiet.

"Billy Draper told you about my meeting."

His throat shifts as he swallows. He nods once.

"And Billy heard about it from Freddie."

"Yes. I know I should've said something—"

"That would've been nice, yeah. If you'd told me the truth any of the times I directly asked you, or any of the times Billy's name came up today." He had *so many* chances. That's what kills me. Like, I get him not telling me first thing this morning, when we were still in competition mode. We were hungover, and reeling from last night, and we didn't trust each other yet. But after that? After everything we went through today? After everything I told him about my job, and what Dempsey meant to me?

"I . . ." Adam shuffles a bit closer. "I wanted to tell you. When we were talking, before the newlywed game, I almost told you."

I raise my brows. "Oh, did you? That's so helpful, Adam. You should definitely get points for *almost* doing the decent thing before fucking me."

"Hey, come on—"

Adam reaches for me, but I step back and cross my arms. Adam's teeth rake over his bottom lip. He doesn't reach for me again. Instead, his fingers curl into a fist that he presses against his own thigh.

"Eleanor, please. I should have. I'm sorry. I just didn't think it would help, at that point."

"You didn't think it would be helpful for me to know that I literally never stood a chance?"

"That's not true." He gestures behind him, in the vague direction of where we left the band. "Freddie wanted to take other meetings, but obviously they aren't all on the same page."

It's a fair point. But it doesn't make me feel any better, because now the whole thing seems doomed for a different reason. The band is fighting. No matter which of us they sign with, we'll know it wasn't a unanimous decision. That someone in the group is pissed off about it. I'm not all that psyched about the prospect of working with Freddie Dempsey when he's obviously opposed to working with me.

"I feel like I made an idiot of myself." My voice is brittle. I've held it together pretty well today. But I think about the look on Freddie's face when I walked into the brewery, and I feel pathetic, and humiliated, and the press of tears grows hot behind my eyes.

Adam sighs through his nose. "You did not make an idiot of yourself."

I scoff wetly, and suddenly Adam is right in front of me, catching my chin with firm fingers and forcing me to meet his gaze. "You didn't. And I'm sorry I wasn't more forthcoming with you." His touch gentles even more, thumb swiping along my jaw. "I won't make that mistake again, I promise."

Adam's brows are knit close together, his mouth in a miserable line. He looks like he regrets his entire existence in this moment, all because it eventually led to upsetting me. I'm finding it pretty impossible to stay angry with someone who looks so wrecked, especially knowing it was never his intention to hurt me.

I believe him when he says he won't withhold information from me again. It's just—Billy. Adam has had a decades-long history with the man, and it's clear he's filled some sort of hole in Adam's life left behind by Atlas. I understand that. But I can't pretend it doesn't bother me, this loyalty Adam has toward someone who has very publicly said some very unforgivable shit in the past. Who prioritizes his own success over basic professional decency.

Never mind Billy's friendship with Griffin. Considering how many mutual acquaintances we have, it wasn't the easiest thing to distance myself from Griffin. But I did my best to evict him from every corner of my life, and I don't love the idea of inviting a connection to him back in—even if it is several degrees removed. I can only imagine the kinds of things Griffin would have to say if he found out I was seeing Adam. Things Billy probably wouldn't hesitate to pass right along to

Adam, thinking he was doing him a favor. I let Griffin damage my relationship with Iris and my friendship with Tyler before. I don't want him tainting this too.

My jaw is sore from clenching my teeth so hard. From biting back so many ugly emotions. Adam's hand falls away from me. He frowns, gaze flickering around my face like my uncertainty is written all over me.

I'm searching for a way to voice my concerns without making it sound like some kind of ultimatum, but I'm distracted when Fiona walks into the room.

"Eleanor, there you are." She offers me a tired smile. "Could you come with me, please? Sheridan would like a word."

I nod numbly. She steps into the hall again, but I hang back long enough to send a bemused look Adam's way. He smiles, so reassuring and *proud*, and it makes me flustered, makes me want to cover his mouth with my palm. It's only Sheridan—not the whole group. We don't even know what she wants yet.

Adam leans in, slow, like he thinks I'll pull away again. He presses a kiss to my temple, and my eyes close as he whispers one last piece of encouragement in my ear: "You got this."

CHAPTER TWENTY

ADAM

Alone in the greenroom, I'm not sure what to do with myself. Whether I should wait right here for Eleanor to come back, or go check if the rest of the band is still fighting, or maybe find Jane and see if she knows what kind of food they'll serve at the wrap party.

If they're even having the wrap party anymore.

I drag both hands down my face, scrubbing my palms against my scruff, and snag one of the bottles of water lined up on a nearby table. I sit down on the couch across the room and take a drink, then fiddle with the cap for a few seconds.

Nervous energy twists through me, and it has very little to do with the band. I'm glad Eleanor is talking to Sheridan, and I genuinely hope it's good news for her. Eleanor needs this deal more than I do. She deserves it more too. They'd be stupid to go with anyone else, me included. But I do wish Fiona had come by a few minutes later. Given me enough time to figure out what was going through Eleanor's head.

Something changed when she found out about Freddie and Billy. It's not just that she was pissed—Eleanor had every right to be upset with me, and I deserved a dressing-down. But it wasn't anger I read on her face before Fiona walked in. It was doubt. Like she was second-guessing starting something with me, trusting me, all of it.

I blow out a breath and lean forward to brace my elbows on my knees and hang my head.

Which is how Freddie finds me a moment later.

He sweeps into the room and collapses onto the couch next to me with a groan. "What a shit show, huh?"

No response to that seems particularly safe, so I lift my head and simply nod.

He stares up at the ceiling for a beat, then pushes himself forward to mirror my posture. "Anyway, this isn't how I wanted to do this, but whatever. We want to sign with you, man."

Ah, fuck.

A dozen competing emotions hit me at once, all of them tangled together and lodged behind my sternum. ". . . The whole band is on board with that decision?"

Freddie's face scrunches up in an irritated way. "Wasn't *exactly* unanimous. I don't know what's going on with Sher tonight, but she'll come around. I can talk her around."

It sounds like he's trying to convince himself as much as me. I look down at the plastic bottle in my hands. My thumb scrapes at the paper label, shredding it. "Look, man . . . I appreciate the opportunity, but I'm going to have to pass."

Freddie blinks owlishly at me for several seconds before he turns away with a scoff. He turns back, looking even more incredulous. "What do you mean, you have to *pass*? You made us the offer."

"It's no longer on the table."

Oh, Eleanor is going to kill me. She'll think I'm turning this down for her, which is only partly true, and not really something I see a problem with. It's simple: I want to be with her more than I want to work with any one band. Beyond that, I don't particularly want to work with this asshole anymore.

I mean, hell, after what I witnessed tonight, I'm not even sure how legitimate Freddie's decision is. He's always been sort of the default leader of the group, but why is he the only one in here right now? Where are the others?

Freddie's jaw ticks. "Come on, Shaw. Just like that? Billy said you—"

"Billy Draper doesn't speak for me."

I set my water bottle down on the side table and push to my feet. Clearly, the option to stay here and wait for Eleanor is no longer viable. Things just got real awkward, and Freddie seems frayed thin. His knee is bouncing and he's cracking his knuckles. He looks like he's a heartbeat away from hitting something. And I've already been punched in the face once today, so I'm out.

"I'm sure you'll land somewhere great," I tell him as I walk away.

Not twenty minutes later, Billy is calling me.

I'm standing on the sidewalk outside the venue, already staring at my phone, when his name pops up on the screen. Eleanor hasn't come out yet. I've been out here racking my brain, trying to figure out a way to prove to her that I mean what I say. To convince her I'll never lie to her or hide anything from her again.

Funnily enough, the only solution I'd come up with was talking to Billy. But I hadn't quite figured out what I wanted to say to him yet. Now he's calling, and there's no point in putting it off.

"Hey," I answer.

"What's this I hear about you walking away from Dempsey?"

I huff a dry laugh and run a hand over my mouth. "What, did Freddie call you? God, he's such a little bitch."

Billy snorts on the other end of the line. "He is. But yeah, he called. Because *I'm* the one who connected you two. Do you not see how bad this makes me look?"

Guilt stabs through my stomach. I hadn't thought of it that way. But then, why would I have? The decision wasn't about Billy. It's *my* career. My call.

"I'm sorry it didn't work out. It just wasn't a good fit."

"A good fit," Billy repeats, like it's the most idiotic thing he's ever heard. "We've been over this. They're on the precipice; their next album could be massive. You had it in the fucking bag, Adam. What the hell happened out there to make you walk?"

"Look, the band's politics are a mess right now—"

Billy cuts me off with a huff. "So, what? You're going to hand them over to Eleanor Thompson on a silver platter?"

Groups of concertgoers are scattered around me, some waiting for rides while others loudly debate where to go next. But it all fades to nothing, drowned out by my own pulse roaring in my ear.

My grip tightens around my phone. "Why do you care?"

"Excuse me?"

"I know this was a potential opportunity for you too. But

from the way Freddie talks about it, you have a good shot at getting hired as their new manager regardless of what label they land with. So why does it matter whether she's the one who signs them?"

Billy makes a petulant noise. I can picture him angrily pacing around his home office, shelves lined with music memorabilia and relics of his glory days. "I'm just trying to figure out why you'd throw an opportunity like this away. And don't give me that bullshit about the band's *politics*."

My jaw twitches. "I need you to be straight with me, Billy. Did you send me here specifically because it was Eleanor's meeting?"

"No. What the fuck? I told you this morning, I never mentioned it was her because I didn't think it mattered. Clearly, I was wrong about that."

This last part is muttered under his breath, and I can't let it bait me. I remember Eleanor's reaction, when she asked me not to call Billy to ask for his help earlier. How worried she was that word would get back to Griffin. I don't want to drag her into the conversation . . . but I have to know.

"So Griffin Hastings didn't put you up to this?"

"Put me up to what?" Billy is getting pissed now. I hear a cabinet door slam in the background.

"Coming to Vegas. Going after Dempsey . . . Going after *Eleanor*."

"Jesus, kid. I don't know where you're getting this stuff, but no. I sent you there because Freddie wanted to meet with someone else and I thought they were perfect for your list."

I pinch the bridge of my nose. Billy wouldn't use me as a pawn. But he might, if he didn't realize Griffin was using him as one too.

My hand falls back to my side, and I tip my head back, staring up at the dark sky. What little of it I can see, past all the bright lights of the city. "So he was never involved in any of this? You never spoke to Hastings about Dempsey?"

Billy hesitates. "We had lunch a few weeks back. It came up. But I still don't see what the issue is here."

Goddamn it.

I sigh and stare down at the pavement beneath my feet. I can't tell Billy about Eleanor, but maybe that's fine. Because none of this is really about her. It's about me and Billy, and about the changes I need to make moving forward.

"The issue is that this whole thing has felt underhanded," I tell him.

Billy scoffs in my ear. "It's just business."

"Don't you ever get tired of hearing yourself say that?" I snap. "It's like your catchphrase. Every time you get called out for doing something shitty, you say *it's just business*, like it excuses any and all bad behavior. But it's not the only way to do business, Billy."

For *years* I've told myself Billy is a good guy. Or maybe a not-so-good guy, but one I could always find a way to defend because without him, I wouldn't be where I am. But clearly, I can't be as objective about Billy as I thought. Me standing here is proof of that.

"You know I care about you, man. And you know how grateful I am for everything you've done for me in my career." I toe the sidewalk and swallow thickly. I picture his face on my graduation day, the pride, the loud, embarrassing whistle he let out when they called my name. He's taken his clients leaving so hard, and I never wanted to be one of the people who hurt him that way.

Then I picture my mom, giving me that look she's been giving me my whole life, every time I drag my feet around a difficult decision. The raised eyebrow and pursed lips that say, *you already know the right move, so make it.*

Another inhale, and I force myself to spit it out: "I want us to have a relationship, but I can't work with you anymore. And I don't know if you'll wanna be in my life if we never talk shop, but I hope you will be."

Billy's quiet for long enough I check the screen to make sure he hasn't hung up on me. My heart inches up my throat, and for a moment I feel eight years old again. Just . . . hoping.

"You're the closest thing I've got to family, kid."

I wince and open my mouth to try to soften the blow, but nothing comes out. It is what it is.

"If that's how you want things, then that's how it'll be. Besides"—he huffs a laugh—"I probably don't have many years left in the industry."

Guilt and relief battle for top billing inside me. "I don't know about that—"

"Hey, I've had a good run. But I know I'm no one's top choice anymore." He sighs. "I want you to succeed, Adam. And I want you to do it better than I did, you know? Figure out a way to succeed and not wind up alone, if you can."

My gaze lifts to the stage door along the side of the venue. To where I've been waiting for Eleanor. "That would be nice," I manage. "Thank you for understanding, Billy. We'll talk more when I'm back in LA, yeah?"

"You got it, kid."

CHAPTER TWENTY-ONE

ELEANOR

Fiona leads me down the hall to a dressing room where Sheridan and Curtis are waiting. Sheridan is perched on top of the Formica counter that spans the entire length of the room, with the mirrored wall to her back. Curtis stands right at her side, but when he sees me walk in he squeezes her hand. "I'll leave you to it."

Sher shoots him a grateful smile and waits until Curtis closes the door behind him before flicking her gaze over to me.

"Hey. Thanks for sticking around."

"No problem." I glance to the side—the room is pretty much empty, aside from a couple of tote bags stuffed into one corner. A few chairs are tucked in at the counter, and I tug one out to sit in, trying not to feel weird that it positions me several inches lower than Sheridan. "How are you?"

Sheridan shrugs, slow and exaggerated. "I've had better days."

She grabs a can of Diet Coke that's sitting next to her and

takes a sip, then presses her thumb into the can. The dent releases with a *pop*.

"Freddie has decided he won't sign with an indie label," she says, and even though I saw it coming a mile away, the sting of rejection still hits me square in the chest.

"Yeah," I manage. "I figured."

"I love my brother, but . . ." She shakes her head and gestures toward the door. "I fucking hate whoever that guy is. His whole persona."

Hard to argue that, after the display I witnessed out there. Still: "A lot of bands go through rough patches. It's a tough transition, going from unknown artists to a group with a large fan base. Comes with a lot of pressure—"

Again, Sheridan shakes her head. "It's been a problem from day one. I don't know if it's because he's older than me, or maybe it's just because he's got a dick and I don't, but I've always come second. I've always been referred to as the *female* lead singer of Dempsey, while he somehow gets to be the front man. When we've disagreed on album decisions, I've always ended up deferring to Freddie, because it's obvious that's what the rest of our team wanted. At least, at the label. Curtis and Ralph are a bit more diplomatic, to be fair."

I may not be in the public eye the way Sheridan is, but I do know a thing or two about having to sacrifice control over your public perception in order to make it in the music industry. And about allowing men to dictate the terms of your own career.

"I really wanted to give you more control," I tell her, almost as a condolence.

She sets her Coke can back down. "I know. Which is why I'd still really love the chance to work together."

My confusion must be written all over my face, because Sheridan smiles.

"Did you mean what you said back at the brewery? About taking me on as a solo artist?"

"Uh . . . yeah." My brows are just about at my hairline. "Yes. Absolutely. If that was something you wanted to pursue, then I'd definitely be interested."

My thoughts scatter in a million directions—how I'll pitch this to Josie, how Sher's PR team will have to break the news of Dempsey's split, and when to reveal she's going solo. What her album would sound like and how I could leverage her existing fan base.

All of which is getting ahead of myself.

"Is the solo track something you want to do in addition to Dempsey, or—"

"No. I can't be part of this band anymore. And I know that if I want to have any kind of relationship with Freddie down the line, it's for the best. We'll kill each other." She pushes herself off the counter, and I stand too. "Besides, Ralph wants to start a family. He's talked about taking a step back. Curtis said he'd play backup on my album if I needed him to." She gives a nonchalant shrug, but I get the sense Curtis would follow her off a cliff if she asked.

While a part of me is sad that one of my favorite bands is breaking up, I have to admit this is the best possible outcome from that situation. As long as I can hold up my end of the deal.

"Full disclosure," I say, willing myself not to seem flustered. "I'll need to get the head of the label's approval before I can officially offer a contract. I've . . . lost some of my sway with her this past year. And as you know, launching a solo career is a different animal than promoting an established band."

A tiny crease forms between Sheridan's eyebrows, but she nods seriously. "I understand. You'll keep me posted?"

"Absolutely."

With a parting handshake and a promise to reach out as soon as I've spoken to Josie, I make my way through the maze of hallways backstage, moving on autopilot until I find an exit.

Someone calls my name almost the moment I step outside.

I look up to find Adam, and have to suppress a smile at the idea that he was standing here, watching the door like a hawk waiting for me. Now that intense gaze is roaming over me, and I must still look a bit shell-shocked, because he's wearing a frown.

"Hey," I say as I make my way over to him. "You waited."

"Of course." He shrugs. "Talked to Billy, while you were in there. I, uh . . . cut ties with him. Professionally speaking. He's still a friend, but . . . I realized I needed that separation."

"Oh, wow." I'm too stunned to say anything more for a moment. Admittedly, I'm pleased with this development. But that almost feels sort of mean? It was the smart thing for Adam to do, but I can't imagine it was easy. "You okay?"

He nods. "Yeah. Had to be done." He waves his hand, as if to wave the subject away. "What happened with Sheridan?"

I glance around. The venue isn't in the heart of the Strip or anything, but there are still a fair amount of people milling about. The last thing I need is some kid to overhear me talking about Dempsey and start live streaming it. "Let's get a cab."

We head down the block to hail a taxi, and a few minutes later we're en route back to my hotel.

"It would seem Dempsey is breaking up," I tell him. "And Sheridan Dempsey is going solo."

Adam's eyebrows rise. "No shit."

I nod. Glance out the side window, then back to Adam. "She wants to sign with me."

"No shit," he repeats, this time with a great big grin on his face.

I laugh. "Yeah. I think she really likes the idea of being with a female-led label."

Adam tips his head. "I think she really likes the idea of working with *you*." Then his expression turns a bit more serious. "Do you think it'll satisfy Josie?"

That is the million-dollar question. "I hope so. I told her I'd check in with her after the show, actually."

"Okay. You want to practice what you're going to say?"

I grin and tip my head onto Adam's shoulder. It's been a long time since I've had this—someone I could lean on and come to for help with my work or whatever else I'm struggling with. That's my own fault. Iris has been there. Josie has told me her door is always open. I was just too stubborn and proud to take them up on the offer.

I'm going to do things differently from now on. "Yeah. That would be great."

I make Adam wait in the hall while I call Josie, too nervous to allow him to eavesdrop but too infatuated to send him any farther away.

Alone in the room, I take a moment to silently freak out before dialing. I hate myself for putting this off for as long as

I did, because Adam was right—it would've helped my case to show her I was open to her suggestions. And considering she has ten years of experience on me and has probably seen plenty of bands on the verge of breaking up, if I'd told her about the tension in the group when I first caught wind of it, she likely would have come up with a better strategy than showing up to the brewery uninvited and asking them to please pick me.

But Adam is almost as good at giving pep talks as Iris, and I know what I'm going to say.

I hit the call button and as soon as she picks up, I blurt out: "I'm sorry it took me so long to touch base."

"Better late than never," Josie says, and her voice is wry, but I know it likely did irritate her to have to wait.

"Things have been very hectic out here. To make a long story short, it looks like Dempsey is breaking up, and Sheridan Dempsey is going solo. I'd love to hear your input on signing her."

Understandably, Josie takes a beat to process this. "That . . . is not the update I anticipated. Have you already pitched her?"

"She approached me, actually. I told her I was interested, but that I'd need to speak with you." I lick my lips, and continue before Josie has a chance to cut in. "Listen, Josie . . . I know my performance this past year has left a lot to be desired." I've started pacing around the room, and I stop in front of the window. The Strip sprawls out below me, showy and artificial. "I know I have some bad habits I need to break, but I really, *really* love this job. I love working for you."

Josie sighs on the other end of the line. "I've loved having you on my team as well, Eleanor."

My stomach plummets. *Past tense.*

"I have to say, your lack of communication on this trip hasn't exactly reassured me that you're willing to implement my feedback."

"I know," I say quickly. "I know that. But I am willing—I'm *more* than willing to work on my approach. It just . . . took me a minute to understand what you meant when you said I needed to be a team player."

Because most of what I know about the music industry, Griffin taught me. He taught me to play by my own rules, and I buried my head in the sand and ignored Josie's advice for so long because Griffin also taught me it's dangerous to put too much trust in someone else. For years I've been afraid of failing, and equally afraid to ask for help.

It's infuriating, after all this time, still to be confronting ways that relationship fucked with my mindset. But I see it now, which means I can change it.

"I meant that I need you to come to me when you aren't sure how to handle something."

"Yes," I say, nodding vigorously even though she can't see me.

"And to trust that the policies I put in place are there for good reason."

"I do," I tell her. "I do trust you."

A long, deep breath fills the silence. "Come to my office first thing on Monday. We'll draw up the offer for Sheridan together."

I squeeze my eyes shut and pull the phone away from my

mouth as I flail around for a second, totally exhilarated. "I'll do that," I tell her, sounding a bit breathless. "See you Monday."

I hang up and blow out a shaky breath, then grin down at my phone for another moment before spinning on my heel and heading for the door.

Adam is right there when I open it, sitting on the carpeted floor right next to my room. He lowers his own phone and lifts his brows. "How'd it go?"

"We have some things to hash out on Monday, but . . . I still have a job. And she's green-lit my offer for Sheridan."

He breaks into an eye-crinkling grin and pushes to his feet, drawing me into a hug as soon as I'm within reach. "That's awesome."

I sink into his chest, pressing my face into the hollow of his throat and inhaling that woodsy scent I've already grown so fond of.

"I'm so happy for you," he says with his chin propped on top of my head.

"Thank you," I mumble into his chest.

I pull back and push the door open wider, wordlessly inviting him back inside.

I heave a great big sigh of relief and collapse onto the bed, then reach with grabby hands for Adam to join me. He kicks off those ridiculous boat shoes and climbs on, propping himself up on one elbow.

"When we get back to LA, I want to take you out to celebrate."

"Well, I did agree to dinner."

He smirks and rolls on top of me. "Maybe I want to take you to the botanical gardens first."

"Hmm," I manage, distracted by the feeling of his stubble against my neck.

"I want to take you to dinner, and the movies, and the zoo, and the beach, and a million other places. I want more than one date."

"I don't know if I mentioned, my sister is getting married in a couple weeks."

Adam pecks my cheek, then pushes himself back to gaze down at me. I run my hands up his arms, gripping his biceps. "Yeah, I think I remember something about that."

"So you probably recall that I don't have a date."

"What about Iris's dog?"

"Oh yeah, she will fully be a third wheel. So you want to go with me?"

Adam shifts his weight so he can grab my left hand, lacing our fingers together above my head. He dips down to kiss me, soft and slow, and when his answer comes, it's in a whisper against my lips:

"I do."

EPILOGUE

ELEANOR

I'm not entirely sure how I was convinced to come back to Las Vegas. One would think after my last experience in Sin City, I would have had the good sense to stay away. And yet. Here I am. In the strip club, no less, sipping on a cocktail Tyler ordered for me. I'm not sure what's in it, but . . . a lot of vodka, would be my first guess.

At least this time I'm not going to spend half the visit stuck inside a conference hall and the other half running around the city on the knife's edge of an anxiety attack.

No, this time I am here to have fun.

Which I am. I'm having a great time. I'm surrounded by all of my closest friends, watching a dancer who is legitimately one of the most attractive people I've ever seen in real life slide down the pole wearing only a pair of mesh boy shorts. I'm pleasantly buzzed, but not too far gone—I won't be making that mistake again—and for once, everything feels like it's falling into place.

I have a job I love, working for a woman I respect. I have a new apartment with floors that are only a little bit crooked, and a new roommate who has become my very best friend in the world. And I'm on vacation, staying in a posh hotel suite Iris booked, using some combination of sweet talk and sorcery to get us an unbelievably low rate. She acquired this negotiating superpower while planning her wedding, and she jumps at any chance to put it to use.

The point is, everything is exactly how I want it to be. Exactly how Iris and I planned it. So I have no good reason to feel so restless.

While the woman onstage collects her tips and the DJ introduces the next dancer, I pull out my phone. I keep it low by my hip, so that none of the bouncers see it and confiscate it. So that Tyler doesn't confiscate it, for that matter.

I bite my lip and find Adam's name. Take another sip of my cocktail.

I miss you, I type out, and hit send.

I stare at the screen as three dots appear, hovering at the bottom of our text chain. I wait, ignoring the new dancer who comes onstage, even as Iris and Tyler lose their minds over her impressive climb up the pole.

The three dots disappear.

I frown and shove my phone into the pocket of my dress. I'm not supposed to be texting him, anyway. And it's ridiculous for my attention to be diverted when there's a perfectly good striptease going on right in front of my face.

I settle in and try to enjoy it. Try to remember this is supposed to be a celebration, and that Adam and I both agreed we were going to do our own thing for a little while.

A moment later, someone slides into the empty chair beside me and presses in close. I look over, expecting it to be Tyler with another round of drinks, but instead find Adam grinning back at me.

"Miss you too."

A wide grin splits my face and I practically lunge over to kiss him. "We're so gross. Can't even watch strippers without you."

Adam shrugs. "This is kind of our spot. Besides, what's the point of a joint bachelor-bachelorette party if I can't come over and kiss you now and then?"

I hum in agreement and tip my head onto his shoulder. He nuzzles the top of my head for a second, then pulls back to whisper in my ear.

"You wanna get out of here?"

I cock my head and eye him. "What'd you have in mind?"

"Thought we'd pay an old friend a visit." He matches my grin and downs the rest of his drink. "Meet me out front in five."

I watch him head back over to the second stage near the back of the club and say something to his friends, all of whom seem entirely unfazed when Adam walks away again. I didn't see him say any goodbyes, so I take my cue from him, and tell Iris that I'll be right back.

When I step outside, Adam already has our limo waiting at the curb.

He opens the door for me and I slide into the back seat, waiting for him to get in after me. "You sure they won't miss us?"

"I can't speak for your sister, but I'm pretty sure the guys won't even notice we're gone. Anyway, this won't take long."

Adam tells the driver our destination, then turns to look at me. "What do you say?"

I curl my lips between my teeth and nod. "Yeah."

Adam laces our fingers together, and I rest my head on his shoulder, grinning into his shirt over the sheer ridiculousness of this decision. But it pretty much epitomizes the past year of my life: learning to trust my instincts without veering into reckless or irresponsible territory. Learning to be a person who is fully capable of doing things myself, but who is okay with letting someone else take the lead now and then.

We pull up to Happily Ever After and look out the window at the neon sign.

"You're sure you want to do this? You only get married once."

I snort and elbow Adam. "Three times if you're lucky."

A month from now, I'll wear a white dress with a sweetheart neckline and a small train that made my mother cry the first time I tried it on. We'll exchange vows on a hilltop overlooking a vineyard. It will be the intimate wedding I've dreamed about, and it will be perfect.

But coming back to this spot where everything changed for Adam and me feels perfect too.

Adam slides out of the car and I follow him across the leather seats. Out on the sidewalk, with the night air cool against our skin, Adam takes my hand and we turn to face the chapel.

"What do you think the odds are that Beatrice remembers us?" I ask.

"Slim," Adam says. "Five bucks says she tries to upsell you on a photo package."

"Ten says you're the one who caves."

"I'll take that bet."

I grin and give Adam's hand a little tug, steering him toward the entrance. As we walk inside, I think about the last time we were here, how it felt like I'd just made the biggest mistake of my life. How it's always a gamble, taking the plunge and putting your trust in another person. Putting your heart in their care. But it's a gamble I can't wait to make, every day for the rest of my life.

I'm all in.

ACKNOWLEDGMENTS

The idea for this book came to me a few hours into a cross-country road trip, sitting in the cramped back seat with my six-month-old daughter strapped in beside me. The premise excited me, felt fun in a way my work hadn't been for a while. While my daughter napped, I texted my friend Mackenzi Lee to pitch her the idea, fully expecting her to tell me to finish the book I'd already started drafting. Instead she replied, "I fucking love that" and immediately began to brainstorm with me. Thank you, Mackenzi, for being my biggest cheerleader around this project. Without you, I would never have made it across the finish line.

Thanks also to my dear friends RuthAnne Snow and Victoria Lee for being my soundboards, accountability buddies, and sources of endless patience whenever I find a plot hole to spiral over.

To my lovely agent, Elizabeth Bewley, thank you for believing in this book and for always championing my work. You are such an utter delight to work with and I am incredibly lucky to have you on my team.

Thank you to my editor, Lara Jones. I knew from the first time we spoke that our visions for this book aligned, and that it would be a blast working on it with you. I can't tell you how much I appreciated your thoughtful approach and brilliant insights into Adam and Eleanor's story.

I'd also like to thank the rest of the Atria team who helped make this book its best and get it into the hands of readers: Libby McGuire, Emily Bestler, Dana Trocker, Zakiya Jamal, Megan Rudloff, James Iacobelli, Paige Lytle, Shelby Pumphrey, Annette Pagliaro Sweeney, Davina Mock-Maniscalco, and Nicole Bond.

Finally, thank you to Jim for being the best partner in crime, and to my daughters for being surprisingly chill on long car rides.